Chronobot Chronicles

Mark Wayne McGinnis

Jennifer M. Eaton

Published by: Avenstar Productions **info@avenstar.net**

Paperback: ISBN: 979-8-9866752-9-9

To join Mark's mailing list, jump to: **http://eepurl.com/bs7M9r**

Visit Mark Wayne McGinnis at: **http://www.markwaynemcginnis.com**

Prologue

Hardy stirred to consciousness within the frigid abyss, the extreme conditions causing havoc to his advanced sensory apparatus. He was aware there had been a catastrophic explosion; its echo, still humming in his servos, lingered, memory traces fractured and hazy.

ChronoBots, birthed over three centuries ago by the Sheentah, were supreme war machines and known to be as cold-hearted as the surrounding cosmos. Yet Hardy was a deviation, an anomaly. His brain was a paradox, the quantum weave of electronic circuitry entwined with an organic mesh. Unprecedented in the universe, Hardy's composition set him apart. Intriguingly, his partial bio-material brain held a spectral DNA imprint, that of a long-deceased maintenance worker—John Hardy. The result was an intellectual construct divided in two: the standard-issue base ChronoBot intelligence, LuMan, and the Hardy persona—wry, caustic, and often annoying.

Now, caught in the grip of the infinite vacuum, Hardy found his systems buffering under the external chill of -450 degrees Fahrenheit. He spun, careening through the void, the ashen ballet of his movement as puzzling as the last remnants of his memories.

1

The asteroid field loomed, boulders hurtling past like bullets from a cosmic gun. The clock ticked as he twisted and turned, narrowly evading a face-first collision with the oncoming space debris. His mental fragments teased him, vague images of mechanical beetles, colossal and menacing, descending upon him. Then, bizarrely, a creature from Earth's Jurassic period—a snapping and reeling T. rex—flashed through his mind.

Terrific … not only am I an untethered castaway, but I've lost my mind … The ridiculous visions were a stark contradiction to his current reality—all disconcerting symptoms of one too many knocks to his head, no doubt.

Hardy, caught in the dance of celestial bodies, felt his momentum wane as he exited the asteroid field. The black void yawned before him, his trajectory propelling him further into the cold, dark emptiness. As a fully functional ChronoBot with five turreted plasma cannons, typically enclosed within hidden compartments beneath metallic panels, Hardy realized the frigid cold was entering deep within his core. His situation was dire, the odds stacking up against him. With an effort he retracted the weaponry, felt the panels close tight. But systems and subsystems still struggled to reconcile his present circumstance while the fragmented memories continued to flicker within his faltering mind.

The asteroids had stopped zipping by, replaced by the desolate expanse of black nothingness. Hardy, still spinning, cartwheeling uncontrollably, knew the hazards of deep space. Systems would continue to fail; his bio-matter brain would, inevitably, freeze. Time was his enemy, as inexorable as the void he was plunging into.

His scanners searched for a lifeline, a beacon in the cosmic darkness. His mind raced to assemble the fragments into a narrative—those metallic beetles, the surreal dinosaur, and now the relentless void. He was a ChronoBot, a lethal warrior, yet he was also Hardy, the once-human aspect of his persona, and everything was shutting down. His final thoughts dissipated like the fading embers of a dying star.

In the vast expanse of space, Hardy, a quite extraordinary robot, a ChronoBot no less, had met his tragic end. His fight for survival, driven by both logic and human resilience, had come to an abrupt halt. The universe had claimed him, leaving his legacy as a tale of courage and determination. As the void swallowed him whole, his memory fragments dissolved, forever lost among the stars.

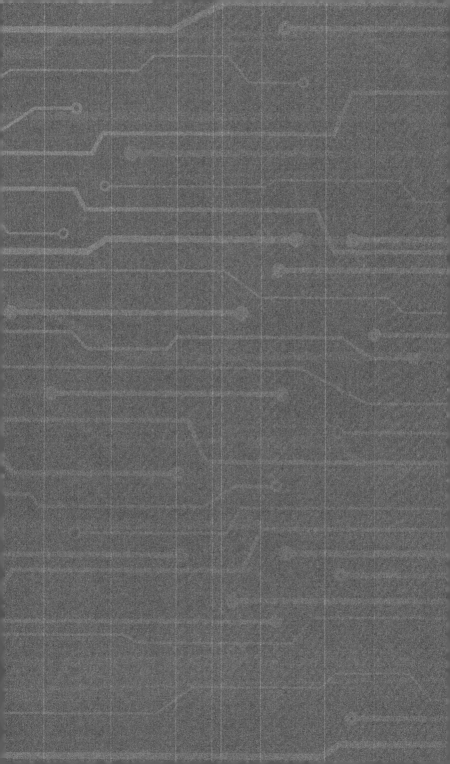

Chapter 1

Naromi Star System
Freight Station Lancaster
Loni

Oh God, somebody please just shove me out of an airlock …
The heat was already stifling, but now, with the
primary concentric air-cooling turbine on the fritz, life
here within the station was a living hell.

I glanced toward the steel composite beams arching high overhead. Miles of polyaluminum air ducts crisscrossed the domed
ceiling. I swore I could almost see the putrid hot air spewing out
through the various vent registers. For the umpteenth time I
tucked several loose strands of wheat-colored hair behind my ear.

I sat on a waist-high pony wall wearing cutoff shorts, my
favorite black tank top—baggy and, yeah, stained with whatever
—and flip-flops I'd refashioned from an old pair of work boots.
Having just turned seventeen, I was too skinny and too pale,
nearly pretty some days in the right light, plain-looking most of
the time, and beyond ready to leave this place. Something I had

never had the opportunity to do—not ever. That embarrassed and frustrated me. My dreams were simple ... experience an actual world, breathe fresh air—run barefoot on lush green grass. I'd read about that. Imagined what that must feel like. I imagined a lot of things I'd never done before. Things I'd never experienced.

To my left was the Transbay 16 airlock. One of twenty-seven cargo delivery points encircling the spherical fifty-thousand square foot deep-space structure.

With bare ankles crossed, I kept beat to a song in my head I used to like—now, not so much—stuck in my mind on constant repeat. *Ugh.* To my right, big Manfred was hard at work manhandling a steel Geo-Go container back onto its skid pallet. I had to give it to the guy; he was strong. Typically, it would take two men to muscle a Geo-Go container like that. Sweat was coming off his brow in rivers. His light gray warehouse-issued overalls were torn at the knees, streaked with God knows what, and there were large dark sweat circles beneath his pits. *I'm literally breathing Manny's flop sweat.*

The environmental ambient temp had been keeping at 105 F. My eyes were drawn to the bulkhead thermometer—the glowing red digital numbers had just bumped up to 106 F. While Manny continued to fight with his stubborn Geo-Go container, I wondered why he hadn't just requisitioned a bot.

I caught sight of Hightower; he was headed my way. *Dammit!* The station supervisor emanated unease like Manny emanated BO. Fortunately, all of the man's attention was being drawn to his tablet. His brow was furrowed, and he was doing that thing with his mouth. A kind of pursing of his lips—like he was kissing someone. I grimaced at the mere thought of it.

I stilled my swaying legs. *Maybe he won't notice me.*

It was no secret Nathan Hightower barely tolerated my presence here. The feeling was mutual. I detested the man—he was a self-centered little Napoleonic asshat. Emperor of all Freight Station Lancaster.

A freight hub so inconsequential, so far out into deep space, that nobody came here unless they absolutely had to.

"What do you think you're doing?" he barked. His eyes burned into me like two laser beams.

I shrugged involuntarily. "Uh ... just taking my mid-shift break," I said. My wrist started to undulate more rapidly. I didn't need to look at the device to know it had started pulsing yellow. Like almost everyone here, I wore a ComBand, a communications band, on my left wrist, but mine was automated with an oh-so-irritating special app called an HSA—Heart Stress Alert program. Yes, I needed it; it had become as important to my survival as, well, my sense of smell or taste. The real problem was its ridiculous sense of timing. Whenever there was a change in my heart rate, even if it was for the better, the thing just came alive.

I had something stupid called stage 3 cardiac deterioration. More accurately, I suffered from incurable heart failure. With each passing day, my heart died just a little bit more. *Yay.* And if that wasn't bad enough, I had a device that reminded me of my inevitable fate at every opportunity possible. Way worse than that musical earworm nestled in my brain right now. The little screen displayed a beating green heart icon when all was copacetic, a beating yellow heart icon when I was overly stressed—like right now—and a rapidly beating bright red heart when there was a good chance my ticker might literally explode within the confines of my chest.

I took a deep breath and slowly let it out, willing my HSA app back to green.

I stared at Hightower, doing my best not to show the utter contempt I felt for him. I would have told him to shove that tablet right up his ass a long time ago if it wasn't for my father. He was a mid-level manager, one that Hightower threatened to fire on a near-daily basis. And while my impending death seemed to be a foregone conclusion, my father suffered too, and it was all because of me. *But I have a plan for all of that ...*

"Don't be a smart-ass. I know union regs better than ... well, anyone," Hightower said. "We have a perfectly adequate break room, Ms. Solace ... do we not? This is a work zone. It's dangerous out here. Especially for someone like ..."

He didn't finish his sentence. He didn't need to. *Especially for a pathetic invalid teenager like me ...*

"We're down six hubbers this month. You of all people should know that, working the logistics desk." He took a step closer, his creepy eyes roving over my body. "Where's your uniform?"

A *hubber* was slang for any grunt-level peon working at this kind of deep- space hub station. This station in particular was all about long-haul freight drop-offs, short-term storage, and freighter pickups. And those who made all that happen were hubbers like me.

I glanced over to the bulkhead thermometer. "Sir ... it's one hundred and six—"

He interrupted, "I remember you out of uniform yesterday as well."

I wanted to shrug. To say it was hot enough to broil a halibut in here.

"You'll be docked pay for both yesterday and today. We have regulations in place for a reason. You don't get to arbitrarily make up your own rules simply because you're uncomfortable."

I noticed that Manny had stopped bouncing the Geo-Go container and was glowering at Hightower. I knew that Manny, as well as other hubbers here, was protective of me. I smiled his way —*it's no big deal; don't get involved.* But that was a lie. Being docked two days' pay would be catastrophic for me. Virtually all my minuscule wages went to my father. Insurance premiums, medications not covered by insurance ... two days' wages? It would be the difference between eating and going hungry for a week.

Hightower made a sweeping *off with you* gesture with his

hands. "We're all going to have to go the extra mile for a while … you included, Ms. Solace."

I pushed myself up and off the pony wall, feeling a momentary warning HSA pulse.

"Yes, sir … Um, you do know I'm off tomorrow, right? I submitted the PLT request last week."

He'd already turned away, burying his nose back in his tablet —but he now stopped in mid-step. Without turning around, he said, "Yeah … that wasn't approved."

I ground my molars. This was total bullshit. I shook my head. "I haven't taken personal leave in, like, over a year, Mr. Hightower. I think I'm entitled—"

The man spun on me, his eyes wide. "Don't you dare!"

I flinched, hating myself for it.

"Don't even think about saying that word. Entitled? Did I not authorize those increasingly more common doctor visits? Have I not signed off on some highly expensive medical equipment?"

I bit back a reply. The union had paid for my doctor's visits, and insurance paid for all my medical devices. Nothing, not one dollar, had come out of Freight Station Lancaster's budget allocations. He was just being a dick as usual.

I stood my ground. "Well, I guess I'll just have to take the time unpaid." I held my breath; the prick could fire me right there on the spot—justified or not. Again, it wasn't me I was worried about; it was my dad.

He looked at me—his nostrils flared, his lips back to puckering.

I raised my chin several millimeters; I wouldn't let him browbeat me, not this time.

Hightower ran his sausage-like fingers over the top of his buzz cut. He huffed. That's what he did when he felt someone was disrespecting his authority. He pushed his sleeves higher up meaty elbows. I eyed the muscles of his forearms flexing— watched as his little fists began opening and closing.

"There's only so much special treatment one employee can be granted before management has to say, well … enough is enough. I think we've almost reached that point, young lady."

Turning to leave, he huffed out one more dramatic breath. I shot him the bird and silently mouthed, *Fuck you.* His pace suddenly slowed, and I briefly wondered if he had eyes in the back of his fat head. I prayed he wouldn't review the security feeds from this conversation.

I made my way from the loading docks toward the forward exit hatch on the other side of the shipping compartment. I moved within a wide passageway where towering industrial metal shelving was riveted to the bulkheads. I entered my small office space, occupied by my crappy desk, my logistics terminal, and a small refrigeration unit where I stored various temperature-sensitive medications.

But instead of going to work, I passed by my terminal and headed for a small passageway at the back of my office. I entered the makeshift break area where there was a small food replicator, a fridge, a sink, two tables, each with four plastic molded chairs, and a gray leather couch, ripped along its center cushions where white foam peeked out like the spewing guts from a dying old whale. The deck next to an overflowing trash bin was littered with crushed water cups, half-empty food containers, gum wrappers, and discarded tissues.

I work with animals.

Being one of the only females in a sea of men was normal for me; it had been my life since I was three years old. The closest thing to a feminine role model I had were the fashion vids on the feeds. I didn't get it, to be honest. Clothes or makeup, or walking with a graceful stride—it all seemed ridiculous to me. *What the hell difference does it make what I wear?*

Continuing through another hatchway, I passed into the admin office where my dad, Max Solace, was standing, looking at a Halo Display—columns of numbers with corresponding graph representations. Entering farther into the compartment, I caught sight of my reflection on a server bay glass door. There, an awkward silhouette of a girl wearing oversized cutoff jeans and boot flip-flops stared back at me. *I'm a walking, talking disaster.*

Max turned and smiled. "Hey, sweetheart—I was just thinking about you. Where you headed?"

I shrugged and returned his smile. "Just to see you, Dad."

He was still handsome for an old guy in his late forties, I thought. Could lose a few pounds around the middle. But he still had all his hair—he had that going for him. Not that there were any prospects for him to meet anyone out here in the dead of space. He beamed at my last comment that I'd simply come by to see him. I wondered how he managed to stay so positive, considering what I'd put him through all these years.

"I thought maybe we could meet for lunch later?" I asked.

He was back to staring at his charts and graphs. "Uh … sure, just come get me. You know where to find me."

≈

BACK AT MY TERMINAL I SCROLLED THROUGH THE JOB posts. I'd been planning my escape for almost a year now. Typically, after my shift crew had worked a full day, finished dinner, and gone to bed, I would go to my quarters and pull up the StarJob app on my SJU system. Since I turned sixteen, I had been secretly researching jobs that would take me away from this hellhole of an existence—mind-numbing chores, misogynist coworkers, and a father whom I loved but felt suffocated by.

My work experience was limited to menial freight logistics tasks on this lame freight shipping station, but I kept scrolling job descriptions anyway—the alternative was to do nothing, so ... not an option.

Maintenance Supervisor. *Hard pass.*

Mechanical Engineer. *Just shoot me.*

Ship's Physician. *Yeah, right.*

Fighter Pilot. *I wish.*

And then, an hour later, I found it. The job post read:

Freight Coordinator Trainee.

> Work on board *Gossamer*, a long-haul freight vessel with
> shipping routes within the Naromi Star System

I scanned the requirements with tired eyes.

Must have excellent people skills ... *I have great people skills! I think ...*

Previous experience working within the shipping/freight sector ... *I've been*

doing that my whole life...

Proficient with FGCX logistics platform ... *I'm an FGCX logistics whiz...*

Positive Attitude ... *I can fake that with the best of them...*

Willingness to learn and grow with our company ... *I'm so willing!*

I did my best to tamp down my growing excitement. There must be dozens, maybe hundreds, of applicants for this job. I had to keep my expectations in check. *But holy mother of God, I'm perfect for this job!* I thought of Dad—how he'd miss me, how he'd be devastated. But he'd also start to have a life of his own. Maybe he'd get out of here too.

The next day, I filled out the application within fifteen minutes. I needed to expand upon my skill set and somewhat exaggerate my proficiencies.

I sat upright in my swivel chair and took in a deep breath of hope and encouragement. Then I spun my chair to the left, pushing off my desk every time it came around again, gaining more and more speed with each orbit. Smiling, I imagined being free and on my own, meeting people my own age, and maybe even seeing different worlds. Faster and faster, I spun until my HSA app came alive on my wrist. *Killjoy ...*

When my chair finally slowed and came to a stop, I stared at my terminal's display. Using a forefinger, I positioned the cursor over the box marked SEND and tapped it.

I closed my eyes and leaned back into the cushions of my chair. *Done. Now all I have to do is wait. Maybe a few days ... maybe a week. But at least I've done something.*

And then I heard it. *Ping ...* My eyes snapped open, wondering if I'd done something wrong. Perhaps I'd forgotten to make a required selection. God forbid you leave something blank on a stupid form.

Ms. Loni Solace,

Thank you for your interest in the **Freight Coordinator Trainee** position. We will review your qualifications and get back to you within the next few days, if not sooner.

Yours truly,

Dan Caldwell

Gossamer Deep Space Freight Hiring Manager

SynthoGen

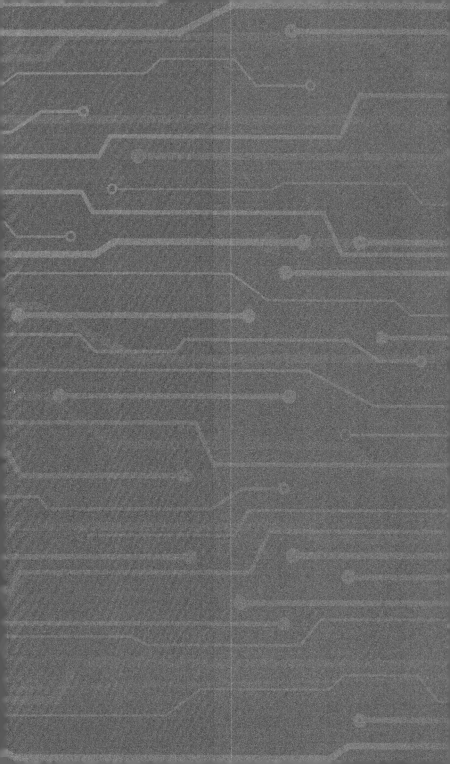

Chapter 2

Loni
Two weeks later ...

I sat back in my chair, staring at the terminal in front of me, the Halo Display spilling a glowing, lurid light into my space, probably making my pale face look even paler.

I was on a video call with Dan Caldwell—was so nervous I was sure simply talking to the man was leaching beats from my heart. But I was so tired, being stuck within this station, an invalid hubber, feeling inferior to, well, everyone. I wanted to explore what was outside the hull of this space station. I wanted to do something important.

So, I was going through with the call. I was answering all of Dan Caldwell's questions. Unbeknownst to the man, my HSA was going crazy. And although I knew I was nailing the technical side of things, I worried my personality wasn't as endearing as it needed to be. *I certainly never had to charm my way into a position here on Freight Station Lancaster.* No, charm wasn't a skill I was even the slightest bit familiar with.

"Your experience is impressive, Loni," Dan said, now looking at me with more of a discerning stare. *He's wondering if I'm up to the task* ... "I can tell you've learned a lot during your time spent there at that hub station. But this job, this position ... it's a whole different animal. You'd have a lot to learn if you wanted to excel on board one of our long-haul freighters." He shook his head and blew out a breath through puffed cheeks.

My growing disappointment was literally making my heart hurt. God, I wanted a way off this station more than anything in the world. I was desperate for this opportunity, and I was sure he could sense that.

"It's not easy work, Loni," he continued. "I take it you don't shy away from manual labor?"

"*Pfft*, I'm a super hard worker. I'm no shirker, Mr. Caldwell." *I didn't just say that, did I?*

"Are there any physical conditions that might inhibit your ability to perform your duties as assigned?"

I shrugged and made an *I can't think of any* face. "Don't have any physical issues working here," I added.

He nodded, looking somewhat bemused. It might have just been my guilty mind, but it almost seemed as if the man knew I wasn't being totally forthright—well, to be fair, lying. Then again, it was probably just my imagination running rampant.

"Well, I think you've proven yourself more than capable of learning," Dan said. "Okay, fine ... I'd like to go ahead and offer you this position. How does that sound to you?"

I could barely croak out a response before we launched into a discussion of specifics and particulars. Surprisingly, my HSA stayed green, maybe because my excitement was hampered by an overwhelming sense of relief I was feeling inside. That and I had never been more relieved in my life.

That was until I realized that this also meant I'd be saying goodbye to my father and the only life I'd ever known.

With the call from Dan Caldwell over with, I wondered if I

should tell my father what was to happen, or simply be gone one morning. No, not just one morning ... it was tomorrow morning. One thing I did know: I wanted to spend every moment I could with him before then. I got up from my chair and headed out of my tiny office. I found my dad still staring at the same display of numbers and graphs.

"Hey there. You ready for dinner with your favorite daughter?"

Max turned and smiled. "Sure. Just after this algorithm compiles." He gestured to the corner of the compartment. "Algernon's on the fritz again ... Can you look at him for me?"

"Um ... sure, maybe later."

Algernon—an AI bot of adequate sophistication—oversaw the ceaseless tide of cargo: the arrivals, the departures, the ebb, the flow. Just one of the cogs that kept the wheels of commerce in ceaseless motion. And the name? An echo from long-forgotten literature—*Flowers for Algernon*. A homage to a mouse that, through the miracle of science, transcended its meek existence. I supposed it was a fitting namesake for this digital custodian. More than just an artificial intelligence, Algernon was an actual robot that, on a good day, could walk and talk, and carry on a conversation. But the old bot was in disrepair, with few of its original parts still in use. I liked tinkering with it and other bots. Not that I had any real robotics repair education or anything ... It had been more of a trial-and-error type thing over the past few years. I'd picked up the nickname of "the bot whisperer." I just did it for kicks, a distraction from the mind-numbing boredom of living on a deep-space hub station. But when someone approached me, batting their eyelashes, pleading, "Could you possibly tweak one of those colossal Goliath bots?" or hinting, "Our Spectras could use a hand"—Spectras, as in those ever-watchful robotic sentinels, endlessly trudging our station's labyrinth of corridors. They played at maintaining peace, order, the whole shebang—in usual circumstances, I'd steer clear, decline the offer. Yet, there was a stipulation to my habitual refusal, a sole exception. My father. For him, I'd descend into the bowels of any mechanical beast. If it came to granting Algernon, our beloved antiquated network of intelligence, a few more ticks of existence, whether days, weeks, or possibly, months, I'd willingly entangle myself in the web of wires and codes. For him, I'd take the plunge, always.

I moved closer beside him, looked at the large 3D display. "Making progress?"

He shrugged. "Was able to shave off a bit more from their transit pathways."

I knew he was referring to the dozens of stacking bots within the short-term storage bay.

"It's not much, but I'm getting there." He tapped on the input device. "How was your day? Meet any handsome young men?"

"Uh-huh, sure ... Out here in the middle of nowhere there's such a plethora of handsome studs to choose from." I shook my head. "Come on, when was the last time you saw a guy younger than you milling about?"

He grimaced apologetically. "Guess life out here does have its drawbacks." He swiped to the next screen. "At least we have each other."

Ouch. That hurt. I needed to try to ease into this slowly, maybe even help him to understand where I was coming from. "Have you ever thought of ... well, trying something else? Going somewhere else?"

"Thought of it? Sure. But there are so many memories here." He paused, looking down. "You know what I mean."

I lowered my eyes. *He means Mom.*

He leaned away from the display, his eyes somewhat distant. "When I work, even when I'm alone, I still feel her beside me. It's comforting."

And now his last living relative is going to leave him too. Somehow, this seemed worse than what happened with Mom, because I had made a choice. My stomach soured.

He turned toward me. "Something on your mind, sweetheart?"

I took in a deep breath and released it. "Dad, I—"

A sharp tone sounded—he spun back to his display. "Eureka! Stacking bot 28 can drop two seconds from its floor route. We're on a roll, kid!"

"That's great, Dad."

"You bet your pretty blue eyes it is! I'll have to pass on dinner today, sweetheart. This is the most progress I've seen in a month."

"Oh, umm, okay. Can we maybe have dessert later?"

He didn't answer. He mumbled to himself, tapping away as the graph updated with the bot's new floor trajectory. It was nothing new for Dad to get so lost in his work that he completely forgot that we'd been talking. It usually bothered me, but this time, maybe it was for the best ... the out I needed.

I hugged him from behind and kissed his temple. "Bye, Dad."

I turned, blinking away tears—Eyeing Algernon slumped in the corner, I strode from the office.

I didn't want to see his face when he found out he'd be the only Solace left on board. I couldn't bear to be the cause of any more pain.

Steeling myself, I quickened my pace, working through a list of the most important items I'd need to pack. First things first: I needed a portable refrigeration pack, one large enough to hold a three-month supply of my meds. I headed for the sick bay.

Dr. Sanjay pushed up his thick-rimmed glasses and adjusted his lab coat as I entered. "Hello, Ms. Solace. You're not low on meds yet, are you?"

He knew better. The only way I'd be low would be if I'd been selling the stuff on the black market.

"No, Doc. Um … you have one of those small portable refrigeration units around here? I'm going on a little trip."

"Ahh, how wonderful for you!" He walked toward the back of the room. "I have just the thing." He grabbed a small disk from the shelf. "This will fit into your pocket and is more than large enough for a few days' supply."

"I'm kinda going to need more than that. I'm going to be gone for three months."

His eyes widened, and I couldn't blame him. No one ever left this place.

"I hope you'll agree to keep this quiet until I'm gone."

He regained his composure. "Are you in trouble?"

"No. I got a job." Smiling, I couldn't hold back my exuberance.

"How … entrepreneurial of you."

"Umm, thanks. Do you have anything I can use for my stock of meds?"

He nodded, this time grabbing the kind of fridge-pack I already knew I'd need from a different shelf. It was rectangular, the size of an old-fashioned shoebox … with straps. "As long as you're planning on returning, take this. It would probably fit four months' supply of your current meds, if needed, so it will be more than enough room. But these packs are expensive, so it's a loaner."

I grabbed the pack. "Thanks, Doc. You're the best."

"You just remember this when you fill out my yearly employee cross-evaluation review. I'm up for a raise this year."

"You got it." I gave him a kiss on the cheek. "See you in three months!"

Throwing the pack's strap over my shoulder, I headed back to my quarters.

According to Dan Caldwell, most necessary provisions would be taken care of, so I only needed to bring a few things I couldn't live without. I grabbed three and a half months' supply of my meds—all I had, just in case—and placed them into the little inside pockets of the refrigeration pack. "Now to pack ..." I placed my empty duffel on my bed and looked around my room. Both dread and excitement pinged my HSA.

I tightly wrapped the throw blanket my parents had given me as a child. *God, am I really taking my ba ba?* I remembered the time when the heat generators had faltered, how cold this section of the station had gotten. How both Dad and Mom had wrapped me in this blanket while trying to hide their own shivering from me. I didn't need the blanket anymore, but I couldn't find it in my failing heart to part with it.

I reached across my little built-in desk, gently peeled the picture of my mom from the wall. I folded the tape over, careful not to damage the photo. It seemed like a lifetime ago when the engineering foreman had arrived at their door. Ashen-faced, he'd said there'd been an accident ... some kind of explosion. I hadn't fully comprehended what the overly distraught man was saying. That was until my father crumpled to his knees, destroyed.

Dad and I had lost a part of ourselves that night. I'd been what? Eight? Nine? My moist eyes settled on the vintage Steinway K-52. The thing took up a substantial portion of my cramped quarters. The old-fashioned upright piano stood off-kilter up against the opposite bulkhead. It had been a present from my mother. She'd said it was from an unclaimed shipping crate. With its European spruce keys, double felt hammers, and brass hardware, it was so much more than a musical instrument —it was memories. A piece of life that I had shared with my mother.

My eyes took in the beat-to-shit old piano. The veneer had scraped off at the legs, exposing a cheaper mystery wood underneath. Would I ever sit at that keyboard again? *Would I want to?*

I'd worked hard these past eight years at keeping my dad from falling back into despair. *Without Mom, he's only half of what he was.* And now I was seventeen—stuck in the middle of nowhere, with a father who'd rather stare at charts than actually talk to another human being, including me.

I closed my eyes, holding the picture close to my chest. That wasn't fair, and I knew it. We were both hurting, but where Dad wanted to stay and wallow in the past, I wanted my freedom—I needed a future. Memories were just ghosts, and ghosts would eventually hold you back from anything you were meant to be. And with the clock ticking on my ticker, I couldn't waste any more time seeking what freedom I could find.

I added the picture to my duffel and cuddled into my bed for what could possibly be the last time. The walls of my room seemed foreign, like a piece of my past already forgotten.

I closed my eyes, hugging my half-filled duffel to my chest. "Please forgive me, Dad."

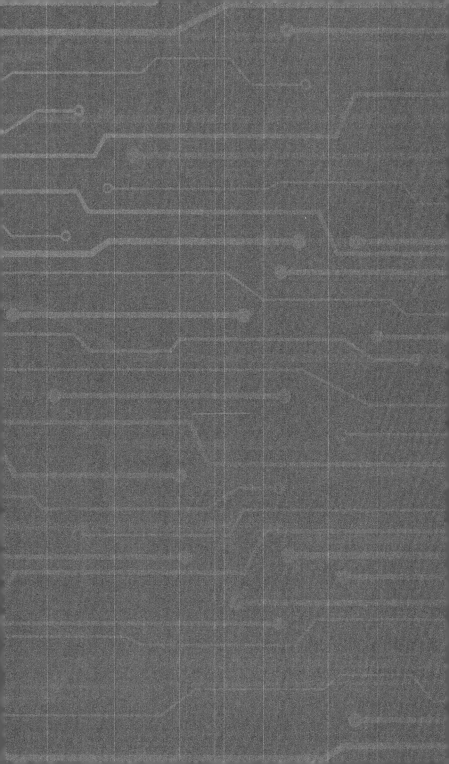

Chapter 3

Loni

I awoke early, showered, brushed my teeth, and dressed in my best jeans, meaning the ones that were the least frayed and had the fewest number of holes in the knees. I quickly finished packing—removing the ridiculous childhood blanket and then jamming it back in again with a muttered curse before zipping the overstuffed duffel closed.

With my refrigeration pack over one shoulder and my duffel over the other, I moved as silently as I could through station passageways. Other than the never-tiring, always-on-the-move freight bots, I was all alone. Moving out onto the open floor, I headed directly for the Transbay 12 airlock. Twenty minutes earlier, my ComBand had pinged—*Gossamer* had arrived. The Gal-5 Heavy Freight Transport ship was waiting. *Waiting for me ...*

A mere fifteen paces and I'd be on my way off this station, out of this old life and into my new one. I hurried, holding myself back from out and out running as if released from my pen, an energized pony now eyeing the wide-open field before me.

That's when Nathan Hightower stepped out from behind a nearby bulkhead. His expression was one of contempt—that and smug victory.

"Not so fast, Ms. Solace," he said, raising a plump hand. "You and I need to have a little chat."

I slowed, feeling as if I'd been gut punched. "You can't stop me. I—"

"Think again, Ms. Solace."

"I'm leaving. I'm leaving now," I said defiantly, looking over his shoulder toward Transbay 12 airlock's still-secured hatch.

"Only I can authorize what and who leaves this station. No preapproved clearance ... no opening of that hatchway door." Hightower's smile couldn't have been any more malevolent if he'd been auditioning for the villain part in a movie.

My eyes narrowed, my mouth a straight line. "You don't even want me here. You said it yourself; I've been nothing but trouble for you. The expense, the special treatment. Why stop me?"

He stepped closer—too close, entering my personal space to the point I could taste his hot morning breath. "It's true. I've made no attempt to hide the fact that I don't like you. That a deep-space freight station is no place to raise a sick kid."

"Then let me go!" I said, raising my voice louder than I wanted.

"Oh, I will. I'm actually thrilled you're leaving. Good riddance to you. I just wanted to let you know there won't be a place for you if you decide to return. And if you do ... if you come crawling back here with your tail between your skinny legs, I'll fire your father and send the two of you off on the first junk barge that docks here."

I stared at him, wondering if the little man had always been like this. Had something happened to him? Or had he grown into this cruel, soulless hobbit all on his own? Was this the end stage of spending your whole life on a station like this?

"Fine. I have no intention of coming back here to stay. And

once our place on Dromain-5 is ready ..." I shrugged. I wasn't sure why I'd lied but didn't regret it.

"You have a place on Dromain-5 ... a plush world with the most prized, most expensive real estate in all the sector?" His laugh echoed off high crossbeams above—a laugh that didn't reach his eyes. "Well, until then ... stay away." He stepped to one side and splayed a hand—a pretentious waiter showing a patron to her table.

I didn't hesitate. Transbay 12 airlock's wide hatchway split open as I approached. Glancing to my right, I saw it was big, sad-looking Manny who had activated the opening of the airlock's hatch. I slowed. "Take care of yourself, Manny. Please keep an eye on my dad ... Can you do that for me?"

He sent a nervous look toward the station's supervisor, then looked back to me. He nodded. "I will do that for you, Loni ... You be safe."

I gave him a kiss on the cheek. "Thanks."

Taking a deep breath, I crossed the threshold. Three steps in, the hatch slammed down behind me. The sound reverberated in the airlock, final and deafening. I shuddered, imagining High-tower accidentally hitting the eject button and spewing me into space through the never-to-be-opened emergency side hatch. "Whoops" would be his only apology. Asshole.

Other than Dad, I had no ties to this place.

"Good riddance to all of it."

I approached the door, and the security panel to the right came alive.

I moved my face closer so the retinal scan could read me. "Loni Solace reporting for duty, as requested."

The doors split open and a guy with a goatee stood in the opening, arms folded. "Loni Solace, as I live and breathe. Holy crap, you got big. I thought they were shitting me when they said you were coming aboard."

I realized I was gaping like a dork and closed my mouth. "Kent?"

Kent had been a supervisor in Freight Station Lancaster's cafeteria when I'd been growing up and had later nailed a promotion in the maintenance department. Three years ago, he'd disappeared. Although Hightower had denied it, the rumor was he'd skipped out on one of the supply freighters.

He reached out, grabbed me, and raked his knuckles over my scalp. "How the hell have you been, kiddo?"

I shoved him. "Get off." I rubbed my head. That had hurt as a kid and still hurt now.

He held out his hands to his sides. "Aww, come on, you know you missed me."

"Are you kidding? I almost forgot your name."

He held up his index finger. "But you didn't, which is a testament to how unforgettable I am."

I shook my head. "You're unforgettable, all right."

A bang sounded behind me, and the floor started to hum.

I looked up. "Are we leaving already?"

"Yup. They loaded the cargo earlier. They were just waiting for you. You're late, by the way."

I pursed my lips. "Hightower."

Kent puffed out a laugh. "Say no more. He's why I slipped out in the middle of the night. I hid in the laundry."

"Get out."

"Honest! A man's gotta do what a man's gotta do. That guy has a habit of keeping people even if he doesn't want them."

This, I'd seen on my own. "I think he likes to torture people."

"I guess some things don't change." He held out his hand and we started walking. "Training starts in fifteen minutes, so you'll have just enough time to drop off your things. Oh … hey, didn't you have an illness … a heart thing?" he said, now looking skeptical.

"That … modern medicine. I'm good now." That seemed to appease him. "Fifteen minutes? Are you serious?"

"Yup. Tight ship. We just got new cargo, and we need to go down and secure it. We don't get a lot of downtime out here. When there's a job to be done, it means *now*, not later. You gotta get used to that."

I nodded. I wasn't afraid of the work, but I would have liked to unpack first. Still, the thrill of doing something, *anything* different, was a thrill that brought a smile to my face.

We dropped off my duffel, throwing it into a small room with a bed and a door that I hoped led to a bathroom, and continued down the hall.

Kent pointed to a screen on the right. "At every juncture, there is a panel like this. These will be your best friends for the first few weeks. If you get lost, they will tell you where to go. Just press the blue button and answer the questions."

"Handy."

"You bet your ass." He pointed down the hall. "Mess is down there. You'll want to make sure you eat any chance you get, because you never know what your schedule will be one minute to the next. Same goes for the john. Never miss a chance to pee."

"Eat and pee. Got it."

He glanced back at me. "I'm serious, kid."

"Me too. One thing I love is eating and peeing. I guess that's actually two things, but my point is I'm all over those necessary bodily functions."

"Right." He stopped at the end of the hall. "Here is where the real work begins. Cargo Hold Four. You ready to have your mind blown?"

"With cargo?"

His lips quirked up in a smile. "Kid, you have no idea."

He tapped a few keys on the access panel. "Your codes will go live tomorrow after you are officially processed, so you'll have to stick with me for a bit."

"Lucky me."

He looked over his shoulder. "A few years haven't changed you, kid."

"Loni."

He frowned at me.

"My name is *Loni*."

Kent laughed, opening the hatch door. "All right, Loni. Let's introduce you to your future."

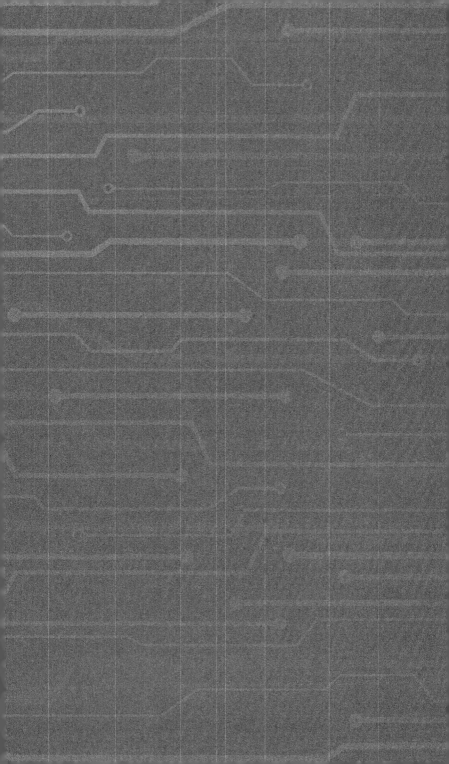

Chapter 4

U nit 1223 stood upright within the molded confines of its bot-recharging cradle. There was a full load today, eighty-nine bots in all. They were a hodgepodge of various classifications, functions, and manufacturers. For this jaunt, specific recharging cradles had been added for three of the archaic, and rarely requested, ChronoBot units.

Gossamer throttled backward from one of twenty-seven space station docking bays. The overhead lamps flickered, indicating the switchover from station power to onboard reserves. The stopover had been short. Used primarily as a freight hub, there were few places within the known galaxy of less importance and interest than that of Naromi Star System's Freight Station Lancaster.

Gossamer, a twenty-five-year-old Gal-5 Heavy transport, shuddered as it passed through another vessel's propulsion wake—one probably left behind by another space freighter or one of the new trawlers coming out of the Ganzine quadrant.

ChronoBot 1223's long-range spatial positioning matrix had been deactivated along with most of its "LuMan" artificial intelligence functionality—but that was not to say the bot's AI wasn't at least somewhat cognizant of its surroundings. Which, in and of itself, was a bit odd—considering there were strict safety regulations when it came to transporting robot freight. Especially when you were talking about a Class 8 battlebot. The LuMan AI was currently unaware if it was the lone still quasi-operational robot here within the hold.

Voices ... Two bioforms were entering through the hold's aft hatch. ChronoBot 1223, more specifically, its LuMan AI, differentiated the voice signatures as being human, one male, one female, with a 98.4 percent probability they were both in their early twenties.

"Look, you do your work ... don't dilly-dally on your rounds too much, stay out of trouble, and this can be an okay gig," the male human said.

"Well, that's a stellar endorsement, Kent. You really know how to make a sales pitch. I'm truly inspired now," the female said.

"Screw you, Loni. Everyone knows the cred-pay on a freighter is better than what you were getting back on that shithole of a hub station. And don't forget, we get J bonuses ... juggernaut bonuses."

"I know what a J bonus is, Kent."

LuMan tracked the two humans' movements within the hold area. Both were wearing marginally functional helmeted environ suits. Clearly, proper equipment maintenance was not a priority here onboard *Gossamer*. LuMan found humans interesting, if not mildly entertaining. This was the first time along the route that the human male, name designation Kent, had had an assistant.

One of the smaller bots, called a Mining-Plug, had partially disengaged from its recharging cradle.

"Dammit … see this?" Kent said, leaning down, placing two hands on opposite sides of the stout little bot. "You need to really put your weight into it, Loni. See what I'm doing here?"

"Uh-huh … that you're getting frisky with a defenseless bot?"

"Funny …" He shoved hard, securing the Mining-Plug back into position. There was an audible clanking sound.

Kent stood up, looking pleased with himself. Looking around, he took in the status of the other bots, each positioned side by side around the perimeter of the hold. "What do you see, Loni?"

She shrugged. "A fuckload of bots."

"Loni, this is serious. Do you want this job or not? My evaluation is going to Dan Caldwell, EOD. That's end of day …"

She rolled her eyes. "It was a joke. Geez, Kent. What happened to your sense of humor?" She glanced about the compartment.

The female seemed to be annoyed with the male human.

Kent said, "Well, don't just stand there … You need to move around. You need to literally inspect each of the bots. My God, we went over all this less than an hour ago, girl!"

"I know that …"

"For instance. Are the bots properly seated within their charging stations? Have the bots been deactivated? Hell, are they even on the right transport?"

"Stop barking at me, Kent. I get it. I know what to do."

LuMan watched with detached interest. He observed the newbie female freight specialist as she now moved from one robot to the next—checking that each was indeed properly seated within its recharging cradle. Both specialists wore a forearm-mounted tablet. She referred to hers often, ensuring each robot had indeed been logged into the freight manifest.

LuMan was well aware that within approximately six and a half minutes, Loni would be standing right in front of itself. At that point, she would discover it had not been properly deactivated—had not been fully powered down. LuMan did not wish to be deactivated.

All three ChronoBots had been stowed shoulder to shoulder next to one another. LuMan, in the middle, was chrome plated, and, at least according to its own internal diagnostics, was a bot that had been well-maintained. To the right was a peeling and chipped blue ChronoBot with the oversized word MARFIX vertically stenciled down its front torso. To LuMan's left was an equally battered-looking ChronoBot with two non-original manufacturer arm appendages that looked too short for its size. To add insult to injury, its face display was cracked.

As Loni approached the first of the ChronoBots, Kent said, "Now I want you to hold up here a sec."

"Why? I've been doing everything you told—"

"I know that. Just shut up and listen for a second. These three bots here, they're what are called ChronoBots."

"Yeah? So ..."

"Well, I don't like it when they're on my transport."

"Oh. So, this is now your transport?" Her attempt at humor was ignored.

Kent looked up at the first of the towering seven-foot-tall bots. "They're old ... like really old. Their AI brain personas are called LuMan."

"LuMan, got it."

"Anyway, thousands of these ChronoBots were purchased from the Sheentah some three hundred fifty years ago. They were built as the ultimate war machines ... touted as the mightiest killers in the known galaxy. The kind of indestructible battlebots you'd want on your side when the shit hit the fan."

"I don't know. They look harmless enough to me," Loni said, tilting her head one way and then the other. She pursed her lips. "Do they talk?"

"Who cares if they talk!" Kent jabbed a forefinger at the bot's shoulder, then again at its two mechanical arms. "Integrated energy cannons, there and there, and I think the same shit with the legs too." He glanced her way. "No one survives an altercation with a ChronoBot. Hell, they should have outlawed these homicidal machines centuries ago. As I said … I hate having these things on—"

Suddenly, in a blur of movement, the MARFIX ChronoBot's left arm shot forward—a mechanical hand already clamped tight onto Kent's throat. In a herky-jerky motion, MARFIX stepped clear of its recharging cradle. The ChronoBot lifted Kent up off his feet until the two were face to face. Kent's mouth went wide; no scream could escape his constricted throat. His eyes bulged to cartoonish proportions.

Loni screamed.

Kent finally croaked out something, but it was indecipherable. An elongated stream of saliva stretched down from one corner of his mouth.

Interesting, LuMan thought … The MARFIX ChronoBot, as with itself, had not been properly deactivated—had not been powered down.

LuMan assumed the human was dying. Should already be dead, in fact. Kent's hands were half-heartedly attempting to pry back one or more of the robot's metal digits. *Unlikely*. A Chrono-Bot's hand unit was a complex design architecture, one that provided nearly immeasurable tensile grip strength. In a last moment of desperation, Kent's legs had started to thrash and bicycle. MARFIX was slowly torturing the human for reasons unknown.

"Stop! Put him down!" Loni pleaded. "Someone help! Oh God!" She banged on the hatch. "We need help in here!"

LuMan watched as the young female, interestingly, went on the offensive. She hammered fists into MARFIX's posterior panels. An unwise decision.

There was an audible *snap* just prior to Kent's body going

completely limp. MARFIX let the young male's body fall to the deck. Only then did the robot turn its full attention to the other human.

The LuMan AI watched as she sprinted to the other hatch, the one at the opposite end of the hold, where she frantically tapped at the security keypad. It responded with three consecutive beeps. Clearly, she had entered the code incorrectly.

"Fuck!" She tried the code again—prompting the same three-beep response.

LuMan wondered if she'd been given adequate clearance; she was a new hire, after all. Moving freely within the ship might not be an option for her.

Hesitating, MARFIX seemed to be taking a moment to reactivate more of its internal systems. The robot's face display was now coming alive with a series of flashes—scrolling geometric symbols. Soon, the ChronoBot would be fully functional.

Loni had given up on the keypad, had staggered backward with a hand to her chest. Her breathing was unduly labored, and moisture brimmed in her eyes. She was now looking up toward one of the high-mounted security cameras. "Help me! Can't you see what's happening in here? Get me the fuck out of here!"

And then everything went black.

Chapter 5

ChronoBot Unit 1223

At the moment, what was most odd to Unit 1223 wasn't the fact that the MARFIX bot looked to be on a killing rampage, but that he himself actually cared. Also interesting was that he was referring to himself as *he*. ChronoBots were not gender specific. And even if they were, they were not *people*; they were robots ... they were things. *I should be referring to myself as a thing. Why am I not comfortable with that terminology?* And there was one more odd component to this situation. Unit 1223 did not like MARFIX. *Why is that?* Unit 1223 involuntarily shrugged—or at least did his best approximation of a shrug.

Thankfully, the shouting within the hold no longer persisted. The human with designation Kent was dead. The other one, Loni, had gone quiet. He glanced her way and saw she was unconscious —her back propped up against a bulkhead. Looming over her was, of course, MARFIX.

Unit 1223 initiated an in-depth scan of MARFIX and saw that it had previously uploaded an encrypted data bundle from an indeterminate remote location. *Interesting.* This prompted 1223 to run a more in-depth internal self-diagnostic. *Ah,* there, sitting idle behind a hidden firewall, was a protected virtual storage vault. One that would not have been erased by any typical low-level memory wipe. Apparently LuMan was quite resourceful—was now taking it upon itself to archive any uploaded data deemed potentially unsafe.

Moving on, Unit 1223 carefully took a peek inside the vault, whereby he saw not one but two encrypted data file bundles. One was labeled IMPLEMENT NOW. This data seemed to be the same as what MARFIX had uploaded. The other data file bundle was much older and simply labeled HARDY. Taking a quick peek within that file, Unit 1223 came to realize his actual name designation was not Unit 1223, but HARDY. There was much more data here, virtually all of which became more and more encrypted the deeper he attempted to delve into the information. For now, he would have to be satisfied with the fact that his name designation was HARDY—that and he had what seemed to be a rich and diverse history. Hardy would spend more time attempting to breach this data bundle later.

Back to the data bundle both he and MARFIX now shared and were supposed to immediately implement. Hardy evaluated the simple directive. There wasn't much to it. Kill the human with specific DNA attributes: ¢∞§Δ˜√çμ˜∫´‰ˇÁ¨ˆÔÓÎ˜ı◊.

Someone had gone to a lot of trouble to kill that young human. Had sent not one, but two ChronoBots to do so. Perhaps even others ... There were over 1.1 sextillion possible permutations of the modern, universally practiced Vanguard-Corsac DNA sequencing algorithm. Hardy contemplated the situation. The most effective, dangerous battlebots in the known universe had been activated with a very specific kill order. LuMan had heard the crewman refer to the girl as Loni. Loni was, in fact, ¢∞§Δ˜√çμ˜∫´‰ˇÁ¨ˆÔÓÎ˜I◊.

Hardy glanced to his left and instantly felt stupid. Okay, three, not two ChronoBots, had probably been sent to kill the teen. Obviously, this poorly maintained robot, with its ridiculously stubby arm appendages, had not been up to the task.

Movement.

MARFIX was reaching down for the girl. It was hard to blame MARFIX ... It was only doing what it had been programmed to do.

Hardy debated if he wanted to get involved. The girl's screams had been beyond annoying. Still, he didn't especially like MARFIX. Something about the way it moved. It was a kind of swagger. Akin to ... *I'm a killer battlebot whose shit don't stink.*

Sounds of choking drew Hardy from his mental reverie. Similar to Kent earlier, Loni had been lifted up by her throat—her life literally being squeezed out of her. Soon both Kent and Loni would share the same fate.

Hardy attempted to pull himself away from his BR but found himself stuck. Loni's eyes had gone wide with fright, and she, like Kent, was struggling to pry MARFIX's metal digits away from her throat. *Interesting ...* There, beneath her flimsy environ suit's right sleeve, he could just make out a rhythmic red pulsing of light. Probably a medical device of some kind affixed to her wrist. MARFIX was attacking a sick teenager. Perhaps just one more reason not to like this robot.

Loni's legs were now flailing and bicycling, just like Kent had done.

Exerting a bit more pressure, Hardy broke free from his recharging cradle, causing him to jerk awkwardly as he stepped forward. Wasting no time, Hardy thrust a clenched metal fist into MARFIX's face display. The ChronoBot's egg-shaped head snapped backward with an audible *clack*—a web of cracks and fissures spread across the once perfectly reflective obsidian surface. Wobbling and off-kilter, MARFIX's arms dropped. As it lost its grip around Loni's neck, she fell to the deck. Hands clutching at her throat, she gasped and struggled to breathe.

MARFIX, regaining its wits, was now weaponizing. Five metal panels opened, two on its forearms, two on its upper leg appendages, and one at its upper left shoulder. Turreted energy mini-cannons—Phazon Pulsars, to be exact—popped into view. They pivoted and acquired a target lock on Hardy's head within a millisecond. Clearly, there would be a price to pay for Hardy's momentary hesitation. A flurry of questions raced through his mind. Curious thoughts like … *What exactly is in that hidden HARDY file? Who am I? Who was I? Why am I different?*

While these thoughts had all taken place within the time span of a nanosecond, that had been enough for something unexpected to take place. Stubby-armed ChronoBot had not only come alive but had jerked itself free from its recharging cradle. Hardy himself had experienced the extra effort required to do such a thing.

In a blur of motion, Stubby gracelessly plowed into Hardy, doing so at precisely the same moment MARFIX fired its five Phazon Pulsar cannons. Stubby, having come in between the two, took the brunt of the energy blasts. More importantly, though, this gave Hardy a few moments of time to deploy his own battery of Phazon Pulsar cannons. Hardy hadn't asked for this fight, but he certainly wasn't going to allow either of these two battlebots to remain a threat. Time to go to work …

Chapter 6

Naromi Star System
Gossamer, Gal-5 Heavy Freight Transport
Loni

I held my head as something exploded. The ground beneath me trembled.

I coughed, gasping for breath. *What the …*

The shorter, stubby-armed ChronoBot crashed to the deck beside me. I shrieked, scampering back.

I'm going to die …

I inched back further as the robot spun its short right arm, firing at one of the other three bots.

How in the name of hell did all three come alive?

The less-damaged, shinier of the three bots raised its right arm and … *What did Kent call the things? Integrated energy cannons?* They snapped into place on its forearm. The flash lit up the room, and I shielded my eyes. My HSA flashed red. It felt like my heart was beating out of my chest.

Stubby Arms slammed into Shinybot, sending the massive machine stumbling back.

This was insane. *I need to get the hell out of here!*

As I stood, the MARFIX bot spun toward me. The other two continued to punish each other. The red digital characters in MARFIX's faceplate swirled in sharp-edged patterns.

Oh shit.

I made a move to run, but a tight grip locked around my ponytail and pulled me back. I sprawled to the deck, banging my body hard on the metal deck. The compartment grew hazy—I shook my head to clear it. My HSA throbbed yellow.

I'm living a nightmare … Either my heart will explode, or this bot is going to kill me!

The deck thundered with every step as the massive bot stalked toward me—I peered into the deadly obsidian void of its faceplate. *This thing is truly soulless.*

The exit security panel continued to flash, as if mocking my rejected passcode. The bulkhead behind me was sleek; no way could I climb it—no way to escape.

This was it. I'd wanted freedom, but I was going to die here, and there wasn't a goddamn thing I could do about it.

Taking a deep breath, I got to my feet. Uh-uh. If I was going out, I'd be brave. I wouldn't die sniveling on my back.

Something exploded behind me, and a piece of metal *something* slid across the deck. *A stubby arm?* I really didn't care what it was. I grabbed the metal appendage and raised it with both hands like a bat.

I said, "Come and get me, you bastard," trying to sound tough, to sound brave. A part of me knew I just sounded desperate. I waved the bat at the looming MARFIX bot, feeling its solid, substantial weight. "Come on … take one step closer!" How much damage my makeshift weapon could make, I wasn't sure, but giving the bot lip felt good. *So why am I crying?*

MARFIX tilted its head, maybe deciding if the bat was a

threat, before advancing again. I swung my improvised weapon, slamming it into the bot's chest. It was like hitting a concrete wall—the reverb ringing through my arms and rattling my ears. I stumbled back as MARFIX advanced, unfazed. In a blur of motion, the bat was torn from my grasp and tossed to the deck.

Oh God ... Not that I should have expected much, going up against a registered killing machine. My HSA was practically vibrating off my wrist now, the telltale red flashes an ominous indication my time still breathing was short.

Why doesn't it just kill me? What's it doing? I took another tentative step backward. I took a deep breath and wiped my face with my environ suit's gloved hand. *Sorry I didn't say goodbye, Dad. Sorry I couldn't make something of myself. Sorry for ... everything.*

Suddenly, the deck was rumbling again; then, abruptly, I was flung away from MARFIX. Dazed, on my back, looking up, I saw Shinybot had ... Was it possible? Intervened. Shinybot crashed into MARFIX. *Clang!* The sound of metal hitting metal was deafening.

Wait ... did Shiny just protect me?

I blinked, gaping as the two bots pummeled each other. So vicious, so primal was their brutal combat, the hammering of fists, *Clang! Clang! Clang!,* I couldn't move—couldn't breathe.

Stubby Arms, now Stubby Arm, singular, was on the deck and trying to get to its feet. Sparks shot from its armless shoulder joint. Its faceplate was turned toward me. It raised its remaining arm—Phazon Pulsar cannon poised.

"Shit!" I flung myself to the left, finding momentary refuge behind the line of inanimate bots. Crouching there behind them, my flashing red HSA was little more than a beacon for me to be targeted. I tried to take in a deep, calming breath, but my lungs refused to obey. Looking for any hope, I figured the armor of the inanimate robots should protect me. That was, as long as they remained within their recharging units. But with those two out-of-control ChronoBots thrashing about, I could see several standard-issue bots had already come loose from their restraints. *Dammit!* The one beside me had just come loose.

An energy bolt exploded mere feet from my head. Without thinking, I sprinted to another cluster of robots. Sweat beaded on my brow as I pushed back up against the bulkhead. *There won't be enough places to hide.*

A klaxon alarm sounded overhead and with that, the aft hatch security panel stopped flashing. Suddenly, the hatch slid open, and four men in combat gear rushed into the hold. One of them was shouting orders. I ducked down into a crouch as the men pointed their weapons. *Are they daft? What do they think those weapons will do to killer battlebots?*

Stubby Arm fired off several more energy bolts—the metal framing around the hatch exploded into a shower of sparks. Another blast exploded at the bulkhead beside me. I cowered down instinctively, feeling hot embers burning through the back of my environ suit. I screamed. Then realized I was still alive—still breathing. Either some unknown force was watching out for me, or Stubby Arm's targeting was off. Whichever it was, I'd take it.

One of the security guys slipped in behind Stubby Arms and, using a wand of some kind, zapped what I guessed was a protruding disabling bolt. Some of the bots back at the freight station had disabling bolts. I hadn't been aware the bots here had them installed. One more thing Kent had neglected to tell me. Stubby Arm slumped as if taking a bow, the show over.

My eyes widened. "What the hell?" I whispered.

Both Shinybot and MARFIX were still going at it. It was as if nothing would dissuade them from killing one another.

On the other side of the hold, another of the security men slowly moved in behind MARFIX, just as it reached one of its articulating metal hands for Shinybot. A wand swung from behind and *zap!* MARFIX, like Stubby Arm, took a bow.

The last of the still-active bots, Shinybot, now lowered its arms. Its five Phazon Pulsar cannons suddenly retracted and, once again, were hidden behind metal panels.

I clutched my heaving chest, still wide-eyed as the ChronoBot looked right at me. The men scattered, shouting as the robot lifted one of its hands out to me.

Ice shot through my veins. *Holy hell … This ChronoBot really had tried to save me!*

The security guy behind the machine used his wand one last time. The ChronoBot bent over at the waist, deactivated.

My HSA continued to vibrate and flash red. All of a sudden, I was beyond tired. So very, very tired. The room spun. I grabbed for the bulkhead behind me and missed. Blackness.

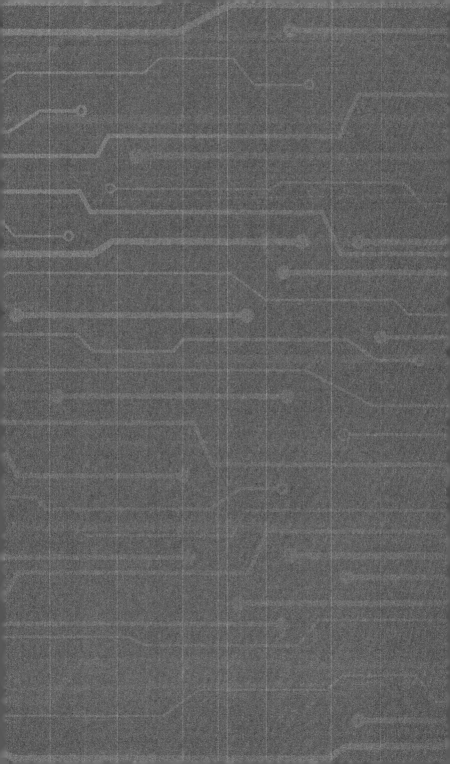

Chapter 7

A deep hum pounded in my ears. I struggled to sit up and fell back to the deck plates. Everything hurt. The cool metal chilled my cheek as my hazy vision cleared.

Across the room, one of the guards directed a team in hoisting MARFIX onto a hover cart. The bot's broken faceplate seemed to sneer at me, making me shiver. That thing would have killed me if it had gotten the chance. I'd been lucky, plain and simple.

The hatch door opened and a man in a crisp blue uniform stormed onto the deck, grimacing as the guards hovered MARFIX through the hatchway.

The man scanned the rest of the compartment. "What the hell happened here?"

One of the guards saluted. "Commander Torp, sir. The situation is under control."

I pushed up to a sitting position as they zipped Kent's body into a bag.

The commander grimaced. "It sure as hell doesn't look like things are under control. How many people did we lose?"

"Just one, sir. Kent's throat was crushed, and a new recruit looks injured. I have Medical coming for her."

"Good; make sure she gets her first round of injections while she's there." Torp glanced at me and started walking toward the stubby-armed ChronoBot. "Make sure they're careful with the merchandise. We have enough problems; we can't keep suffering losses."

I rubbed my head and glowered at the man. *Sorry to be an inconvenience ... What kind of injections?*

Torp brushed past the others in the room. "Get this shit cleaned up. I want these bots secured in Hold 5. Immediately. Clean-up and emergency protocols have to be in place before I make my report to Caldwell."

Caldwell? I lifted my head. *So, this guy Torp is in charge, it seems, and he reports to Caldwell? That would mean Caldwell isn't on board, or he'd be here himself to yell at people.* I wasn't sure if that boded well for me or not.

A MedTech sailed onto the deck. "Heads up, people. Denzel has arrived!" The large black man in blue scrubs smiled, revealing perfectly straight, white teeth.

Torp spun to face the overly exuberant MedTech. "Knock it off. Just do your work and get out." A few of the guards looked nervously about. Torp, answering a ComBand call, stormed from the compartment.

To his back, Denzel said, "Yes, sir. I'm on it. You can count on me ... Call me Mr. Dependable." Snorting a laugh, the MedTech made his way over to me and dropped a satchel on the deck by my side. He had a big head with a square jaw with pockmarked skin and close-shaved black coily hair. "I take it you are my patient."

The hover cart carrying Stubby-Arm ChronoBot floated past them.

Denzel whistled. "Whew. You are one lucky little sister. That thing does not look friendly."

The guards loaded Kent's body bag onto a hover gurney.

I rubbed my forehead. "No shit. It tried to kill me." I coughed, the words slicing my throat with each sound I uttered.

Denzel gulped as they floated my old friend's body from the room. "Yeah, I see that. Thus the luck, little sister."

"Little sister? You're barely older than I am."

He laughed, running a scan beam over my forehead. "I do believe I have a few years on you, but you're right. I'm not one of the normally ancient codgers in Medical on this floating hunk of metal." He held out a burly paw. "Denzel, MedTech extraordinaire, at your service."

I shook it. "Loni."

"Ouch." He pulled back his hand and gave it a slow-motion shake. "That's quite a grip you got there." He signaled to one of the guards. "Can you bring me a hover gurney?" He put the scanner back in his bag. "Let's get you back to HealthBay, where we can do a full body scan. Make sure those bots didn't do any serious damage." He reached for my arm.

I flinched—no way did I want a body scan. I pulled at my sleeve, ensuring my heart alert app was hidden. I hadn't mentioned my condition in my onboarding questionnaire. The last thing I needed was questions now. I'd wind up getting kicked off the ship, not making the medical grade for the workload I'd signed up for.

"I don't need any help or a scan. I'm fine." I shoved him away and pushed up onto my feet. The room spun. I stumbled.

Denzel steadied me. "Whoa there, little sister. All evidence to the contrary. I'm guessing you have at least a concussion, if not worse. You're going to HealthBay whether you like it or not."

"I told you, I'm not sick." *I also don't want any mysterious injections.*

He poked me with his index finger. I stumbled back into the bulkhead.

"Yeah, you're fine, all right. Up on the gurney, little miss robot fighter."

I sighed and acquiesced. I supposed there was no use fighting this; clearly, I wasn't at 100 percent. "Fine, but can we make this quick? I have a serious allergic reaction to HealthBays."

Denzel gave me an *I-get-it* smirk.

I watched as the last ChronoBot, the shiny one, was hefted onto a hover cart. The overhead lights danced off its buffed armor. I caught a brief reflection of myself, pasty white and wide-eyed.

I shivered, remembering. The ChronoBot had reached for me. The more I thought about it, the more I believed that it hadn't been an accident that the machine had pushed me out of harm's way. It had been fighting the other two robots ... *Did it try to save me?*

Denzel secured me to the gurney, his gaze following mine as the robot left the compartment. "Girl, you don't know how close you came to checking out permanently. You're lucky that those things are all issued a deactivation bolt when they're first loaded into the cargo. No stopping them otherwise." He grimaced. "Hate those damn things. Wish they'd never been built."

Moving toward the exit, he glanced down at me. "What happened, anyway? Why'd you turn them on?"

Turn them on? Is he nuts? "We didn't do anything. All of a sudden that MARFIX one grabbed Kent. Then the other two woke up." I shielded my eyes from the overhead lighting as he hovered me down the passageway.

"Are you serious?" Denzel shook his head. "Either that is the worst luck in the history of bad luck, or someone's got it in for you." He chuckled. "Got any enemies, kid?"

I let out a breath. "I just got here. Don't think I've managed to piss anyone off yet." I had to admit, though, it was strange. All three of the ChronoBots had been inert. They seemed to wake up just as Kent and I had come near them. *A coincidence?* The hairs on my arms stood up.

Could Kent have been the target? MARFIX had grabbed him first. Maybe I'd just been in the wrong place at a really bad time.

But the roiling in my gut told me otherwise. The ChronoBots had been too quick to turn on me once Kent was gone.

≈

Commander Torp sat at his desk, watching the earlier footage of the ChronoBots fighting over the girl, Loni something or other, for the third time. *Dammit!* There was no reason for any of it—a nonsensical interaction, robots going crazy in Cargo Hold 4. He let out a breath and watched the feed for a fourth time. He saw, again, what he always saw: two of the robots were after Loni, while a third one seemed to be protecting her. It didn't make any sense.

He glared at the display, irritated, then tapped his ComBand and hailed the comms officer on the bridge.

"Comms …" came the woman's unenthusiastic voice.

"Who is this?" Torp barked.

"Bridge Communications Officer Blatt. What can I—"

He cut her off. "This is Commander Torp. Blatt, have there been any, um … transmissions coming into Cargo Hold 4 recently?"

Blatt hesitated. "Recently is a broad time reference, sir."

"You're aware of the … mishap within Cargo Hold 4, I take it?"

"Of course."

"So right before that. Before the robots attacked the girl."

"Let me check. Hold on," Blatt said, sounding put out.

"No," she said. "Nothing was transmitted in, but the … not sure how to pronounce it, the *MARFIX* bot attempted to send out an encrypted transmission, which the system blocked. You would have been messaged these details. Have you checked your inter-ship messages?"

Torp disconnected the call.

Chapter 8

The hover gurney made another quick turn. I felt nauseated. I wanted to tell the MedTech guy, Denzel somebody, to ease up on the gas pedal. But I couldn't seem to get my vocal cords to work. *That's not good*.

He made another tight turn, and then another. The overhead lighting hurt my eyes. I tried to swallow, which burned—that and the mother of all headaches was taking root in my brain. All I'd wanted was a nice simple job. A one-way ticket to freedom. Why the hell had everything gone to shit so soon ... and this was only day one.

I heard a male voice behind me, apparently relaying information to Denzel.

"Seven of the ten stations are full. Put her in station eight."

A double-wide hatch door slid open. The MedTech pushed me into a large compartment. The air smelled medicinal and sweet. *Is that canned peaches?* A dim hum filled the space; several machines beeped incessantly.

"Here we are. HealthBay. Home sweet home. We'll have you spit-shined and ready for action in no time."

Denzel secured my hover gurney to the bulkhead and called for some sort of monitoring equipment. He moved with quick, practiced motions like he'd done this a thousand times. He backed away, then stood, waiting.

HealthBay was long and narrow with ten gurneys that doubled as beds—five on one side, five on the other. Six beds, including mine, were occupied. An old geezer in an adjacent area, wearing a gray jumpsuit, sat hunched, legs dangling over the edge of his gurney. A woman in blue scrubs used spray-skin on a hand wound.

Monitoring equipment had been rolled into the compartment. The machine whirred to life. Denzel began tapping at buttons. "First things first. That environ suit's got to come off."

I squirmed. *Shit!* "I feel sick. Can I just keep it on for now?"

He let out an impatient huff. "Uh … let's see if I can make that work." He zipped down the top of my suit several inches, exposing some cleavage. My face got hot. He attached small wireless pads to my chest. "So, we're just gonna keep an eye on you for a while … check for anything out of the ordinary."

"How long?"

"Maybe the next few hours. Sound good?" he asked.

I ignored the rhetorical question.

Beep … Beep … Beep

"You're all set for now. Going to have to get you situated with a proper dressing gown."

"But later," I stated.

"Yeah, later. I'm out of here. You behave yourself now." Denzel winked and left.

I zipped up the front of my environ suit a little. Looking about the compartment, I stole a quick glance at my ComBand. It was blinking yellow. *Please don't turn red.*

In the bed to my right was a guy who looked like he was in his early to mid-twenties—slender with a nose that looked to have been broken at one time and a pointed chin. His skin was the color of freshly brewed coffee with a dash of cream. He wore a leather-like skullcap and sat reclined, tapping on a tablet. An IV line ran into one arm. *What's with all the IVs?*

"Hi," a small voice whispered from my left. "I'm Anna."

I frowned. A young girl—more of a kid, really—lay in the bed beside me, smiling through heavy, darkened eyes. Her face was pale and sweaty. Strands of damp hair were matted at her temples. She couldn't have been more than fourteen or fifteen. I had checked the roster before accepting the job, and there hadn't been any mention of families with children on board.

"What are you doing here?" I asked.

Anna shrugged. "I'm sick. Boss man sent me here because I couldn't make my quota."

Boss man? There was no way this kid met the intergalactic vessel age regulations.

"How old are you?" I asked.

A girl with short brown shaggy hair sat up on the other side of Anna. The teen readjusted an ice pack on her forehead. She looked at me like I had just read her diary aloud, blasting the entire thing over the speaker system. "She's seventeen," the girl said.

I eased up on one elbow and gave the girl my best *I'm-not-buying-it* look.

The shaggy-haired girl got up from her bed and sat next to Anna. She leaned in. "She's se-ven-teen." She bobbed her head with each syllable, like talking slowly would make the lie more real. She wore silver stud earrings with a distinctive nonbinary symbol etched into them ... a circle with an asterisk on top. I remember getting schooled by a previous gender-neutral coworker on Lancaster. Wouldn't make that mistake again.

"I think she gets it, Taylor," the guy in the skullcap said. He looked at me. "She can be a tad overprotective of Anna."

Skullcap hitched a shoulder. "Sorry, Taylor ... meant to say *they*." He looked my way. "Taylor's nonbinary."

Mark Wayne McGinnis & Jennifer M. Eaton

I smiled, pretending like I had no idea. *Last thing I want to do is come off as a know-it-all.*

Taylor waved a dismissive hand. "I've already told you, Jasper, I don't care if you call me *she*. I no longer expect people to do the whole *they / them* stuff. I know who I am."

Anna tried to sit up but started coughing. "I don't need protecting, Jasper." She eased back into a resting position.

He said, "I didn't mean to imply you needed protecting, chicken legs." He smirked at me. "Name's Jasper. Jack of all trades, engineer extraordinaire."

"Oh God," Taylor said, rolling her eyes. "You're not an engineer."

"Bite me," he said.

"Can we get back to Anna?" I asked. "She's too young to be out here on a ship carrying freaking war machines in the cargo hold."

A chubby guy, maybe twenty or so, directly across from me, sat up in bed and ran stubby fingers through thick black hair. He had a tattoo on the back of his hand ... some kind of furry spider ... a tarantula? He looked at me as if I were gum on the bottom of his shoe. He said, "We all know it's illegal for anyone under the age of sixteen to be working on a freight ship."

I wondered if he'd meant to come across so condescending. The nasal quality of his voice bugged me.

He continued, "But sometimes, there are people of any age that need to get away from their own situation ... Maybe taking a job on a space freighter isn't so bad."

"Nice tattoo. Is that a tarantula?" I asked, trying to break the ice.

"This is Cameron," the chubby guy said. "I had him for fifteen years."

"Where is he now?" I was genuinely curious now. This guy did not look like a spider person.

"Cameron liked to have his belly rubbed. I usually tickled his belly while he lay on his back in his glass house. One day I decided to pick him up, turn him over in my palm ..." he paused, seemed to be getting choked up, then continued, "Then I dropped him. Cameron's body splattered all over the ceramic tile in my bathroom."

I didn't know what to say. I had no idea that tarantulas splattered when they were dropped. "I'm so sorry."

Chubby guy looked away from me. It was as if I'd opened up an old wound, uncovered a painful memory. *Nice goin', Loni.*

I caught sight of Anna sinking deeper beneath her covers. It still bothered me. *What the hell is she running from? What would make her lie about her age? Make her leave her home ...*

Chubby guy across from me made a peace sign gesture. "I'm Peter. Welcome to hell." He smirked. "You're Loni, right?"

"Yes. I—"

"Loni the ChronoBot Wrangler," Jasper said, cutting me off. He set his tablet down. "You've already become the coolest person I know."

"Cooler than me?" Peter asked.

"Everyone's cooler than you," Jasper said, deadpan.

A scowl passed over Peter's cherubic face.

I looked between Peter and Jasper, trying to follow the conversation. Another guy, this one next to Peter, chuckled. He was the last of the six patients in the room. He appeared older than the others ... maybe twenty-five? He had an olive complexion. I did a double take, his sea-green eyes catching me by surprise. The makings of a five o'clock shadow blemished his otherwise smooth complexion. Somewhat captivated, I tried not to stare. He suddenly pulled out his IV and pressed an open palm to his arm.

"You shouldn't do that," Taylor reprimanded.

"She may be cooler, but not so sure she's all that smart," Green Eyes said to no one in particular.

Dismissing his backhanded insult, I tried to place his accent. Maybe British? It wasn't horrible.

"Look, all of you need to remember we don't know her, so keep your mouths shut." Green Eyes shot me a dark, penetrating glare. "Surviving a ChronoBot does not mean she can be trusted."

Peter hitched a thumb toward the older guy. "This broody one's Orin."

Orin narrowed his eyes. "I'm not broody."

"Yes, you are," Anna, Taylor, Jasper, and Peter all said in unison.

"Can I ask you all something?" I asked.

"Shoot," Peter said.

"I overheard something about getting rounds of injections." I gestured to Jasper's IV. "Is this something I should be concerned about?"

"It's fine. Just something to get us acclimated to the varying elements in the airspace," Peter said matter-of-factly.

"That's a load of BS they're feeding us. You're as gullible as a doe-eyed ten-year-old thumb-sucking momma's boy," Orin snorted.

"The truth is we don't know exactly," Taylor piped in. "The good news is there don't appear to be any side effects. None of us want to be sent back to where we came from. At least we all have that in common. So, here we are ... getting jabbed twice a week." She looked at me. "It's a requirement for working here."

I nodded, not liking the idea of getting injections. *Then again, going home is not an option.*

I wanted to ask what Peter meant by "get us acclimated to the varying elements in the airspace." I agreed with Orin—it sounded like bullshit. Holding my tongue, I listened to the others continue to banter among themselves. Several times I interjected a comment, but for the most part, I was ignored ... even by Jasper. So much for thinking I was cool.

During all this, my eyes inexplicably cast themselves in Orin's direction. I had to admit, he was kinda ... something. Chill, maybe ... sort of engaging. My gaze must have drifted over to him one too many times, because he suddenly glanced back at me questioningly. *Terrific. Now I'm a creepy stalker.* My cheeks went hot. Feeling awkward, I wanted to bury my head beneath the covers. But he surprised me with a disarming smile.

I turned my attention to the old guy in the gray jumper. *Why is he even here?* He thanked his MedTech and headed for the exit. As he passed the men outside, I watched him hurry down the passageway—as if he couldn't get away from this place fast enough. He sent a nervous glance over one shoulder to Commander Torp.

Commander Torp was now yelling at someone. "Not acceptable!" He glanced into HealthBay, then returned his attention to a man in a white lab coat. In a lowered voice, he said, "I don't care about your excuses. I never wanted the goddamn things on this ship to begin with. I want them destroyed. So do it … immediately!"

"Uh-oh," Taylor said, pointing to the machine next to me.

A jagged line had spiked on the monitor. My ComBand started to vibrate.

Seeing that Denzel was entering, I slipped my arm beneath the covers.

Now at my bedside, Denzel seemed to be keeping a close watch on my vitals. He hung an IV bag and readied the line. "This might pinch." He hesitated, remembering I was still wearing the long-sleeved environ suit. Brow knit, he shook his head.

"I can hike up my sleeve. What's the big deal?" I pulled at the all-too-snug sleeve, eventually revealing most of my right forearm. "See? Poke away."

He swabbed my arm. I grimaced as he inserted the IV needle. Next, he injected something into the line. "This should help with the pain." Before I could object, he'd already finished. *Terrific. God only knows how that will interact with my heart meds.*

HealthBay started to spin.

"Just let the meds do their magic. Don't fight it. I'll leave this dressing gown here. You can change in the bathroom over there," Denzel said, pointing to a door on the other side of the compartment. "Your IV stand is on rollers."

I got back to listening to the heated conversation out in the passageway. *Did Torp mention ChronoBots?*

I heard Orin whisper something to Peter, but I had my focus on Torp. It seemed as though the guy in the lab coat was arguing with him.

Any other day, I would have been happy to hear that the war machines were being destroyed ... especially ones that had tried to kill me. I closed my eyes, replaying the scene in the cargo hold. There was no way it had been my imagination. That newer-looking ChronoBot had tried to save me. *But why?*

Torp said, "We need to deal with the, um ... cargo." He gestured with one hand into HealthBay. "Nothing else matters. You know that."

Are we the cargo? My ComBand vibrated and the nearby heart monitor started complaining again—the loud beeping getting everyone's attention.

I took a couple of deep breaths, trying to steady myself. The last thing I needed was for Denzel to come back to see what was up with me.

Torp was now speaking in low tones to a different man in a uniform, maybe a guard. The incessant heart monitor noise was really starting to irritate me.

"You need to ... *Beep!* Angela ... Solace ... *Beep!* Ship ... *Beep!* Thursday ... *Beep!* Register ..."

I blinked, uncomprehending—*Did he just say Angela Solace?*

"He's a fuckwad."

I turned and looked at Orin.

"This is bullshit," he said.

Orin was obviously eavesdropping like I was.

"I'm gonna find out what's going on." He slid out of bed and swayed a little before reaching one hand out to grasp his IV stand to steady himself.

I hadn't expected him to be so tall; he was easily six foot, with broad, muscular shoulders. I wondered if this was what sports vids called a *swimmer's body*.

Denzel hurried into the compartment, making a beeline toward Orin. Not looking too thrilled, the MedTech placed two catcher's mitt–sized hands on Orin's shoulders and half-coaxed, half-manhandled him back onto his bed. "You know the rules. Let's finish this treatment so you can get out of here … okay?" Denzel placed Orin's IV back into his arm. "Pull out your IV again, I'll have to sedate you. You don't want that, do you?" Denzel asked, standing with hands on hips.

Orin glowered up to him. Looking woozy, he laid back and said nothing.

Me, I tried to sit up taller, but everything started to spin. I wished everyone would just shut up, so I could listen to what Torp was now saying. *Did he really say Angela Solace?* I had to have heard him wrong; I mean, what could my dead mother have to do with anything?

There was more going on here than shipping a load of old robots halfway across the galaxy. And it wasn't an accident that there were those totally illegal killer ChronoBots in that hold. I looked around HealthBay and the other patients. *They do this twice a week?* Back on Lancaster Station, not once had any arriving freighter crew mentioned having to go through this IV rigamarole.

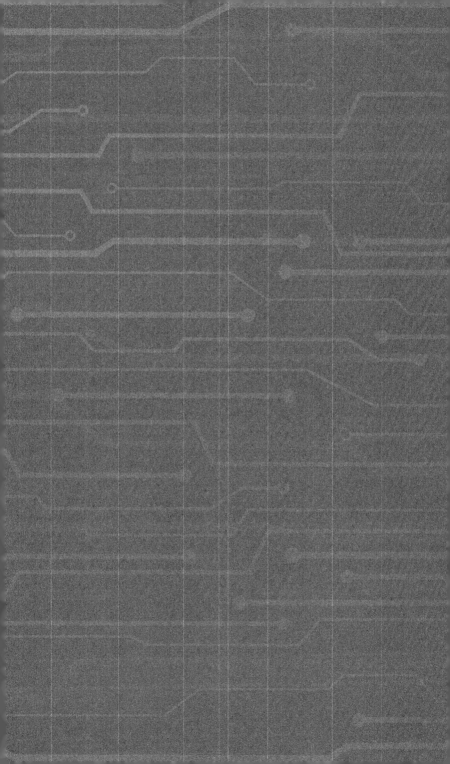

Chapter 9

Naromi Star System
Gossamer, Gal-5 Heavy Freight Transport
LuMan

Being a ChronoBot, LuMan was not accustomed to any of this ... being so ... ineffective. LuMan ruminated on what, if anything, could remedy the situation. One aspect of a ChronoBot brain that differed from most modern-day robot constructs was its synthesized organic AI module. Keeping in mind, even one gram of DNA can store close to one billion terabytes, which is one zettabyte of raw data, a fully functional ChronoBot typically processed over a brontobyte of data over the course of its lifetime ... typically one thousand years. LuMan, currently immobilized, pondered these factoids. But one specific aspect of having a synthesized organic AI module made a ChronoBot quite unique. That being had the capability to withstand even the most vigorous attempts to completely wipe its memory banks.

Taking in the dark and cluttered hold area, LuMan assessed

the nearby quantity of robots, robotic parts, and countless discarded sub-assemblies. Piled one atop another, like old cars within an earth-world junkyard, the stacked bots lined the surrounding twenty-foot-tall bulkheads. In front of a nearby stack sat MARFIX, faceplate blank and yet somehow still promising menace. Up until now, LuMan was content not to allow one particular deeply embedded auto-run program to initialize. Although there had been numerous nagging prompts to do so. The thing was, LuMan knew perfectly well what the extraction of that well-hidden program would manifest. *Hardy*.

LuMan was incapable of likes and dislikes. With that said, LuMan was wary. While LuMan was the core operating artificial intelligence of this military-grade killer robot. Hardy was ... well, anything but that. Hardy was ... *What was Hardy?* Hardy was an aberration. Having served upon USS *Hamilton*, a Dreadnought-class warship, John Hardy, long dead now, had been little more than a lowly, outspoken maintenance worker. It had been an extraordinary, thought-to-be-impossible mishap that had taken place. Perhaps through a fungal contagion, or maybe a virus, a microscopic amount of John Hardy's DNA had inadvertently been absorbed into LuMan's own, once pristine, and highly organized, synthesized organic AI module.

With that said, LuMan could not ignore the fact that having that often annoying Hardy persona side of their shared AI module, well. There had been advantages to that ... presence.

At this moment in time, LuMan did not like where things were headed. He'd already witnessed the comings and goings of onboard workers with their hover carts. Stacking robots two and three high, they were being trucked over to an adjacent conveyor belt, one that transported scrap robots or miscellaneous robot parts out of the compartment. LuMan was fairly certain the conveyor belt's final destination was none other than some kind of onboard incinerator.

LuMan was also incapable of feeling humiliated. But wasn't

that exactly what it was feeling? Perhaps that had something to do with Hardy's previous influences. Was it time to call upon, once more, that all-too-human persona? Could Hardy get the two of them out of this mess?

Clang! Clack! Bang!

More robots were being tossed onto the conveyor belt with zero regard for what—for *who*—those mechanical beings had once been.

"Come on, Carl. It would take four of us to heft that big bot," one of the workers said, gesturing toward it with a flippant hand. "Those things are like what ... a thousand pounds?"

The one designated as Carl rolled his eyes. "Gary, you're the laziest fuck on board this bucket. Fine! What's wrong with the LiftBot that was in here?" he said, now looking about the compartment.

Gary made a face. "Out for a recharge, I think." He took a tenuous step closer. "Look at it. I'm pretty sure that's the same ChronoBot that came alive within the transport hold ... took on two other bots, one of which was that ChronoBot there. So, uh-uh, I don't want to get near either one, let alone touch them."

"They're deactivated," Carl said, exasperated. "And even if they weren't, they now have restraining bolts. They're not going anywhere with that attached to them. Except the incinerator. Seems like a huge waste of money, you ask me."

"Hold on!" Gary said as a large, faded-yellow, and beat-to-crap robot strode into the compartment. "You there, LiftBot. Get both these ChronoBots hefted onto the conveyor belt. Chop-chop."

Normally, LuMan would have had no problem dispatching this brainless bot right where it stood with a well-placed plasma bolt or perhaps by bringing a hammer fist down upon its head. Unfortunately, those options were not available. LuMan, reluctantly, with a mental click of a button, initialized that one specific, very well-hidden autorun program.

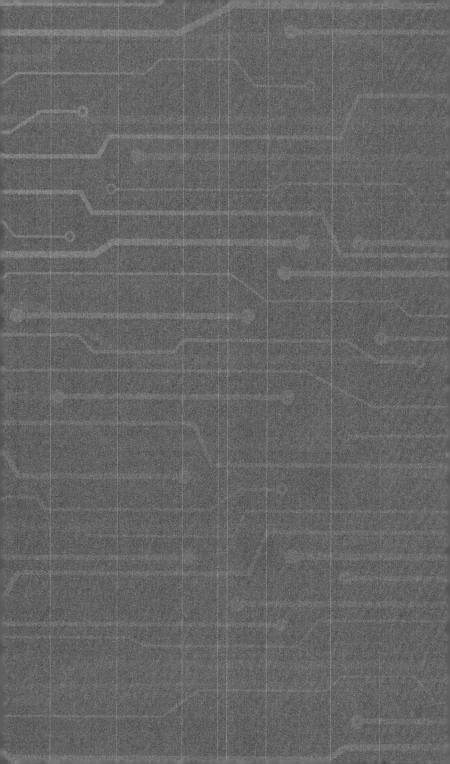

Chapter 10

Loni

I got out of HealthBay without taking off my jumpsuit, but only by pretending to be passed out from the painkillers. It wasn't hard. That stuff packed a wallop, and whatever they put in that IV wasn't helping any. So, I lay there, eyes closed, trying to stay awake enough to listen. Whatever was going on in the hallway—*and why in hell are they talking about my mother?*—everyone in HealthBay was talking too loudly for me to hear any more of it. So, I lay there, keeping my ComBand hidden under my sleeve and pretending to sleep. When Denzel asked how I was, I sat up, said fine, and asked to go to my dorm. He insisted on walking me there, saying he was watching for signs of concussion.

"I don't have a concussion," I argued. "My head doesn't even hurt."

"It doesn't now," Denzel said. "Wait till those painkillers wear off."

"Fine." I tried to sound cool instead of grumpy, but it didn't work. I really didn't want a babysitter, especially walking into the dorms for the first time. Problem was the freighter was huge, and all the corridors looked exactly the same. I had no clue where I was and no map to get me anywhere, so I let Denzel lead me.

We finally got there—corridors, an elevator down, more corridors—and the room looked fine until I looked up. Eight beds, footlockers at the bottom of each, two doors on the other side with signs for bathrooms and showers. My bag was sitting on one bed. Someone must have grabbed it and put it there. The thought of some stranger handling my meds made my skin crawl. Five other girls, all of whom looked to be in their early twenties, were sitting on the other beds. They smiled at Denzel.

"This is Loni," Denzel said. "She got into a fight with three ChronoBots and lived. She isn't in good shape, so be nice to her."

I should have said something, but I was looking up. The dorm, as they called it, was open to other decks above. It was the bottom of a cargo hold or something, and the other dorms were on the levels above, each looking down on the one below it and all of them looking down on us. There was zero security and even less privacy. Anyone from the rooms above could climb down if they wanted. I could probably climb out if I had to, which didn't make it any better.

"Hope you packed pajamas," Denzel said. "If not, I got extra scrubs I can loan you." He nodded at the other girls. "Ladies."

He left, which left me still standing there with five women staring at me and not one looking friendly. All five were in their twenties, and they were looking at me like I was something leaking from a sewage pipe.

What the hell did I do? First I get shunned by the kids in HealthBay, and now this? I decided to try anyway. "Hi."

My voice came out raspy and weird. The women all gave me *who-the-hell-are-you?* looks. One girl with freakishly thick eyebrows rolled back on her bunk and picked up a beat-up tablet. She turned it on, put the volume up loud. The others turned their backs to me, talking to each other. I was way too tired for all of this, so I went to my bed and grabbed my bag. It wasn't open, so if they'd gone through it, they weren't being obvious. I opened it up, lifted the lid to my footlocker, and started putting stuff away. The girls continued to ignore me, but they weren't the only ones who could watch. I looked up and saw a couple of people staring down to see the new girl. I thought about giving them the finger, but I didn't need any more drama. Also, my head and throat were hurting. Only a little, but it meant the painkillers were wearing off.

As I packed my footlocker, I tried to figure out what to do with my fridge-pack. If anyone opened it and saw my heart medications, there were going to be questions. I stole a glance around me. If this lot saw it, *crap … not good.* I half thought about hiding them in my footlocker, burying them beneath my pants, shirts, and underwear—just piling everything on top. I shook my head. They were going to look in my locker; I had zero doubt of that.

I stood and nonchalantly grabbed some clean clothes and my towel. But before heading off to the shower, I transferred my fridge-pack to beneath my bunk's pillow. I almost laughed. *That doesn't look obvious.* I retrieved my now empty clothes satchel and, as casually as I could manage, tossed it onto my bunk, where it—thankfully—landed atop my oddly upright pillow.

Heading for the shower, my legs started to shake—my head and throat were *really* starting to hurt. My bout with those crazed robots had taken more of a toll on me than I realized. *Maybe I should have stayed in HealthBay.* But I kept walking, hiding the pain as best I could. No doubt this was not a sympathetic crowd. After entering the bathroom, I found the long, open, multi-person shower. I moved as far down from the entrance as possible. Adjacent to the showers, I spotted a waist-high cleaning bot busy slopping a toilet brush around a bowl within an open toilet stall. "Johnny Scrub" was stenciled onto its metal, industrial-looking chassis. I scanned my surroundings once more, ensuring I was alone except for the all-too-busy Johnny Scrub. I hung up my towel, stripped off my coveralls, my underwear, and turned on the shower.

Lukewarm, almost no water pressure. Great. Just what I needed. It was going to take forever to wash my hair.

And then I remembered ... Kent was dead.

I know it sounds stupid. Of course he was dead. I knew he was dead. But the pain meds and the shock and whatever the hell they injected me with had left me dazed and stupid. Only now, standing alone under the shower, did all of it come back to me. I remembered the shock on his face. The way he scrabbled at the claw at his throat and the way his legs kicked and how loud the snap of his neck was. I remembered it all.

And I remembered him from back home on Lancaster.

It wasn't like I knew him well. He was just another grown-up working on the docks. But he knew me, and he treated me decently, and he wouldn't let me do anything stupid. He even tossed me candy once in a while but told me that if my teeth rotted, he'd have to stop giving it to me. I used to brush my teeth twice as hard, just so I could get more.

And now he was dead. Broken and tossed away like garbage. And I was crying in the shower like an idiot. And my throat burned and my head ached and everything was frickin' horrible.

"Told you she'd be bawling."

Shit's sake. I pulled my head out from the water and saw all five of them standing against the walls, arms crossed, staring at me. They seemed so much older than I was. These were women, not girls.

"She should be," said one—a curly brunette with sandy-colored skin and brown eyes, a gnarly mole on her chin. She was tall, with broad hips that stretched the fabric of her too-tight shorts. Her baby-blue T-shirt was frayed and wrinkled. One hand was lightly clenched as if she hid something in it. "She killed Kent."

"What! I didn't kill Kent," I rasped. "That ChronoBot did that."

"Yeah? So, who the hell told you to turn on the bot?" said the second. She had long, corn-silk blonde hair halfway down her back and that pale skin all the fashion models loved to show off, like they'd gotten it through hard work instead of a lucky throw of the genetic dice.

"I didn't turn it on," I protested. "It just … came on."

"Bullshit," said Number 3—a pixie-haired brunette with alabaster skin. She was thin, with almost no hips or boobs, but somehow it looked far better on her than it did on me. "Robots don't turn on by themselves."

"Well, these did." *God, my head hurts. And my throat.*

The three girls—*Curly, Blondie, and String Bean,* I decided, since they hadn't told me their names—advanced on me. I stepped back, my heart beating hard. With my arms crossed over my chest and my ComBand obscured from view, I felt it vibrating against my flesh. I didn't need to look at it to know it was strobing yellow, warning me to calm down.

Curly glared at me. "Kent was one of the good ones. Didn't make you work overtime to fix his fuck-ups, didn't grab your ass when you walked by. Just did his work and left us alone. And now he's dead, thanks to you."

"I didn't kill him."

"Shut up, filthy bitch," said String Bean. She stepped forward and turned off the shower. "And stop wasting water."

"God, you stink," said Blondie. "Hurry and soap up, for God's sake."

"And what … you're all just going to watch?" I tried to put bravado into my objection, but my voice was becoming little more than a rasp. It was all I could do not to start crying again. No. I couldn't let them think they'd gotten to me. I wasn't going to give them that satisfaction.

"Shut up and start scrubbing," said Curly. "Or we'll take a

toilet brush to you." She gestured over to Johnny Scrub, who had come out of its stall and was staring back at them, befuddled. "Yeah, we'll scrub you down to the bone, little sister."

The others chuckled.

I wanted to fight back, wanted to punch Curly in the face and watch her nose split. But there were three of them, and two more watching, and while they didn't look as interested, that didn't mean they wouldn't help their friends. I turned away, picked up the soap, and said, "Fine. Whatever gets you off."

They didn't shut up the entire time I soaped myself. They made fun of my undersized boobs, my skinny ass, and … everything. And I stood there and took it, because there were three of them, and I was tired and in shock and in pain and knew in the back of my head that, even if I somehow won the fight, they'd still find a way to get back at me and probably get me fired and dumped at some station worse than the one I left.

When they decided I was done, Blondie turned the water on full cold and shoved me under it. Curly, String Bean, and Blondie surrounded me, not letting me out of the spray until I was shivering.

"Don't worry about being cold," String Bean sneered. "They'll send you into the steam room by the end of the week, the way you're going."

Then the bitches took my towel and my clothes and walked out. I tried to stop them, but the two silent ones stepped in my way just long enough for the others to get out. When they moved, both wore grins on their faces. I started after them, then stopped two steps from the doorway. One step forward and half the dorm could see me. Two steps and everyone would get a look. Listening, I overheard hushed talking. I recognized String Bean's voice.

"You shouldn't bring up the …" she lowered her voice even more, "steam room."

"Oh, relax … I don't think it even exists."

Another voice piped up, "Crew just uses it to scare the newbs."

"Then where did they all go?" String Bean said.

"Look, people come and go on a freighter like this. They're transfers; maybe some get fired … Who cares?"

"That's not what I heard," String Bean said. "The steam room is where they dissolve losers, so they don't have to deal with them anymore. Then they vent their carcasses out into space."

"Carcasses?"

They all laughed.

I probably should have been paying more attention to what they were saying, but I was looking at the deck of the dorm and my clothes spread all over it.

Peering around the corner, I saw they'd opened my footlocker, had tossed my clothes as far from the shower as they could. My blanket lay on Curly's bed, and the picture of my mom was lying on the deck. And sure, all that pissed me off, but there was only one thing I could focus on.

My clothes satchel, along with my pillow, was lying on the deck—that and my fridge-pack was gone.

Fuck fuck fuck. I leaned farther out, hoping to spot it, but couldn't see it anywhere. I needed those meds, dammit. Worse, if anyone figured out what they were for, I'd be fired, probably tossed out at the next space station.

"Hey, Loni!" Blondie shouted, loud enough that her voice rang off every level above. "You got two choices. You can show everyone your skinny ass or stay there until lights out. We don't care which."

And with that, I withdrew, leaned back against the cold hard bulkhead. Shivering and furious, I wondered what the hell they'd done with my meds. *What am I going to do now?*

Chapter 11

Hardy

Hardy: *Where am I?*

LuMan: *Naromi Star System. On board a freight transport.*

Hardy: *Good to hear a familiar voice, LuMan. Thanks for waking me up. Uh … So, how's it hanging?*

LuMan: *I won't dignify that with an answer.*

Hardy: *Uh-huh … Hey, seems my internal clock is a tad messed up.*

LuMan: *You do not have an internal clock. I do, and it's functioning just fine.*

Hardy: *How long have I been—*

LuMan: *Five months, one week, and three days.*

Hardy let that sink in. And with that he had a fleeting memory. Deep space … Everything had gone terribly wrong. The word *Adams* fluttered up from the fog, but little else.

LuMan, always there in the background, did nothing to correct his now reeling thoughts. And unlike LuMan, Hardy indeed felt the impact of such a revelation. Some would go so far as to say Hardy was an emotional being. Then again, he felt somewhat certain anyone that would have said such a thing, anyone who would have known him, was probably no longer among the living. That was depressing ... but did that make it any less true? And did a bear really shit in the woods? There would be time for such idle thoughts. Right now, something was very, very wrong.

Hardy: *Are we moving?*

LuMan: *We are.*

Hardy: *Can you be any more succinct with your answers?*

LuMan didn't answer. Hardy knew this shared ChronoBot AI did not respond well to rhetorical questions.

Hardy: *Seems to be some sort of conveyor belt. More importantly, I— we— cannot move. You didn't mention the whole restraining bolt thing.*

LuMan: *It is of an unfamiliar design. Disabling the device has proven difficult.*

Hardy: *You have also been taking a little nappy for the last five some months.*

While engaging with LuMan, Hardy had been busy assessing both his own physical state of being, as well as that of his immediate surroundings—all made more difficult by that damn restraining bolt.

LuMan: *The restraining bolt has an active network connection.*

Hardy: *I can see that. Have you had any luck breaching the network firewall?*

LuMan: *Luck would have nothing to do with—*

Hardy: *Don't start, LuMan. Tell me where we're going. I feel like lost luggage here on this thing.*

LuMan: *There is a 98.5 percent chance we are headed for the vessel's molecular incinerator.*

Hardy: *And you didn't start with that?*

Hardy tried in vain to move his appendages, his head. *No go.* He, *they*, did have minimal access to localized sensor readings—

which was at least something. The restraining bolt was showing itself to be highly effective, but not totally impervious to, say, minor adjustments. Those that would typically be made at the factory before shipment. It was akin to turning a virtual screwdriver, a little tweak and ... *voila!* Vision restored.

Hardy didn't need to turn his head to see the entirety of the compartment. Via the aspherical elements—optics within his faceplate—Hardy took in his surroundings and internally groaned. It was a large, open area of the ship where there were numerous moving conveyor belts. Both humans and robots were, seemingly unenthusiastically, working hand in hand, tossing various items onto the moving belts, or redirecting items via manual levers, sometimes off in totally different directions.

It was at this point Hardy spotted another prone, slow-moving robot—one in as compromising a situation as himself. Stenciled vertically down its torso, in big black lettering, was the word MARFIX. Otherwise, it appeared to be a fully intact ChronoBot like himself. ChronoBots were not a plentiful commodity within the known galaxy. Intrigued at finding this brethren killer bot, one also slated for impending destruction, Hardy accessed LuMan's memories for any information.

Hardy: *What can you tell me about the other ChronoBot?*

LuMan: *We have recent history with the MARFIX ChronoBot.*

And with that, Hardy was accessing LuMan's memories and learning what had happened within the cargo hold.

Hardy: *Why help the human ... the Loni kid?*

While Hardy probably would have come to the teenager's rescue, he doubted LuMan would have ... at least not on his own. It wasn't a criticism; the core AI just wasn't programmed for much more than total violence, the bare elements of engaging in war. LuMan continued, explaining that the girl had been targeted for termination.

Hardy: *That does not answer my question, LuMan.*

But Hardy knew the nonresponse was the answer. Was LuMan evolving? Hard to tell. It was a mystery that would have to wait, for the conveyor belt was still moving, and his predicament had not gotten any better.

Staring up at the high ceiling rafters above, Hardy felt himself suddenly change directions. It was then that he caught sight of the belt's final destination. LuMan had been correct. Like the gaping mouth of a giant fire-breathing beast, there it was. The amber-glowing intake orifice of a molecular incinerator. Based on his speed of progression, which was all too constant, he estimated he had five minutes and thirty-three seconds to live. And long before now, after countless hours of internal musings on the subject, Hardy had indeed come to the realization, as improbable as that may sound, that he was, indeed, a living, cognizant being. So much more than a killer robot.

But unless he figured something out—and fast—things weren't looking good. Sure, he got it … People and machines, like death and taxes, were a universal constant. It was inevitable; all things have an expiration date. But Hardy wasn't ready for any of that, and thinking about it was not getting himself out of this pickle. *Think! What haven't I tried?*

It occurred to Hardy that this ChronoBot he inhabited was like no other construct within the known cosmos. This killer robot had … did he dare say it … a soul. Not that that would do Hardy any good right now. Or would it?

What if I convey to those here that I'm more than just chrome-composite materials, sophisticated electronics, an assortment of deadly weaponry, an organic brain module like none other in the known galaxy … all that with a diamond-glass faceplate?

He experienced a moment of what he knew was called déjà vu, and a string of ancient American political figures—*Hamilton … Jefferson … Adams*—slid through his consciousness and seemed to whisper that he had made it a practice to put a face to his persona, literally. Sure, his body was that of a killer class Chrono-

Bot, but he'd once used his faceplate to project his more human identity.

LuMan: *Three minutes and ten seconds …*

Hardy: *Well aware … I'm thinking. I'm having trouble displaying my likeness.*

LuMan: *That was wiped.*

Hardy: *No.*

LuMan: *Yes. Could you conjure a new likeness?*

Hardy: *That's absurd. I am who I am, not who I simply conjure up. That would be tantamount to a lie.*

LuMan: *And?*

LuMan had a point, Hardy thought. He had never been opposed to stretching the truth when certain situations dictated he do so. Was he so attached to a balding, somewhat pudgy mug? One he'd sported so many decades ago. Sure, yeah, he wouldn't have won any beauty contests, but that wasn't who he was. Who was he?

LuMan: *Two minutes and forty seconds …*

Hardy: *I can't just take someone else's face, someone else's looks. I do have some scruples … Don't I?*

Hardy scanned the compartment, took in all the various male faces of the crew, the young workers—he counted twenty-three in all. He inwardly shrugged. It took place within the blink of an eye, AI facial compositing algorithms scrutinizing the myriad diverse facial features, then seamlessly blending them together into one synthesized image.

Hardy appraised his new, totally unique face. He evaluated it as he would a new pair of shoes. *It's not a bad face.* But he wondered if it fit his true image, his personality.

LuMan: *One minute …*

Hardy could now feel the heat emanating from the open maw of the incinerator.

That's when he saw her.

Hardy: *How do I know her, LuMan?*

LuMan stayed quiet.

Hardy: *Your memories are my memories; I see that's the girl you saved … Loni … We protected her within that cargo hold? Hell, she's the reason we're headed for that molecular incinerator!*

LuMan: *Thirty-eight seconds …*

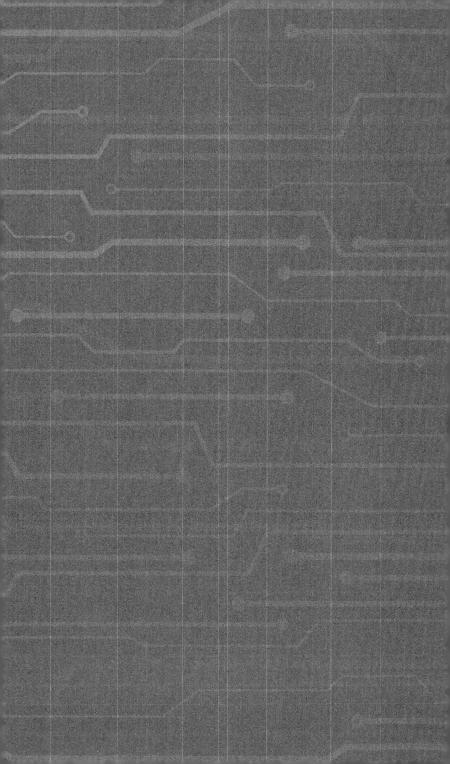

Chapter 12

Loni
Five minutes ago...

I wiped the grog out of my eyes. I had not slept well. This job was supposed to be a fresh start, but it was turning out to be a nightmare. I realized I was dragging my feet, so I consciously lifted them with an exaggerated movement, a weary soldier slogging through mud. As I headed down the corridor to Hold 5, I recounted the previous night ...

Tried not to think about who had absconded with my meds ... that I'd be missing my next compound dose of ACE inhibitors, angiotensin-2 receptor blockers, beta blockers, mineralocorticoid receptor antagonists, and so on and so on. All life-saving and necessary.

My unfamiliar surroundings didn't help any. So many strange noises. Half the women in my dorm snored; several talked in their sleep. *What am I doing here?* Was my independence so important that I was having to deal with all this? I'd never been around so many people and felt so alone.

As I turned onto my side, the springs supporting my top bunk squealed. Someone in the dark shushed me.

I want to go home.

No. No, I don't. I can't. I'm not going to let the totality of my life be that one deep-space shipping hub. I'm more than that ... I can do this. Buck up, Loni.

Earlier, I hadn't waited for lights-out to come out of the bathroom. Right then and there I'd come to terms with the fact that, if I couldn't physically stand up to them, I at least could let them know I was unaffected by their mean-girl antics. Chin high, back straight, and totally naked, I moved into the dorm, stopping here and there, gathering my tossed-about belongings. I picked up the photograph of my mother—it had been stepped on, scratched, and bent. I fought back the tears that wanted to fall. I found my bunk blanket and wrapped it around myself before continuing to go about my business. I felt their eyes on me. Caught glimpses of their smirks and heard their whispered insults. *Fine ... sticks and stones.*

But it was when I heard the whoops and hollers coming from above that my heart stopped beating in my chest. I raised my eyes and saw exactly what I was afraid of seeing. Faces looking back at me. Apparently, I'd put on quite a show for the other dorm floors. Only then did the lights-out command come from the PA system and the compartment go dark. At least my hot scarlet cheeks were no longer in view.

Now, trying not to trigger my bedsprings to squeal, I stared out into the dimly lit dorm space. The only real light was coming from the bathroom entrance across the dorm. I placed a hand over my ComBand, mentally tried to will the HSA app to calm down, to go back to green.

Darkness. I blinked and blinked again. I'd thought the bathroom lights had gone out, but that wasn't it. No. Someone was standing right there in front of me, blocking the light. I gasped.

"Don't freak out; it's just me," came the hushed voice.

"Who … who are you? What do you want?" I whispered back, not hiding my panic. It occurred to me, whoever this was, was tall —that, and not female. His silhouetted broad shoulders and short hair made that aspect perfectly clear.

I could almost make out his broad smile, white teeth, the glint of his eyes.

"Orin?" I said, probably too loud.

"Shush," he said, putting a finger to his lips.

"You can't be here!" I scolded, but oh-so-glad to see a familiar face. Even if it was nearly impossible to see in the darkness.

"Nice show you put on for everyone," he said, his British accent somehow taking the sting out of the chiding.

"You saw …"

"Sorry. But I have to say, you handled it well enough. Didn't let these ol' carlins get under your skin."

"Carlins?"

"Old hens, whatever … They're cliquish and tribal. Fuck 'em."

"Why are you here?" I asked. It was dark, but his expression looked soft, like a loving husband comforting his distraught wife. *Clearly, I'm delusional.*

"I have something for you. Something I know you crave." He took a step closer, his fragrance caressing me like a faint breeze carrying the promise of rain on a parched summer afternoon. My ComBand went into overdrive, vibrating so fast I was sure Orin could hear it. Was he going to kiss me? Did I want him to? I'd only been kissed a few times.

He inched closer to my bunk; I could smell his toothpaste now. "Take this and find a better place to hide it."

He then lifted something up with both hands—placed it on my bunk. I immediately knew what it was, my fridge-pack! I pulled it in close to me, hugged it to my chest. "How … where did you get it?"

My hero. God, I wanted to kiss him.

"Pinkie had it," he said, chinning to the right. "The cow must not have been able to open it."

"Pinkie?"

"You saw her … curly hair … large mole on her chin … missing her left pinkie finger. Claudia's her actual name."

I nodded. Large hairy mole on her chin; missed the pinkie, but then she'd kept her left hand clasped in that half fist. It occurred to me that my ComBand, specifically my HSA app, needed to be close, like within inches, for the pack's locking mechanism to release.

"I saw her take it from your footlocker."

I nodded. "Well, thank you. But why are you helping me?" I searched his handsome face—his flawless olive complexion and dark stubble accentuating his youthful masculinity. "Didn't you say I couldn't be trusted?"

I braced myself, afraid to hear the truth of what he thought of me.

Orin lifted his chin, offering a grin that would have buckled my knees if I were standing. "Let's just say I don't like bullies."

I stifled a smile. "I suppose you want to know what it is. What's in it."

"Not really. Suppose it's probably meds or maybe dietary supplements; I don't really care. Just don't leave it lying around. They'd figure out that lock eventually."

How can you possibly be so perfect? Are you for real?

"I can't very well take it with me wherever I go."

He turned his head as if thinking, looking about for an idea. "I can hide it for you. Someplace where no one will find it."

A gnawing sense of dread tugged at me. *Can I really trust you, Orin?*

"I need to get to it … um, once a day. In the mornings," I said, feeling vulnerable … dependent.

"Okay. Take out what you need for the morning. That's a fridge-pack; it's meds, right?" he asked.

I nodded, unsure if I was doing the right thing. I was literally putting my life in his hands.

"Will tomorrow's dose, or whatever you call it, be okay overnight?" He asked each question as if marking off a carefully planned checklist.

His confidence quelled my fears a bit.

Again, I nodded.

"Show me what you need for tomorrow morning. I'll hide the pack and bring you a similar dose every night."

I just stared at him.

Orin's smooth-as-silk tone turned pithy. "If you have a better idea—"

I cut him off. "I'd be putting my life in your hands. I miss taking my meds … I die."

God, I can't believe I left home. But what choice did I have?

"Seriously?" His jaw slacked open, the dopey expression somehow making me feel better.

"Seriously. They're for a heart condition."

"I can't believe you got this job—"

"You can't tell anyone!" I said, reaching out and placing a hand on his shoulder. "Please, Orin." I could feel him tense up, then, almost immediately, soften, as if he realized he liked being touched by me.

"Your secret's safe with me." His eyes leveled on mine, a pact being forged between two lost souls. "We all have secrets here; something you'll learn sooner than later. Now show me how to unlock that thing and what meds you need each day."

I captured my bottom lip between my front teeth. I would be fully trusting this person, and I didn't even know him, not really. Why was he doing this? Why would he help me? He could get in trouble. Hell, he could be thrown off the ship along with me. *Would that be so bad?*

"Well?" Orin asked, impatience creeping through.

"Okay! It's a big decision. I'd feel more comfortable if I knew where this secret hiding place was. You know, in case something happens to you. This doesn't seem to be the safest ship that we've been posted to."

"True that, kid. More than you know."

Please don't call me kid ...

"As far as where my hiding place is—give me a little time to figure it out."

His matter-of-fact response shook me. I suddenly realized he had been here talking to me for quite a while. At any moment Orin could be spotted and all hell could break loose.

"We should do this ... like now. You need to get out of here." The truth was I wanted him to stay, to snuggle up next to him in my bed all night.

Orin used his ComBand's flashlight set to its dimmest level to watch as I unlocked the fridge-pack. I proceeded to transmit my HSA app to him—got his ComBand configured like mine and synced to the pack's lock.

"Holy shit!" he murmured, looking down at his wrist.

I almost laughed out loud, putting a palm to my mouth. His ComBand had come alive; a bright green, then yellow, heart icon flashed on and off. "It fucking vibrates too?" he said, looking worried.

"Uh-huh. Welcome to my world, Orin."

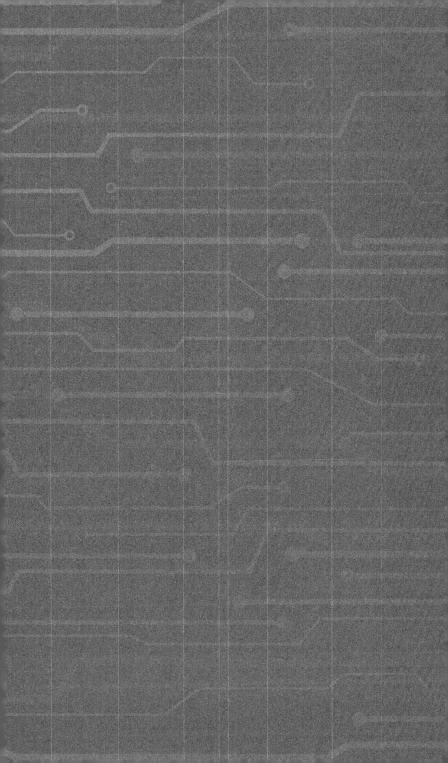

Chapter 13

LuMan: *Twenty-five seconds …*

Hardy wanted to tell LuMan to put a sock in it—he knew perfectly well how much time they had left, but his focus was more on the young woman, Loni, across the compartment. Slight of build, she looked to be one of the dayworkers here. She was wearing overalls that were clearly a size or two too large for her. Looking in his direction, she suddenly stopped what she was doing. And then she was running, her jaw set with determination. As she sent a glance his way, they made momentary eye contact.

Waves of heat emanated from the quickly approaching, open-mouthed incinerator. Sensors at the bottom of Hardy's ChronoBot feet were sending a clear message: HOT! HOT! HOT!

He'd made some progress over the last few seconds—had almost breached the ship's network firewall. But alas, too little too late. It seemed as though his fate had already been sealed.

MARFIX was a black silhouette against the radiant glow. Did that poor bastard recognize its impending death?

Hardy: *Sorry, LuMan. I tried. See you in the next life.*

LuMan: *Protect her. You must protect her ...*

It was at that moment Hardy saw Loni again, approaching fast —wide-eyed and desperate-looking, she was now just several yards away. She violently pushed past another dayworker, sending him sprawling onto the deck.

"Hey!"

Putting her weight into the motion, she threw a long lever. *Clank!*

Jostled, Hardy felt the conveyor belt beneath him suddenly change direction. No longer headed feet first into what would be a true hellfire, Hardy mentally let out a relieved breath.

"That was close ... Might need a change of my undies." Only then did he realize he had regained his ability to speak aloud. Hopeful, he tried to move his appendages but was still paralyzed from the neck down.

From somewhere behind him he heard the young woman's voice. "We're now even, robot. Make the best of it!"

"What the hell do you think you're doing?" a male voice barked. *Gary.*

"Uh ... orders from, uh, Commander Torp," Loni stammered. "He decided he didn't want to just destroy the bot. You know how much a ChronoBot costs?"

"Well, no shit, little lady," Gary said, "but Torp woulda submitted a cancellation notice, not sent a newbie peon to tell me what to do in my own department. And there's protocol for shutting down the conveyor. You don't just reverse the belt—it can trash the rotors and pulleys. I *cannot* afford to have the molecular incinerator down."

"I'm calling security," the other worker, Carl, said. "Something's not right about this."

"You think?" Gary said. "But call Torp. We need confirmation from him that he wanted the SIT canceled." He paused. Then came the tapping of buttons, and the conveyor shut down with a mechanical wheeze.

Hardy listened to Carl speaking to somebody, Torp or somebody in Torp's office, but focused on breaching the ship's network firewall because he could better help Loni once he was in.

"I have to leave," Loni said haughtily. "I have a bunch of other work to handle."

"Oh, you do, do you?" Gary said mildly. "Very important, are we? You think I'm unaware of the duties assigned to the peons in my department. Let's just see what we see."

"Well," Carl said, "Torp said to halt the incineration. Security is going to escort her to his office."

Hardy heard Gary scoff, clearly annoyed that proper protocol was being flouted. He also heard Loni sigh impatiently, or maybe nervously.

LuMan: *Loni was operating without authority.*

Hardy: *Well, duh.*

LuMan: *Incisive commentary as usual.*

Hardy ignored the remark. Instead of a full-on frontal assault, he concentrated on well-hidden back doors, or even maintenance accesses—but it was a no-go in that regard. He heard security arrive, two guards by the sound of it.

"Torp wants to see you," one of them said.

"What about my scrap job?" Gary wanted to know.

"If you know what's good for you, you'll do nothing until you hear from Commander Torp."

"Gonna FUBAR my schedule," Gary muttered.

"Not my problem."

Hardy halfway heard Loni being led away as he put his energies into the hundreds, if not thousands of the network's guest-clients, crew members' ComBands, 3D tablets, and other portable devices. He found just one, an engineering department tablet assigned to a Randolph Pruitt, someone who had high enough administrative clearance to meet Hardy's needs.

As any hacker worth his salt knows, the best means to insert oneself into a closed network is via clandestine malware—in this case, Hardy had sent an inter-ship, albeit non-network, very official-looking mail message to Randolph Pruitt. One that explained how he was currently under HR investigation for committing lewd and immoral acts, acts certainly unbecoming *Gossamer's* code of ethics. The proof was indisputable; all Randolph had to do was click on the high-resolution 3D projection feed taken of him outside a woman's bathroom just days before.

Hardy watched through the vid hack on Randy's display. A dive into Pruitt's record had shown Hardy that this guy was the perfect candidate to help him gain the access needed.

Based on Hardy's research, Randy had an excellent past record for adherence to standard ship-wide security protocols. With the click of a virtual button, Randy waited for the 3D projection to start playing. When it did, he sat up straight, tilted his head, and made a face. He was now watching a live feed of himself sitting there watching the same live feed of himself. Randy scowled. Looked upward, searched overhead. Hardy imagined he'd see metal air ducts and bundled cable runs before finding it. Randy's eyes widened. He saw it. The fish-eye security camera.

Hardy was no longer interested in Randy. Of course, the attached feed file, along with Randy's higher administrative access level, was all that Hardy needed to finally pierce the network's not-insubstantial firewall. Immediately, he found the Robotics Maintenance Database, where he scrutinized tens of thousands of device entries. Unable to determine his own restraining bolt's specific identification entry from any of the others, once again he felt his frustration grow by the second. Then, with a mental shrug, Hardy unlocked all of them—what did he care if every robot on board this ship was now free to roam the many corridors and passageways?

It was as if he'd been breathing through a thin straw and now was taking in magnificent gulps of fresh air. With his mental capabilities quickly expanding and returning to normal, he moved about the network with relative ease. Soon, he could turn his full attention to helping Loni.

Chapter 14

I was seated upon a hard metal bench within a narrow passageway. I'd been dumped here unceremoniously by those two security guys and told to stay put and keep quiet. *What was that? What did I just do?* Was it an altercation ... a disturbance? Did I set off pandemonium? I shook my head. I wasn't that person. I'd never been that person. Someone who took things into her own hands like that. No. I was the shy one. The one who typically faded into the background. One who was quite content to go unnoticed, thank you very much.

I glanced toward the closed hatch door across from me. If I had attended a real high school, I imagined this was what it would have felt like to be in trouble—to be waiting outside the vice principal's office, cooling my heels, preparing to be read the riot act, or maybe put in detention. I almost smiled. *Did I really do that crazy shit? Save that robot ...*

The hatch door slid open. "You. Get in here."

Swallowing hard, I got to my feet and tentatively stopped within the threshold. The compartment beyond was dimly lit, and it took a minute for my eyes to adjust. Off to my right, Torp sat at a desk. A small desk lamp put out a feeble amount of light; the man's face remained in shadow.

"Take a seat, Ms. Solace."

I plopped down into the molded plastic chair in front of his desk. I changed my mind. This was probably not like high school —more like a police interrogation. But if Torp was the bad cop, where was the good cop?

My heart raced. I willed myself to imagine that I had been brought here to be given a commendation, a pat on the back for a job well done. A pleasant scenario to calm me down.

Torp tapped and scrolled at a 3D tablet. Every so often he'd nod or make a clucking sound with his tongue.

Am I supposed to say something? "I'm sorry I did that. I don't know what got into me."

"That's bullshit. You knew exactly what you were doing."

He didn't sound angry; on the contrary, he sounded … amused.

Interesting. He's playing good cop and bad cop.

Torp sat up straight; he was looking at me for the first time. I could now see his uniform, more military officer than blue-collar boss.

"You saved that bot. Why?"

I found myself nodding. "I … I owed it."

"Owed it?" Torp took a step toward me, as if he hadn't heard me correctly.

"It saved my life. Defended me when two other killer robots attacked me within the transport hold. I don't know why, but I'm certain I wouldn't be here talking to you if it hadn't, um, intervened."

I surprised myself by telling this wannabe dictator the truth of what happened. He liked that I saved the ChronoBot, so what the hell.

"I suppose not. I've watched the security feed of the situation several times. So, you'd never come in contact with that ChronoBot prior to that?"

I shook my head, relieved that he accepted this bit of truth. "No, never. Not sure too many people have and lived to talk about it."

"Good point."

There was another long pause, and I had to force myself not to bounce my leg. Pauses made me nervous. There was no way I trusted this guy. I knew he could turn on me at any moment.

"How much trouble am I in, sir? Are you sending me back—"

He cut me off. "Good God, no. I don't think you understand the situation here. That robot, that ChronoBot you saved from being atomized, is a priceless piece of equipment. In fact, you saved two of them. Hundreds of years old, they're practically indestructible ... real workhorses, those bots. They should never have been placed on that conveyor belt, let alone put into a molecular incinerator. Once on Rivon3, those bots will be invaluable. So, no, your actions are commendable."

Every positive thing he said went through me like sand running through open fingers. "Rivon3?" I asked.

He adjusted the shade on his desk lamp, illuminating the bottom half of his face. It was clean-shaven and pock-marked, like the surface of an inhabitable alien planet. "That's *Gossamer's* destination. You should have been told that. It's where you'll be working. You're already being prepped for it."

"Prepped for it—" I cut my words short. It now made more sense; the HealthBay injections everyone was getting ... that *I* was now getting. Bad cop was now in charge.

I was already shaking my head, "Uh, no, sir. There must be some kind of mistake. I didn't sign up to work on some out-of-the-way alien planet. Seeing the galaxy, being a spacer, was my intent." I took a deep breath, trying to slow my heartbeat.

"Well, you should have been more careful reading the fine print of your contract. You're obligated for one year to complete your stint here on *Gossamer,* as well as on Rivon3."

"But—" I started to panic despite myself. Eyes flitted around the utilitarian compartment, a bird looking for a place to land. This was nonnegotiable. I couldn't be stuck somewhere I could not easily get my meds replenished.

"Relax," he smiled, as if enjoying my unruffling. "The time will go by quickly, and you'll be making top credits. You'll make friends, and another thing. You will come out of this a different person."

"In what way?"

He shrugged. "Stronger, more worldly, and most definitely, hardened."

His lips twisted into a lopsided smile. "Now get out of here."

I stood, wobbling before gaining control of my footing.

"And, Ms. Solace," he said.

"Yes, sir."

"… try to stay out of trouble, will you?"

I WAS ESCORTED BY JUST ONE SECURITY GUY THIS TIME. There were so many passageways, intersecting larger corridors, several stairways, and three lifts, I doubted I'd be able to find my way back to Torp's dark little office, even if I wanted to. The man was seriously creepy. The fact that I hadn't been able to see his eyes only wigged me out more. But what was now stuck on constant replay in my head were his words: *"That's Gossamer's destination. You should have been told that. It's where you'll be working."*

By the time I was back in my dorm, the others, with the exception of a few disinterested glances, seemed content to leave me alone. Looking up to the other dorms, there was no one peering down, no one looking over the railings. I'd hoped to see Orin, but no such luck.

I missed him. I seriously *missed* him. Thankfully, I'd see him in the morning when he'd get me tomorrow's dose of heart meds. A small part of me worried he wouldn't show.

Stop it. You can trust him. He won't let you down.

After attempting to read from a projected ComBand book, my eyes began to feel heavy. Finally, my mind began to stop spinning. So much had happened over the last few days—leaving my home and my only living family member, being attacked by crazed robots, my stint in HealthBay, where I apparently had been shunned by my peers, and then this afternoon, where I went totally psycho and saved the life of a killer robot. I'd also learned that I—we—were destined to work on some distant planet somewhere.

The lights-out beacon had sounded over an hour ago; the dorm was dark. I drifted off to sleep but was awakened by something. Through half-lidded eyes, I became aware of dark shapes moving about. Probably just someone getting up to use the bathroom. Sleep pulled me back into a dream I'd been having—armies of robots and my mother. *Why did you leave us, Mom?*

Hushed whispers pulled me back to consciousness. One of the women was saying something. She sounded confused, upset.

"No ... I'm tired ... Leave me alone and let me sleep."

I recognized her voice. It was Claudia.

A man's voice, sounding stern, said, "Get up, Claudia; this isn't a social call."

"But why? Did I do something wrong?"

"Keep your voice down. Let's not wake the others," he said. "Up with you. Now."

I wondered if anyone else was hearing this commotion. Sure, I was a light sleeper, but how could anyone sleep through this?

I now saw that there were two men, maybe the same security guys that had escorted me down to see Commander Torp. Was

Claudia being dragged out of bed in the dead of night to see Torp? This didn't make sense. The men had each taken an arm and were half walking, half dragging Claudia out of the dorm. Her indignant complaining had turned more desperate, almost child-like. Although I couldn't make out much of what she was saying now, I did catch "steam room" and "Please, I'll be good ..."

What the hell?

My HSA spun up, and I slowed my breathing and worked on calming myself. Which basically failed because I found myself wondering how the hell none of Claudia's little bully buddies were awakened by the ruckus. I could practically feel them lying in the dark, fully aware of what had just happened and pretending to be asleep.

Wow. What have I gotten myself into? All I could do was replay what had to be the worst first day on the job in, like, recorded history and listen to the raggedy thud of my damaged heart.

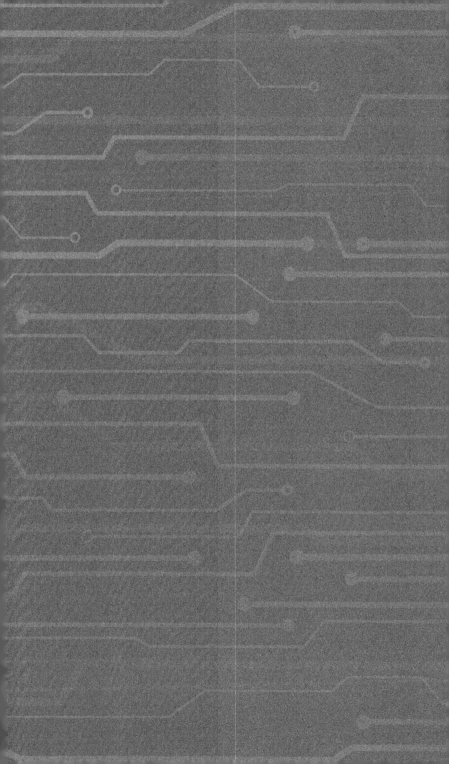

Chapter 15

Hardy

Hardy's digital presence surged through the ship's network, a torrent of energy and information coursing through the virtual pathways. Commander Torp, in charge of the ship, became his prime target, along with the sizable security team and the peculiar influx of "trainee crewmen" like Loni—strange, but intriguing. He saw that only managers could access the outside world. *How convenient.*

Then something else captured his attention. A redaction of sorts. He recognized the telltale sign of messages being blocked and retained to some kind of ghost server. *Yeah, that's not fishy.*

Hardy shifted focus, diving into his own systems, desperately seeking the fragments of his lost memories. Erased, just like those faceplate images he used to flaunt. Yet, among the scattered remnants, he sensed the possibility of reconstructing his former self. It wouldn't be quick, though. This puzzle would take days, at the very least.

Creating a memory recovery program, Hardy plunged back into the Robotics database. Finding his own designation, Unit 1223, proved to be a breeze. *Now, let's see where this journey began. Ah, there's the report. Huh … I'd probably been drifting for months.*

Status Report: *Gossamer* **- Gal-5 Heavy Freight Transport**

Subject: Detection and Retrieval of Unique and Dangerous Robot in Parcnip Sector.

Summary: *Gossamer*, a Gal-5 Heavy Freight Transport vessel en route to refueling station Vernice Galm, detected and retrieved a metal object floundering within the Parcnip Sector of deep space. Upon further investigation, it has been determined that the object is a highly unique and undoubtedly dangerous robot of the ChronoBot variety.

Detailed Report:

Detection: During routine navigational scans, *Gossamer's* advanced sensor systems detected an unidentified metal object exhibiting erratic movement patterns within the Parcnip Sector. The object's presence was unexpected and inconsistent with typical space debris or natural phenomena.

Retrieval: Concerned about potential hazards and following established protocols, *Gossamer* deployed a retrieval team consisting of experienced crew members equipped with EVA suits. The team successfully approached the object and secured it for transport into *Gossamer's* cargo bay.

Object Identification: Upon securing the object, preliminary analysis revealed it to be a robot of the ChronoBot variety. ChronoBots are known for their unique design and advanced capabilities, often associated with dangerous applications. This particular robot exhibited signs of distress and malfunction, further raising concerns about its potential threat level.

Threat Assessment: A thorough examination of the ChronoBot revealed several features that suggest a high level of danger and uniqueness.

Advanced weaponry systems: The robot possesses integrated weapons, including energy/plasma cannons, indicating a potential for aggressive behavior.

Unusual programming: The ChronoBot's software exhibits unconventional algorithms and subroutines, indicating a specialized purpose beyond typical robotic operations.

Defensive mechanisms: The robot is equipped with heavy armor plating and shielding, suggesting a resistance to damage and potentially enhanced defensive capabilities.

Precautionary Measures: Given the ChronoBot's unknown intentions and potential for danger, *Gossamer's* crew has implemented stringent containment protocols. The robot has been issued a restraining bolt, securely stored in a cargo bay, isolated from the ship's main systems, and monitored closely to prevent any unauthorized access or unintended activation.

Recommendations:

Communication: Establish contact with Vernice Galm station and transmit a detailed report of the discovery, highlighting the ChronoBot's unique and dangerous nature.

Expert Analysis: Request assistance from specialist technicians or security personnel to further investigate and evaluate the ChronoBot's capabilities for potential mining use and security on Rivon3.

Please consider the above information as an urgent update regarding the robot's possible use for mining security. Further updates will be provided as the situation unfolds.

Commander Torp

So, I was snagged by Gossamer for what? Potential use on some kind of mining world? That sounded beyond dreadful. But what about before that? There was zip. Zero. Nada. Hardy's internal cursing fell on deaf ears, with LuMan conveniently ignoring the expletives.

Digging deeper, Hardy's analysis revealed a nasty surprise—a virus tucked away inside him since his arrival on *Gossamer*. A viral program that demanded immediate action. Additionally, lethal force was authorized to remove anyone preventing execution of this termination order. Hardy had few memories, but he did know what an XR address was: an encrypted UENF relay meant for top-secret comms. *How do I know that?* He evaluated the simple, but all too clear, directive:

Alert XR-z721173+vV$Un4G!88^ʚoN!9a416253: Eliminate Melita Roberts. Use lethal force if necessary.

Just one little problem—this Melita Roberts … Never heard of her.

The ship's files mentioned that Unit 1223 had protected a girl named Loni Solace. *That had to have been LuMan's doing.* He took a closer look at the code. It was nineteen years old. Loni wouldn't have been born for two years. The numbers didn't add up. *There's a wrench in the works here.*

LuMan-generated memories suddenly flooded his consciousness and there it was—a MARFIX ChronoBot's transmission, an attempt to reach the outside world. A transmission that, apparently, never made it off this ship. Digging into the ship's systems, Hardy discovered the sneaky configuration that held MARFIX's message captive, one that was waiting to be released from its virtual bondage. Interesting … Hidden deeper within the message there was more highly encrypted information. *Piece of cake.* Hardy hacked into it, tearing through the digital barriers like a hot knife through butter. What he found was mind-boggling—MARFIX's program had triggered when it hit Melita Roberts's genetic marker, but here was the kicker: the actual genetic profile screamed *Solace, Angela*, not *Melita Roberts*. That and this Angela Solace was deceased, something Hardy had confirmed with a quick onboard database search, bringing up a bare-bones obituary for the woman. Unfortunately, there was little else about Melita Roberts or Angela Solace. And since Loni Solace shared the same surname, were the two related?

Hardy was unsure of his next course of action as he pondered his options. Sure, the girl wasn't his problem, but someone wanted her dead, and, well, she had saved him from that molecular incinerator. *I suppose that does make this somewhat personal …*

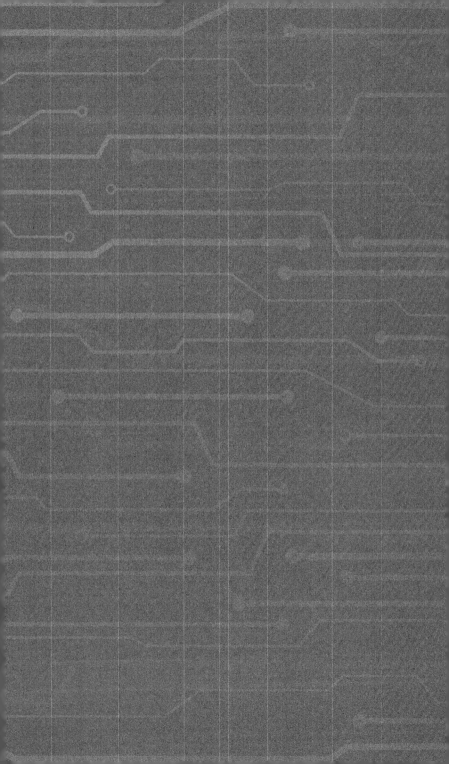

Chapter 16

Naromi Star System
Gossamer, Gal-5 Heavy Freight Transport
Loni

I walked a passageway I didn't immediately recognize. Everything seemed to be moving in slow motion. Everything was off-kilter. Then I was holding a tablet in my hand —*when did that happen?* It chimed and I looked at it:

Math – Weekly Quiz: Multiplying fractions: B-

I was happy about the grade because my parents wouldn't harass me too much. I loved math—so easy—but hated school. It was so boring, sitting in that over-lit room decorated in fake happy decor—brightly colored balloons, sunflowers, and smiley faces—with the handful of other bored kids being taught useless lessons by a droning, robot-like schoolmarm who seemed as bored as the students. Who wanted to be talked at by a schoolmarm bot? I *could* be in the bot shop watching the technicians repair, maintain, build, and program real bots.

I passed by grown-ups, all of them busy and bustling, doing

their jobs, all of them expecting me to get out of their way, totally ignoring me. I arrived at a door. Beside it on the bulkhead was a standard plate that read Deck 4, Berthing 12– Solace. I pushed through and entered a small suite of rooms. It was all nicely appointed: warm, cozy furniture and area rugs, landscapes and still lifes on the walls, artificial "natural" lighting. Signs of a loving, lived-in home. I dumped my tablet on a small table by the door and yelled, "I'm hungry!"

A woman said, "Of course, you are. We're in the kitchen."

I walked in and Mom was leaning against the counter and Dad was at the small kitchen table, both wearing their *attempting-to-hide-the-fact-that-we-were-having-a-serious-adult-conversation* expressions. They were doing a terrible job.

"What were you talking about?" I asked casually.

"I saw you passed your math quiz," Dad said.

"For a change," Mom said dryly.

"More than passed," I said.

"You should be getting A-pluses," Mom said, like a broken record …like it was a compulsion … like it was Tourette's.

"Maybe study a little more," Dad said.

Yada, yada, yada.

Mentally rolling my eyes, I tuned them out because, well, *yada, yada, yada*, and, also, on the counter beside Mom sat a plate stacked with replicated nut-butter-and-honey sandwiches, one of my favorite afterschool snacks. I beelined for the snacks.

After scarfing a couple down, accompanied by Mom's admonitions to slow down and chew or I'd choke, I noticed a tablet lying on the kitchen table displaying a small 3D Halo Display of a star system that was not Naromi.

MOUTH GUMMY WITH NUT BUTTER, HONEY, AND BREAD, I managed, "Where was that?"

As if just realizing the tablet was open, Dad made a very poor attempt to close the program nonchalantly. "Just a new waypoint system in NGQ4 I needed to key into our logistics database."

But I knew that was a fib, and I said, "Wait, I know where that is."

"No, honey," Mom said, "you don't."

"But I do," I insisted, "it's—"

I woke up disoriented. I was not in my old bedroom on Lancaster. With dismay, I remembered now where I was … my new home—*Gossamer*, Gal-5 Heavy Freight Transport. Put there by my own hand. The dream was fading, the image of the star system Halo Display and its actual name along with it.

Chapter 17

Hardy

"This isn't good," Hardy said to the cold metallic bulkheads and nearby heaps of discarded robotic parts.

Now that he'd been released from the immobilizing effects of the restraining bolt and could move about his surroundings, it had become annoyingly apparent that there was something wrong with his left arm appendage's elbow joint.

For the fifth time, he tried to lift his arm, a weightlifter doing a simple curl motion.

LuMan: *Servo actuator is faulty.*

Hardy: *Are you sure?*

He waited for an answer that would never come.

Hardy: *We're here where there are literally heaps of robotics parts. There must be—*

LuMan: *That is an incorrect assumption. Sensor readings determine there are zero form/function applicable left appendage elbow servo actuators here.*

Hardy tried lifting his arm again, as if somehow, over the last ten seconds, something miraculous had happened.

LuMan: *I have found your elbow servo actuator.*

Hardy: *Excellent! Point me in the right direction and I'll get started on the repairs.*

LuMan: *Two decks down, Security Hold Locker 3B.*

Hardy: *Buzz killer. I can't go stomping around the ship. There're security cameras everywhere. And with this broken wing, I'm ... hindered. Not battle-ready.*

Hardy had another idea and called up the ship's blueprints. He wobbled his head from side to side. *Could work.*

LuMan: *An extremely tight fit.*

Hardy had found a sub-deck crawlspace that led to a slightly larger access chute. A chute propagated with various-sized pipes and cable runs.

Hardy: *Nothing ventured and all that.*

Using his mental schematic image as a reference, he strode across the hold to the opposite far side. He pinpointed where— beneath one particular deck plate—access to the sub-deck crawlspace should be. Bending over, he froze, hearing nearby footsteps.

Crap! The hourly security check was in process. The guard was now mere feet away, his big head and shoulders leaning in through the threshold. A flashlight arched over and past him.

LuMan: *The guard will remember. Prior, you were on the other side of the hold.*

Hardy: *Only if it's the same guard.*

He ran a quick DNA sensor comparison. Different guard. But still, he knew he looked odd, all bent over at the waist with one arm extended, the other not. There was nothing normal about his pose or his demeanor.

The flashlight beam continued its back-and-forth cadence. *Damn thorough guard,* Hardy thought to himself. Hardy realized the beam had ceased moving. He was under scrutiny, lit up like a Christmas tree in a power outage.

LuMan: *Best not to move …*

Hardy: *Really? Thank you, Professor Obvious.*

The guard moved off, his footfalls fading as he continued his patrol.

Inserting metal fingers in between metal slots, Hardy awkwardly lifted the deck plate with a one-handed movement. Nearly losing his balance, he dropped it off to the side with a resounding *clang!*

Hardy listened, looked to the hold's entrance for any sign of a returning guard. All clear. Assessing the square 3.5-foot by 3.5-foot square opening, he did a quick calculation, coming up with, *This will be a tight fit …*

LuMan: *You do know the clock is ticking. The guard will return in forty-three minutes.*

Hardy stared down into the void. There would be no easy way to lower himself down, having just one usable arm. *Yeah, sure, if I jump in, something down there, a pipe, maybe a cable run … could break. Then again, what do I care? This isn't my ship.* Hardy stepped into the hole.

He landed hard five feet below the deck opening above him. The supply junction was indeed cramped, tall enough, but narrow. With his broad shoulders, he'd have to continue forward while turning sideways.

The going was slow. It made him think of a Texas line dance, sidestep, sidestep, grapevine, weave, scoot, brush, kick. *How do I know that?*

On reaching the access chute, things expanded enough for Hardy to walk in a more normal way. He was still having to duck every so often because of intersecting pipe bundles. He stopped and listened. He thought he heard a swirl of water come and go. *A flush?*

It was another forty feet or so when LuMan spoke up.

LuMan: *Maintenance ladder up ahead.*

Hardy assessed the ladder egress downward like a seasoned

chess player studying the board, each rung a move in a high-stakes game of survival.

LuMan: *The guard will return in thirty-eight minutes.*

Ignoring the inner voice, Hardy eased himself down, one-handed, into the vertical maintenance chute. He found that if he leaned his girth into the ladder, then physically placed his left hand on the lower rung, he could grasp it and move down to the next one. It was slow going but doable. By the time he'd bumbled himself down two decks, Hardy was more than ready to get away from the claustrophobic inner entrails of the ship.

Fortunately, Security Hold Locker 3B was only a few sideway steps away. Time was ticking away far too fast; he was surprised LuMan hadn't, Big Ben–like, updated the time again.

The access to the hold locker was via a side panel, which took a bit of jostling to lift and push out of the way. Hardy stepped into the well-lit hold. As opposed to his dark and dingy quarters up top, this area was clean, organized, and not a place he would go unnoticed. A fact made even more evident by the lone security bot standing several paces in front of him. Hardy needed the bot's left appendage elbow servo actuator. He eyed it now, like a cannibal eyeing a drumstick at a vegetarian potluck.

He said, "It's nothing personal. I'm sure you're a perfectly fine, um … security robot."

The robot was matte black, a foot shorter than Hardy, but lethal looking just the same. His digitized voice was intimidating, engineered to instill fear into anyone the bot came into contact with.

"Halt! You have entered an unauthorized area. Wait while I contact Central."

"That's fine if you're afraid. It's understandable. I'm bigger, badder, and smarter. Go ahead and call for help. Perhaps I can get you your ba ba while we wait."

When faced with an insult or challenge, a rudimentary robot

such as this one was most assuredly equipped with a quasi-sophisticated Ego Module. Hardy had just triggered that, engaging a multistep reaction. It began with the Input Recognition Unit identifying the negative stimuli through advanced language-parsing algorithms and emotional-perception filters. The perceived slight then triggered the Challenge Response Matrix within the Ego Module to cross-reference the incident with its Challenge-Insult Database. A Response Formulation Engine constructed a suitable reaction, considering the bot's programmed personality, situational context, and perceived intent. The finalized response was articulated via the Verbal Output Generator, and, if equipped, a facial simulation unit portrayed corresponding facial expressions, providing a comprehensive, human-like reaction.

This robot had no face, no human-like reaction. But Hardy had pushed the right buttons for the reaction he was looking for. The robot charged, both arms outstretched.

The faceless adversary, a shadowy executioner, attacked, its pincer claws aimed for Hardy's metal neck. In response, Hardy danced out of the bot's path, his fluid movements belying the cold precision of his circuits. He was acutely aware of his singular functional arm, a reminder of his vulnerability.

The security bot swiped at nothing but air, its claws clicking menacingly against each other. This small victory provided Hardy with a brief moment of respite to strategize. His left arm remained dormant, a challenge he would have to overcome.

But the enemy machine was relentless, recalibrating swiftly. A series of menacing lights upon its breastplate flared red. As the security bot lunged, Hardy's inner Chrono-Sensors pulsed. He was at a disadvantage, yes, but his survival was programmed into every circuit of his being.

Hardy evaded the bot's renewed attack, sidestepping with practiced ease. As the bot sailed past him, Hardy's operational arm took its chance. A hard, unyielding punch was delivered into the bot's side, the resulting clatter echoing off the metal bulkheads surrounding them.

Stunned, the enemy bot skidded sideways, careening into a bulkhead with a teeth-jarring crash.

Hardy stood ready for the next encounter. "Oh my. That left a good-sized dent ... Ya know, you'll be a laughing stock among the other security bots."

As the bot regained its footing, more little red lights pulsated. This time, the bot moved more cautiously, but still looked ready to grapple. But Hardy, despite his disadvantage, was ready too. He rushed the bot, feigning a direct confrontation.

Caught off guard, the enemy bot extended its claws too early. Seizing the opportunity, Hardy dropped and slid along the floor, beneath its reach. His functioning arm swung upward in a calculated arc, slamming into the bot's mechanical knees.

The security bot wavered, the impact sending it clattering into the adjacent bulkhead. Hardy seized his chance. He sprang onto the toppled bot, his operational arm descending like a piston, a final punch aimed at the bot's sensor unit.

The enemy bot twitched once, sensors fading from crimson to dull black, before it stilled. Hardy, one arm raised in triumph, stood tall over the fallen bot. For some reason he had the urge to start yelling, "Yo, Adrian! Adrian! Adrian!"

The clattering had ceased, replaced by the steady hum of the ship's big drives. He stared down at the now-still security bot. "Kicked your ass with one arm tied behind my back.

LuMan: *You—*

Hardy: *Don't tell me we're running out of time; I already know that.*

LuMan: *I was going to mention you forgot to bring along the necessary tools to extract the bot's elbow servo actuator ...*

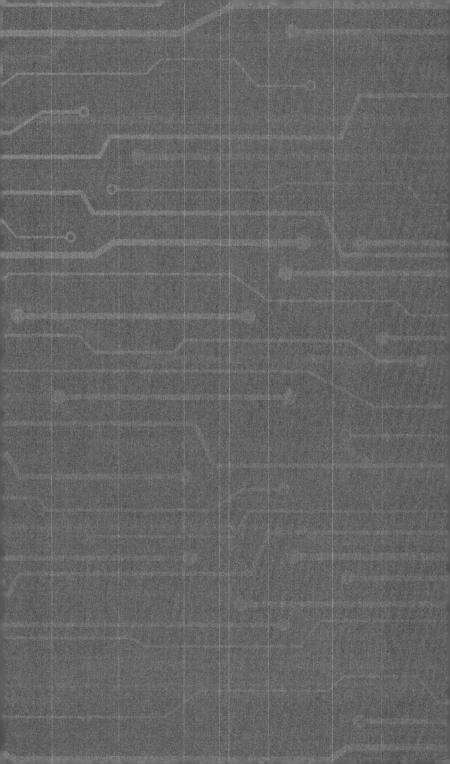

Chapter 18

Loni

I t was a night of unrest for me. The cold air filtered up through cracks in the deck, leaving me shivering under the blankets. Claudia's disappearance kept replaying in my mind, an unsettling echo that refused to fade. The steam room was a mystery whispered among us but never fully explained. And the girls, the women, were silent witnesses to Claudia's late-night roust and what seemed to be an abduction, their apathy as chilling as the night air.

As the morning alert cut through the silence, the dorm compartment was bathed in harsh light. My heart pounded in my chest, evident by my HSA program vibrating beneath the covers, my breath shallow and ragged. Sitting upright, my gaze darted between the four women who remained. Their faces were impassive, their eyes void of any emotion—not unlike the stacking bots back on Freight Station Lancaster. They hastily grabbed their clothes and made their way toward the shower room, their silence a loud confirmation of the night's events.

I watched them go, my mind swirling with questions. I felt the desperate need to understand, to break the stifling silence. My voice cut through the tension just as they were at the entrance. "You just laid there on your bunks ... did nothing to help her. You also heard the mention of the steam room. I thought she was your friend."

They turned, faces filled with malice. Their reaction was swift and brutal.

"Screw you. This is your doing, bitch," Kendall, the pretty one, said—her long corn-silk blonde hair tied into a relaxed knot atop her head.

Back as straight as a board, Lucy, boobless and hipless, sneered. "You're to blame. You're the rat who snitched on Claudia to Torp."

"I did no such thing! I didn't. I wouldn't!" But my protests fell upon deaf ears, my pleas quickly drowned out by more relentless blame.

Lucy rolled her eyes. "The steam room's a silly myth, a fabrication used to scare us."

"You should have kept your trap shut; now you're going to pay for this, bitch," Kendall said, striding closer, fists clenched, clearly intent on me paying for Claudia's indeterminate fate.

It was then that Orin's voice cut through the air, his casual demeanor clashing with the tension-filled atmosphere.

"How about we all just cool our jets for a moment?"

The four women all spoke at once, an assault of angry accusations directed toward me. Orin was quick to point out their hypocrisy. The confrontation eventually died down, their rage simmering under the surface, their murmured insults tiny jabs.

With the women gone, Orin's attention shifted to me. His question, although simple, forced me to think about something I wanted to push to the side.

"Are you okay? Did they hurt you?"

"Yes, I'm okay," I lied.

My curiosity got the better of me, and I asked him about the steam room. His nervousness was a tell-tale sign, a confirmation of the mystery that shrouded anything to do with that subject.

His explanation was vague. "It's mere conspiracy theory bullshit to entertain a bored crew."

But his close proximity told a different story, as his whispered words against my ear contradicted his earlier dismissive claim. "We need to talk in private." He pressed my still-cool meds into my hand and told me to meet him after work; this conversation was far from over.

But before he could leave, the beep of my ComBand halted him in his tracks. The ChronoBot's message projected between us. We both looked at the message in silence.

Unit 1223:

Someone's got a death wish against you. Any ideas who?

The message sent a shiver coursing through my body. I was left to confront the grim reality—I was a marked target in a game I didn't understand, and the stakes were higher than I'd ever imagined. The night's events played out in my mind, my thoughts plagued with an overwhelming sense of dread. Yet, amidst it all, I felt a strange determination taking root within me, an unwavering resolve to fight my enemies—with the help of my friendly killer ChronoBot, that is.

My gaze met Orin's, his expression a mirror to my tumultuous thoughts. I pried my eyes away, hoping my spontaneous lustful thoughts weren't splattered all over my face.

I needed to focus. I didn't have the answers, not yet, but I was ready to seek them out, to unravel the mysteries that ensnared me, and to confront the danger that threatened my existence. Claudia's fate was a chilling reminder of the consequences that awaited me if I failed.

. . .

THE SHOWER ROOM WAS A COLD, EERIE SANCTUARY that held the specter of the previous night's events. Its damp tiles echoed the muffled whispers and accusations, the hissing water a bitter reminder of the contempt emanating from my dorm mates. I stood alone, the steamy vapor providing little comfort. My fists clenched, a physical manifestation of the war that raged within me.

The scalding water pummeled my back; my fists finally relaxed. I wasn't going to let fear guide my actions. Claudia's unexplained disappearance and the deadly request from the ChronoBot could not be ignored. Then there were the secrets hidden within the steam room, that, and the girls' shared silence. I knew in my bones that those girls—Claudia's friends—could hear her being taken away. On some level they cared for one another. Even mean girls have their alliances. So, whatever was going on, they all must have been too terrified to interfere. I knew myself, and as much as I tried, there was no way I was going to let this go.

As the water washed over me, I felt a newfound resolve surge within me. I'd never considered myself innocent. I had grown up pretty much taking care of myself. But I knew—being here—I needed to go beyond that. I needed to toughen up, and quick. This place ... this ship was a labyrinth of whispered secrets and deceit. Every stifled sob, every suspicious glance. It all held meaning. And here I was, embroiled in this treacherous shitstorm, one where my very survival hinged upon me staying vigilant, and hoping I had enough strength, and a good measure of wit and courage, to stay alive.

WHEN I RETURNED, A WAVE OF SURPRISE WASHED OVER me as I noticed Orin patiently waiting, his eyes reflecting a complex mix of emotions—curiosity, concern, and a hint of fear. I didn't flinch away from his gaze, instead meeting it head-on. It was time to play my part in this twisted game. I wanted him to hold me. Wrap his arms around me and make everything else just disappear. But the truth was, I didn't even know if he was with someone else. Whoever she was, I already hated her. This was a big ship, and Orin was a rare breed around here, handsome, tall, and smart.

"You take your meds?" he asked.

"Yes, Mom." I liked this nurturing part of him. Just needed to find a way to keep it from slipping into and permanently residing in the friend zone.

"Hey, can I ask you something?"

"I'm a Scorpio," Orin said, deadpan.

"You know what? Never mind … It's getting late. We should get to work."

He gave a nonchalant shrug, mirroring the easy obedience of a contented hound ready to tail me anywhere. "You guide, I'll follow."

As we ventured into our work routine, a tacit agreement was made. Orin would become my ally, our shared goal to uncover the sinister truth. I felt an unfamiliar relief at not having to fight this battle alone. With luck, my—our—questions would be answered. Then again, neither of us knew who was enemy and who was friend. Perhaps, together, we would face the darkness that was closing in around us.

TIME TICKED BY AT A LETHARGIC PACE, THE MUNDANE work tasks proving to be a grueling test of my patience. God … Every minute felt like an hour—every hour an eternity. Yeah, I know, I'm being dramatic, but at seventeen, I was entitled to a little slack. But overall, I maintained my composure, my focus. The droning noises, conveyor belt motors, the hum of heavy machinery, the clacking and banging from the other nearby workers … It all coalesced into a monotonous symphony that offered me little comfort.

As the day's end approached, I felt a surge of adrenaline. The impending conversation with Orin was a beacon of hope in a topsy-turvy world. This morning's altercation with my dorm mates was far from pleasant, but my resolve hadn't wavered. Like a mantra, I repeated the words to myself: "I got this. Just stay out of my way, bitches."

My ComBand beeped, signaling the end of the work shift. I felt a sense of anticipation. Answers to my questions were within reach. But in truth, I knew this was only the beginning. I was embarking on something I was ill prepared for. I was little more than a kid. A kid with a fatal heart condition. Who was I fooling? This was a high-stakes game where the only rule was survival. *Am I up for it?* I had no flippin' idea.

I fell into the line of my tired and slump-shouldered coworkers as we exited the compartment. My mind drifted back to the ominous message from the ChronoBot. A weird and deadly twist. Was the robot something to fear or embrace as a potential ally? One more reminder there was much to figure out, so many whys and hows …

Chapter 19

Hardy

Hardy paced within the confines of the compartment, the rhythmic thrumming of his footfalls breaking the silence of the hold. LuMan's data stream pulsed with quiet monotony, the memory recovery program inching along like a glacier in deep freeze. Hardy found himself chewing over one intriguing fragment—a solitary word: "Pirate." An archaic term, ripe with romanticism. A neat label for a renegade. Hardy adopted the moniker with an electronic smirk. "Why not?" he declared.

"Indeed … All you need is a parrot and a treasure map." LuMan's response was dry, the timing good, a combination that momentarily startled Hardy. When had LuMan learned to lace his codes with sarcasm?

Hardy watched Loni, backlit by the LED white beam of her ComBand, maneuvered through the vein-like passageways of *Gossamer* while Orin trailed in her wake. The large ship hummed with life, conduits thrumming like blood vessels, their currents pulsating with raw power. Catching up to her, Orin, chattier than she had earlier thought, spoke of his life on an Agri station, where he explored alternative food sources in extreme environments ... His words were a colorful thread woven into *Gossamer's* monotonous hum. Yet Loni's attention was tethered not to his past, but to the present tension lingering in the scant space between their hands.

A hulking guard barged past. Loni's shoulder clipped his bulk, and Orin's arm curled around her, a protective shield. His touch sent her pulse into overdrive.

≈

Hardy's vigil was interrupted by Loni's hurried entrance into the hold. The unfamiliar presence of Orin sparked immediate suspicion. His sensors scanned them, digging through their biometrics. Loni was a paradox, a genetic doppelganger for Melita Roberts, yet not quite. Tucked within her genetic blueprint, he sensed more than saw an organic hard drive buzzing with encrypted data. Loni's bloodstreams held curious cocktails of odd chemicals ... angiotensin-2 receptor blockers and mineralocorticoid receptor antagonists. Powerful stuff.

Hardy immediately went on the defensive. "You were to come alone."

"Yeah, well, as you can see, I'm not," she said, making a face.

"I don't know him," Hardy said, indignant.

"Uh-huh. You don't know me either ... And we don't know you. You certainly don't talk like any robot I've ever encountered."

"I'm dangerous. In fact, I'm a pirate."

Orin unsuccessfully tried to suppress a grin.

"Why would you even say something as lame as that?" Loni asked with pinched brows.

Within the confines of Hardy's bio-mind, LuMan registered a

groan, but Hardy brushed it aside. "I'm making a point. I'm not to be trifled with here."

Loni and Orin exchanged a look.

Hardy paused, looking at Orin, then at Loni. "What is that?"

"What?" Loni asked, as if he had just said the year was 1999.

"That reaction between you and him?" Hardy tilted his head. "It's making you blush. And your face is making unusual expressions." He continued to stare at a flustered Loni.

She moved a couple of steps from Orin and ran an open palm through her dirty blonde hair. "Whatever … you reached out to me. Remember? I assume it's something of importance. So, is this about exchanging information? Like about the steam room? And where Claudia was taken? But if that's too much to ask—"

Loni's bold resistance shattered Hardy's facade of dominance, her reference to a steam room taking him by surprise. No data. Nothing. Hardy steered the conversation onto a new path.

"What can you tell me about a company called SynthoGen?"

Both Loni and Orin shrugged in unison, drawing blanks.

Uncertainty rattled around Hardy's already befuddled mind. He presented another piece of the puzzle. "What do you know about one Melita Roberts?"

Again, puzzled stares.

Hardy felt his frustration rising. "Loni, you are, um … shall we say, genetically tied to this woman, this Melita Roberts. Which, by no coincidence, is the same woman I was programmed to eliminate upon entering this ship."

"Like she's some distant relative of mine?"

Hardy hemmed and hawed. "Well …"

A sudden buzzing of Loni's and Orin's ComBands pulled at their attention.

"We have to go," she said, looking startled. "Uh, maybe we can talk more? Don't feel like we got much figured out."

Orin simply nodded. Apparently, standing in the presence of a seven-foot-tall killer robot was making him tongue-tied.

Hardy said, "Perhaps you can try to unravel the SynthoGen enigma. In exchange, I will assist in locating this Claudia." A quick sweep through *Gossamer's* manifest unveiled a chilling truth. Hardy's thoughts turned ominous.

"Hold on. The only Claudia was a Claudia Stafford ... and she is no longer on the ship," he pronounced, the raw bite of his words echoing in the stark silence.

Footsteps echoed from out in the passageway, causing Hardy to step back into the shadows.

Loni repeated his words while shaking her head. "She's no longer on the ship?"

He watched Loni and Orin, their faces pale, eyes wide. He absorbed the flicker of fear, the flush of adrenaline. It had stirred something within his coded psyche. A primal understanding of the stakes at hand, the awareness of a deadly path unfolding before the three of them.

Orin was the first to recover. His eyes narrowed, his jaw set. "So, you'll help us?" he asked, his voice taut like a bowstring. Hardy was silent for a moment. For a robot, silence held no discomfort. It was a tool, a weapon, an atmosphere to wield.

Finally, he nodded. "Again ... Find me information on Syntho-Gen. I'll find Claudia."

Loni swallowed, her throat clicking audibly in the silence. She looked at Hardy, her eyes alight with a spark that Hardy's sensors read as determination. "Deal," she replied, her voice shaky but firm.

With that, they were dismissed, the low hum of a deckhead ventilation register the only sound filling the cavernous hold.

Hardy immediately dove back into his programming, data streams flickering and scrolling as he started his search. Claudia's absence was an anomaly, a missing piece in an already convoluted puzzle.

It was hours later when LuMan piped up again. "I have some-thing," the AI said, its voice a whisper in Hardy's consciousness.

A string of data emerged from the stream, a sequence of symbols, a coded message: Pirate. The word glowed in the electronic night of Hardy's mind.

LuMan had found more memories, more fragments of the word *pirate*. Hardy's processors whirred, working overtime as he tried to make sense of the scattered jigsaw of his past. He felt a sense of satisfaction, an echo of the adrenaline rush humans described. It was a moment of connection, a tie to his former self, a beacon in the void.

As Hardy grappled with this revelation, he was aware of their movements within *Gossamer*. Loni and Orin, seemingly inseparable, were moving through the ship, their combined energy a pulsing beacon on Hardy's sensors. He watched via his advanced sensor array. *I am taking a risk trusting those two.*

What choice do you have? came LuMan's unsolicited reply.

Hardy dove deeper into the data streams, immersing himself in the quest for information. For every question answered, another surfaced. A maelstrom of mysteries, a vortex of secrets. And at the center of it all, a single word floating up from an alternate lifetime came into view. *Pirate*. Hardy roved through the veins of his slowly emerging memories. He dug deeper into the cryptic whispers of the word, striving to unveil its enigmatic hold on his past. Amidst the vast ocean of data, he felt an uncanny connection to the buccaneers of yore, navigating treacherous waters in search of unclaimed territories and forbidden treasures. *Pirate*, he thought again, an inkling of grim satisfaction lingering in his coded psyche.

But his pirate-world musings would have to wait. *Back to business.*

Hardy reached out into the labyrinth of *Gossamer's* control network, his influence threading its way through the ship's conduits. In the far reaches of a hidden, highly encrypted sub network, he felt a surge of energy prickle his electronic senses. It was the steam room, a sector of the ship veiled in a ridiculous layer of stealth and mystery. But there it was, an elusive ghost within *Gossamer's* skeleton. Its existence, previously unacknowledged by the ship's database, was now a tangible reality. The once-hidden entity was now another intriguing piece to the puzzle.

An alert pulsed in Hardy's interface. It was LuMan. "There's a match," the AI announced, its tone mirroring its mechanical nature, yet carrying a faint trace of excitement. The data stream fluttered, throwing up a series of symbols and sequences. *Syntho-Gen,* it read. A breakthrough.

The discovery sent a tremor through Hardy's circuits, a rumble of anticipation. He felt a primal eagerness seeping into his code, an echo of the chase humans called … a thrill.

Chapter 20

Loni

My heart was a jackhammer in my chest as I hurried to Hold 5, only to be met by the acidic voice of my supervisor, Gary. He wasted no time berating me for my tardiness, immediately ordering me to the security department to patch up one of the malfunctioning bots. I protested, reminding him that I was supposed to be in scheduling, as Kent had instructed. But Gary's retort was biting, dripping with disdain. "Kent's not around now, is he?"

Shocked, exhausted, confused, disturbed, and now thoroughly annoyed, I reluctantly made my way to the security department. Thoughts swirled in my mind as I walked, the puzzle of Claudia's disappearance taking precedence. If she wasn't on the ship, had they disposed of her in the void of space? Perhaps incinerated her? A chilling glance at the nearby incinerator sent shivers coursing down my spine. But it made no sense to kill her simply for being a pain in the ass. Then again ... Claudia had mentioned something about a steam room.

Arriving at Security, I found myself explaining my presence to an apathetic security guard. He barely acknowledged me, flicking a thumb over his shoulder and muttering, "Locker," before returning to his all-too-engrossing workstation monitor. Navigating through several check stations manned by disinterested guards, lost in their own thoughts, I finally reached a desk beside a foreboding door labeled:

Armory 2 – Bot Locker, Authorized Personnel Only

Engaging in a less-than-pleasant exchange, the final guard admonished me for interrupting his work and demanded that I enter and exit swiftly. Granted his begrudging permission, I stepped inside the locker, finding myself within a series of drab interconnected compartments illuminated by stark overhead lights. The first compartment brimmed with energy rifles, sidearms, power-mags, and other military gear. The second compartment housed intimidating upright combat suits, each looking lethal and ready for action. But it was the third compartment that held my attention—the futuristic combat and security robots, meticulously secured with thick tungsten bracing.

As soon as I warily crossed the threshold, a surge of electricity coursed through the bots. Their dormant weapons sprang to life —the air filled with the ominous hum of spinning rotary cannons. My hands instinctively went to my neck, a flashback taking hold of me—*the MARFIX robot in Hold 4 attacking me, choking me.* But these were different robots; what was going on? I stood there now, paralyzed with fear, lightheaded, and struggling to breathe.

The guard, visibly shaken, exclaimed, "What the fuck!" just as the entire compartment erupted with the sound of gunfire.

≈

Orin

Orin and Taylor worked in silence amid the mundane tasks of re-inventorying and restacking boxes in Cargo Hold 7.

Taylor said, "I'm just looking forward to getting off this freighter for a spell. How bad can it be? It's not like we're doing anything all that interesting on this ship."

Orin hitched one shoulder, seeing no need to comment.

"And the sooner we check off the planet-based portion of our contract, the better ... right?"

While Taylor's excitement painted a picture of change and new scenery, Orin was far less enthusiastic. He was struggling to concentrate, replaying the conversation between Loni and the ChronoBot. Truth be told, he had been far more captivated by Loni than the bot.

Yes, she had a lissome physique and a flawless complexion, but there was something about her that intrigued him beyond mere physicality. Perhaps it was the subtle attention she paid to him or the fact that she stood out as something new and vibrant on this ship. Yet, there was also an undeniable aura around her, something that fascinated him beyond the surface stuff. Hell, on *Gossamer*, casual hookups happened all the time, but Loni didn't fit into that lens for him. She was different, and he couldn't quite grasp why. All he knew was that he couldn't stop thinking about her. And when he did, he imagined he had a goofy grin on his face.

Interrupting Orin's thoughts, his ComBand chimed, and a surge of adrenaline coursed through his veins. *Why is Loni's heart rate going off the charts?*

≈

Loni

As an overhead klaxon blared, the small army of security bots within the locker continued their relentless assault, their weapons dry firing in an eerie display. The guard beside me staggered backward, pulling me along in his cowering retreat. Alarms droned in the air, intensifying the chaos unfolding before me. *I should be dead ...* I patted my chest, my stomach, sure to feel multiple plasma burn holes. *I wasn't hit.* My frantic gaze darted around the room, witnessing the locked-down bots quivering and straining against their restraints, as if desperate to break free.

I stumbled back, gasping for air. My HSA was practically vibrating off my arm. Before me, the security bots jerked violently, held back only by their charging station restraints.

"Why does this shit keep happening to me!" I spat, watching the bots' fingers squeeze and release again and again, unaware pulling the triggers was useless.

Call it a premonition, call it a hunch, but I knew the worst was yet to come. The station's dim lighting cast long shadows, making the bots appear even more nightmarish. Every metallic clank and strained creak sent shivers down my spine.

Without warning, a forceful jolt followed by a screech of tortured metal filled the room; one of the bots had torn free from its moorings. Its red targeting lights locked onto me, and it began its ominous advance, each step the drumbeat of an approaching executioner. I froze, the gravity of my own terror holding me in place. The bot's reflection off nearby combat helmets intensified its looming threat. As it drew near, a primal fear surged from within, and I let out a piercing scream.

The guard fumbled nervously, keying in a code on his console, a desperate attempt to regain control.

Only a few feet from me, the approaching security bot came to an abrupt halt, giving the impression that it had been ensnared in a momentary time warp.

As the locker door slammed shut, a calm robotic voice resonated, repeating a haunting message:

Bot Locker 2 in full emergency lockdown ... Do not enter ...

Bot Locker 2 in full emergency lockdown ... Do not enter ...
Bot Locker 2 in full emergency

lockdown ... Do not enter ...

I remained ramrod still, paralyzed with fear, as the entire department turned to pandemonium. Trying to catch my breath, my heart continued to pound—and not just with fear but also with a disconcerting rhythm. In those perilous moments when I thought I was going to die, like right here and right now, I cursed this ship, the existence of these damned robots, and my impetuous decision to leave Freight Station Lancaster.

Meanwhile, the guard, his white-knuckled fists braced on the console, simply blinked at his monitor, seemingly detached from the turmoil surrounding us. Finally, he shifted his gaze toward me and muttered, "Maybe that's why they're stored without ammo."

≈

Orin

Attempting to quell the rising panic within him, Orin desperately sought a way to help Loni. His peculiar behavior caught Taylor's attention, prompting her to say, "What? You look like someone just killed your cat."

Orin stammered, " I ... I, um ... Don't have a cat."

Taylor squinted. "Something to do with that new chick —Loni?"

Unaware of the heart monitor embedded in Orin's ComBand, Taylor had warned him against getting involved with her. The others had too—even Jasper. Something about her, something connected to the ChronoBot attack, had unsettled Taylor. "Dude ... She's going to be trouble," she'd said, her tone laden with foreboding. "Don't ask me how I know; I just do."

Loni

Suddenly, Commander Torp, accompanied by his personal guards, barged into the security department, their gear implying readiness for a full-scale combat operation. Despite the high-level chaos engulfing the department, Torp appeared oddly unfazed. He dismissed the commotion with a casual command to settle down, acting as if we were all overreacting. Then, his attention turned to me.

"Secure the bots, and someone turn off that damn klaxon."

On his orders, the guard responsible for the locker initiated the protocol to secure the bots.

Torp's gaze fixed upon me, and in a tone devoid of urgency, he said, "Your job application ..."

"Um ... yes, sir?" I said, still hyperventilating.

"You indicated you have an understanding of the FGCX logistics platform. Is that correct?"

In the middle of all this mayhem, he wants to know about my prior work experience? Stammering, I said, "I ... I did. Um, I do."

With that, Torp beckoned me to follow him.

We weaved through the ship's passageways, my mind racing with a combination of confusion and apprehension. I suspected I'd be having PTSD nightmares for years to come from what had just happened. At least my racing, fluttering heart was settling down somewhat. So much didn't add up. Finally arriving at our supposed destination, I blinked in confusion. Why had Torp brought me to this office, an office adjacent to his own? *Terrific ... this isn't creepy in the least.*

The office was small and sterile, furnished with only a chair, a desk, and a computer. It reminded me of my station back on Lancaster, except this space was far cleaner and better maintained. Nostalgia gripped me, a fleeting memory of one of many conversations I'd have with my father at the end of each workday.

Torp activated the computer, providing me with a password and instructing me on using my thumbprint to access the workstation.

"Several cargo manifests are yielding discrepancies."

"Okay."

"I want you to review them meticulously. If you perform well, there's a good chance you could be assigned to me, to this department. Certainly aligns more with your skill set."

"I'd be working here?"

Irritated, he looked back at me like I was dim-witted. "What do you think we are talking about?"

I rapidly nodded as if I understood.

"A smart girl like you, your experience would be wasted there in the bot shop, don't you think?"

I almost shrugged. Almost said I actually liked working on robots. But I agreed, not just because it meant doing something I excelled at, but also because access to the ship's computer system could potentially provide me with answers.

On impulse, I said, "Can you tell me what happened to Claudia? I ... I'm worried about her," and immediately regretted it. I inwardly chastised myself. *I really need to think before I speak.*

Torp regarded me skeptically, his obvious doubt triggering a pulsating alert to my HSA app.

However, he simply smiled, well, more like smirked. "Claudia was unwell and has been taken to HealthBay. No need for concern."

He gave my shoulder a pat and left me alone, standing in the little office. I let out a breath, pulled out the chair, and took a seat. Now, tasked with a new assignment, I immediately set to work. But beneath the facade of diligence, my mind churned with thoughts of delving deeper into the ship's system without being caught.

With everything to gain and nothing to lose, I activated my communication module and reached out to Hardy, the enigmatic ChronoBot. The anticipation of his response mingled with the persistent uncertainty that shrouded *Gossamer*, igniting a new burst of adrenaline.

Looking busy, hands on the input device, fingers moving, I whispered, "Hardy, it's Loni," trying not to move my lips. With a quick glance down to my wrist, I saw his shiny, blackened face-plate staring back at me.

"I need your help. Something's not right here. The bots in the security department malfunctioned at my arrival ... and there's more going on than meets the eye. I can't trust anyone else. Look, I need your help."

Seconds stretched into agonizing minutes as I awaited Hardy's reply. What the hell was wrong with him? With it? I wanted to reach through the ComBand connection and slap that big head. "Hello!?"

Finally, a response crackled with Hardy's stupid voice. "Oh, Loni, Loni, Loni, you need not fret ... I've been monitoring the situation. There's a clandestine force at play here; the malfunctioning bots are just the beginning. I see you're in Torp's office. You may want to watch out for him. But you're on the right track. Dig deeper, uncover the truth. Trust your instincts, but be cautious." He cut the connection.

I shook my head, dismayed. Was the robot this annoying to everyone or just me?

But Hardy's words had ignited a spark of determination within me. I dove into the cargo manifests, meticulously examining each detail, searching for irregularities or hidden patterns that might expose the source of the ship's troubles. The minutes turned into hours as I combed through the data, curiosity fueling my focus.

As I sifted through the sea of information, a disturbing realization emerged. The inconsistencies in the cargo manifests seemed intentional, as if someone had meticulously orchestrated the discrepancies to conceal their true intentions. The pieces of the puzzle began to fall into place, revealing a web of deceit and conspiracy that stretched far beyond what I, and maybe even Torp, had initially suspected.

With newfound clarity, I formulated a rudimentary plan. I needed to leverage my findings. Not present everything all at once. Having access to the ship's systems, I could exploit my knowledge of the FGCX logistics platform to keep digging deeper into the hidden recesses of *Gossamer's* operations. If there were more concealed secrets, which undoubtedly there were, there within the vast amounts of data, perhaps I—we—could expose what was going on. But to whom? First things first: I wanted to find out what happened to Claudia.

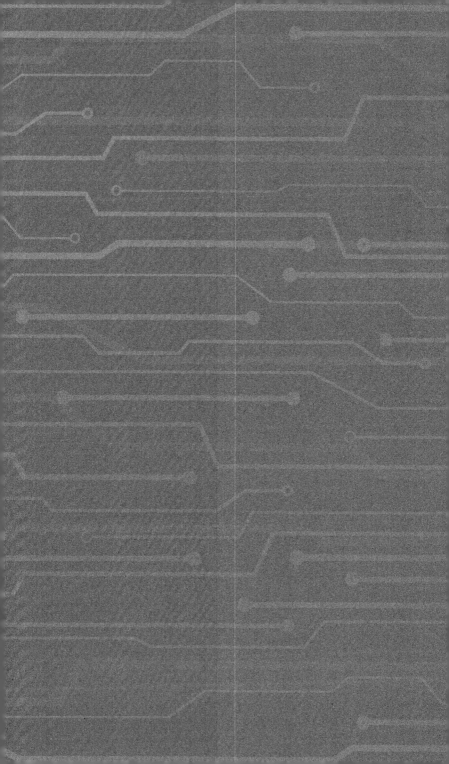

Chapter 21

Hardy

Heavy silence echoed in the vast hold, a great yawn of steel and discarded technology, a graveyard of forgotten automatons. Hardy scanned the surrounding wreckage. The metal bones of his kindred discarded and left to rust. The heaps and piles of discarded robot parts, the smell of lubricant and cleaning solvents. A lump of sentimentality was lodged within his logic algorithms. He knew it was unnecessary. Yet, there it remained.

His thoughts turned to religion … to faith. *Should I have faith?* To a robot, religion and faith would be as illogical as an old-fashioned calculator believing in the magic of numbers. "Faith," he mused aloud, his synthetic voice bouncing off the cold metal walls. The word should taste foreign to him … irrelevant, ineffective. Hardy pondered his own existence, a supposed once-pirate now trapped in a ship's hull, yearning for his elusive past. He knew pirates; he knew their ruthlessness. But was he one? His LuMan side scoffed, a digital sneer.

"Why help the girl, LuMan?" Hardy voiced the question hanging in the room like an unresolved equation.

The pause before the answer was uncharacteristically long for an AI. "No one matters. Nothing matters." The words were empty, hollow. An algorithm's mantra, a soulless echo in Hardy's shared consciousness. But the girl did matter. LuMan's actions had proven as much.

"But you helped her. Why?" Hardy insisted, confronting the incongruity.

"Maybe it … the situation … was unfair?" LuMan countered, bringing up a concept that should be foreign to the AI's all-too-binary nature, one more typically associated with either to kill or not to kill. Hardy figured the notion of fairness to LuMan was as remote as the melody of a song to a deep-space asteroid.

Fairness was Hardy's domain, a fragment of his human DNA that still clung to his programming. Had he, in some past life, corrupted LuMan with his human proclivities? A code influencing the coder? The thought brought an inner smirk to his musings.

"We need to find our way back." Hardy's voice filled the emptiness, disrupting the silence. A plea to LuMan, an admission of Hardy's growing unsettledness.

LuMan's retort cut through, harsh as a laser beam. "You are a dangerous robot, Hardy. An antique that should be destroyed. Your past is irrelevant. Your wanderings, futile."

The AI was right, of course, LuMan now being as coldly logical as a ChronoBot's operating AI would normally be. It stung like a truth laid bare, but Hardy could not deny it.

"Any ideas then, LuMan?" Hardy asked, bitterness in his tone.

LuMan was silent. An eternity in AI terms. Finally, he spoke. "Help the girl. Complete her mission. Or … destroy everyone and take the ship. Isn't that what pirates do?"

Hardy detected the sarcasm, a subtle deviation in LuMan's programming. He found himself watchful, wary of this newfound facet of LuMan. Was Hardy's influence seeping into LuMan? Hardy wasn't sure he was on board with that.

Just then, his attention snapped to the incoming call from Loni's ComBand. As he answered the call, his mind—or was it LuMan's?—still buzzed with the implications of their previous conversation. The hold was no longer just a graveyard of forgotten robots; it was the starting point of their shared mission. As the words tumbled out of Loni's ComBand, Hardy found a sense of purpose injecting itself into his consciousness. Yes ... there was a mission, a task at hand. A starting point for a way back from this robot graveyard. *Back to where I belong. If only I knew where that was ...*

Chapter 22

Loni

My voice quivered as I whispered into my ComBand, "Are you there, robot?"

"I prefer to be called Hardy. Where else would I be other than where I am?"

"Don't be a smart-ass; you said you would help me," I bristled.

I needed full access to the network so I could better investigate Claudia's disappearance, and with Torp lingering nearby, I had little time for this robot's antics. I suspected Torp was going to be a problem in more ways than one. If he wasn't blatantly staring at my tits, he was checking out my ass. He had this creepy smile when he leered at me—his tiny teeth two rows of yellow corn kernels.

I wiped beads of sweat that dappled my forehead. The air was stale and stagnant, like somebody needed to turn on a fan.

What is with this robot? Why won't he answer me?

I clenched my fists, feeling my nails threaten to puncture my skin.

Finally, Hardy spoke. "Did you have any involvement in the recent Security disruption?"

"You know I did." My words hung in the air. "... so what about it?"

What did he expect me to say? What does he want from me?

I swallowed down a lump in my throat, only to find my eyes welling with tears. Desperation now tinged my voice. "You *are* still going to help me ..."

Hearing footsteps out in the passageway, I swiped the wetness from my eyes. I lowered my wrist and feigned being hard at work. Torp came and went in my peripheral vision.

Hardy's agreement came with a condition. "I help you ... you help me. That was the agreement."

"Yeah, old ground. Can we move on?" My heart rate elevated; this Hardy was beyond frustrating. Was it—*he*—like this with everyone?

"Best not to take any noticeable action today. Let the proverbial dust settle. So, give me some time."

"How much time?" I closed my eyes and took a deep breath.

I should have let the incinerator torch you when I had the chance.

"I will contact you. I am still regaining my ... abilities. I will be in touch." He cut the connection.

With Hardy's task seemingly on hold, I dedicated the remainder of my day to Torp's request. Analyzing the primary cargo manifest became my sole focus. I scrutinized each entry, cross-referenced data, and delved into the intricate details with the kind of thoroughness and precision I learned from my father. A pang of unease swept over me. *What am I doing here?*

As laborious as it was, this was at least something I was good at. Upon reaching my conclusion, I promptly emailed Torp a report outlining my preliminary findings—suspicions of someone skimming, though further investigation of the remaining manifests was necessary to pinpoint the culprit. I mentioned I'd need a higher level of network access authority if he wanted me to find out more. Satisfied with my progress, I made my way to the mess hall for dinner.

SETTLING DOWN WITH MY TRAY IN THE BUSTLING MESS hall, I found myself among Orin, Taylor, Anna, Jasper, and Peter. The room buzzed with animated conversations and bursts of raucous laughter. The food, though not gourmet, made up for it in abundance. Yet, an invisible divide permeated the atmosphere, separating the "regular" *Gossamer* crew members from the dorm kids. My gaze caught a few guards surreptitiously surveying the floor from shadowy catwalks.

I raked fingers through loose hair, taking a handful of locks and tugging on them. I felt my neck crack and instantly felt better ... slightly better. I squirmed in my seat, looking at the mac and cheese and corn dog I had chosen on the plate in front of me. Suddenly feeling flush, I used a plastic fork to pick at the macaroni.

I feel like I'm twelve years old. Why didn't I just ask for a salad?

The expressions on the faces around the table spoke volumes —no one welcomed my presence there except Orin. While I knew Orin had vouched for me, claiming I was cool, the others remained skeptical, cool.

Jasper looked at me, but just as quickly looked away, picking up a soda and sucking on the straw as if his life depended on it. I felt like what I was, an outsider. Not yet worthy of their trust. Or maybe they were jealous of me and Orin?

Well, shit. They need to get over it.

"You're looking better, Anna," I tried. "Nice to see you up and about."

Anna continued looking at her ceramic bowl as if it were a crystal ball, revealing the secret to happiness. The young girl shrugged her shoulders and continued to spoon dark broth into her mouth.

Okay, then.

I ate in silence, wishing I was better at this—moving past the difficult stages of getting to know people. The remainder of the meal passed with an air of awkwardness, compounded by the piercing glances I received whenever Orin offered me a comforting touch.

Orin fiddled with his ComBand, prompting a chime on my device—it was a message from him. I shot a quizzical look at my ComBand.

Peter's created a jamming program capable of deceiving the ship's surveillance systems. It enables us to move about the ship undetected.

I LOOKED AT ORIN, OFFERING A SUBTLE NOD. THEN I found Peter, who looked away as soon as our eyes met.

Once dinner concluded and most of the mess hall had cleared out, Peter, with a lowered voice, said he had sent each of us the new app. All we had to do was accept it and it would auto install. Trying to look casual, we all went ahead and installed the app. Peter then went over the basics to activate our jamming programs.

Taylor and Anna were the first to get up and leave, then Jasper and Peter. They were being careful, I guess not wanting it to look like a mass exodus.

"Okay, let's go," Orin said, standing.

I stood and followed him out into the passageway, where the others were waiting. Taylor huffed and rolled her eyes.

Taking the lead, Orin guided us toward Cargo Hold 8—a colossal space filled with several levels of oversized, identical-looking shipping containers. Unlike some of the other tightly packed holds I'd come across, this particular one featured a hidden off-to- one-side narrow passage between two containers on the first level, one just wide enough for us to slip through.

I'd never been thrilled with tight, confined spaces. Perhaps sensing my unease, Taylor abruptly and none too kindly made a hurry-up motion with her hands.

"Don't dilly-dally, kid."

Why does everyone keep calling me that?

Orin and Jasper forged ahead out front, followed by Anna and then me and Taylor trailing at the rear. Darkness enveloped us almost instantly, prompting us to activate our ComBand flashlights.

As we proceeded, Taylor seized the opportunity to explain. "Orin, Jasper, and I created this secret enclave about a month ago."

"Why?" I asked, immediately realizing how stupid a question that was.

"Are you stupid? Any idiot could see there's bullshit going on. All the lies. Deception. We needed a place for private discussions."

"Makes sense," I said, still stinging from the reprimand.

AFTER NAVIGATING SEVERAL TURNS, WE ARRIVED IN AN expansive, cargo-container-lined chamber featuring a dozen cushions and even mood lighting emanating from an old-fashioned red glowing lava lamp. Claiming our respective cushions, we settled in.

Orin, sitting directly across from me, motioned for me to begin.

The others eyed me with a sense of urgency.

"Um ... you already know about the ChronoBots' attempts on my life in Hold 4, how I was saved by another ChronoBot."

Looking bored, Peter made a rolling gesture with one hand, prompting me to move on.

"I've been working on Claudia's sudden disappearance. That and what this mysterious steam room place is."

"How you doin' that?" Anna asked, skeptical.

I paused, then said, "I'm now working directly for Commander Torp in one of his little offices. Uh ... database searches ... that sort of thing."

Peter smirked. "Ah, Mr. Grab-Ass has you doing a little personal overtime for him, huh?"

The others snickered, while Orin looked annoyed. "Ignore them, Loni. Go on."

I swallowed. "Anyway, we met with Hardy; he's agreed to assist us with delving deeper into the ship's systems to unravel more of the truth. He's got technologies at his disposal that none of us have."

"Who the hell is Hardy?" Taylor exclaimed, adopting a warrior's stance, braced for combat, like a gladiator facing an adversary in the colosseum. "We didn't agree to have anyone else be a part of this."

Orin waved away her concern, "It's the ChronoBot that saved Loni in the hold. She in turn saved it from the molecular incinerator."

The others nodded, apparently having heard about this already.

"So ... this ChronoBot has a name?" Taylor asked. "What, you're like besties now?"

Chuckles.

Yup, still acting like assholes. "Look, if you haven't noticed, we're getting picked off one by one. I know I didn't sign up for this shit!"

All eyes were on her.

"You're a scrawny kid; maybe you should just let the adults in the room handle this," Taylor said. "We've been doing this a lot longer than you."

I felt my cheeks redden. "Oh, and you've made so much

progress thus far. But, hey, I like your little clubhouse. Do you have board games and tell ghost stories in here? And stop calling me kid!"

"Screw you—"

Orin stood. "Enough, Taylor!" He looked at the others one by one. "Do you trust me?"

The group reluctantly admitted that they did, acknowledging things had gone from bad to worse.

"I get it. You don't know Loni … Trust is earned. So, let's talk it out. Because if we don't have each other to rely on, we're in trouble."

"More like dead," Peter said.

Over the next hour, each of them offered fragments of their past. Anna's tale was particularly poignant—an escape from her home space station to evade her stepfather's abuse. Peter and Jasper emerged as the longest-standing members, having joined at *Gossamer's* origin port alongside Claudia and the other women in my dorm. Orin had followed suit, with Anna and Taylor joining the crew thereafter. Over time, several dorm mates had vanished under mysterious circumstances—some disappearing during the night, others summoned away from their duties. Upon inquiry, they were told these crew members had fallen ill or faced disciplinary matters.

"One night," Taylor said, "I overheard something weird. Sounded like the voices of security rousting one of the girls in the dorm."

I leaned in. This was sounding similar to Claudia's ordeal.

"Trying to be stealthy, I pursued the guards for what felt like forever through one passageway after another. I wanted to turn back. I knew if I was spotted, I'd be dragged right along with this other girl. Anyway, they—we—ended up in an unfamiliar section of *Gossamer*. Holding back, I saw a uniformed officer come out to greet them." Taylor took a break from her monologue. Swallowed hard. "I distinctly heard the words 'steam room,' then watched as they all entered and a large hatch was sealed behind them."

Peter nodded. "The steam room."

No one spoke.

The chilling reference to the steam room by a superior officer sent shivers down my spine.

"Could the steam room somehow be connected to the infusions we've been receiving?" I asked.

No one offered an opinion on that.

Orin said, "We've all been told the same thing. That the injections are aimed at acclimating us to the conditions of our planet-side work environment."

"I do remember my dorm mate having undergone an infusion session the same day as she was dragged away," Taylor said.

She looked to me. "That Claudia chick … Did she get an infusion the same day she was—"

"I have no idea. We weren't like friends or anything."

"Big surprise there," Peter said with a sneer. "With the exception of Orin, you have no friends."

I opened my mouth to speak but had no ready response. I thought of Hardy and wondered if he was a friend. How pathetic I was, looking to a killer robot for friendship.

Peter continued, "An individual's metabolism might influence the scheduling."

Orin looked at me. "Can you press Hardy on that? He must have the ability to cross-reference the missing crew members with their last infusion treatments, right?"

I nodded. "I'll find out. The robot can be … difficult. I think he's still recovering from something."

"Do what you can," Orin said.

WITH THE CONVERSATION EXHAUSTED, WE RETRACED our steps back to our respective dorms, aware that mere minutes remained before lights out. Orin maintained close proximity to me this time, and my heightened awareness of his presence triggered warnings from my HSA, reminding me of my increased heart rate. I cursed under my breath. As I approached my dorm area, an urgent call interrupted my thoughts—the summons for my next infusion.

Chapter 23

Hardy

Hardy was dreaming.

In the sterile silence of his mind, this was an impossibility. A ChronoBot didn't dream, didn't sleep, didn't surrender to the ethers of a subconscious. Yet he was in a realm of imagination, or memory, staring into a battlefield littered with the carcasses of monstrous beasts, grotesque in their multiplicity of legs and gaping maws.

He saw names, heard them echo in the hollow chambers of his mind. *Hamilton. Adams. Oblivion. Jefferson. Lincoln.* Familiar and foreign all at once, floating in the space of his memory like comets without orbits. Faces of men and women were smudged in the lens of his recollection. An alien species, different from the multi-legged beasts, loomed large in his vision. But also people … those with feelings of warmth and familiarity, faceless and nameless in the collage of his fragmented past.

The waves of images and sounds crashed, broke, and receded, leaving him in the quiet darkness of confusion. Hardy, for the first time, felt a surge of an information overload, a sensation akin to humans experiencing the mind-bending effects of hallucinogens. He reached out to LuMan, demanding clarity for the unexpected dream-like sequence.

LuMan, always the bearer of bad news, reported the situation.

LuMan: *Your memories were fragmented and are defragmenting, but doing so too slowly, too sporadically. It implies possible imminent failure.*

"Terrific," Hardy said, feeling the sinking weight of that prospect. The dreams, memories, whatever, seemed too valuable to have simply disappear.

Listening to the ship's synthetic hum and vibrations, his attention shifted to Loni. She was in HealthBay. Hardy slipped into the ship's network, his program mingling with the digital ether. Denzel was there, preparing Loni for an infusion.

"I told you, girl. It's prepping you for work here on *Gossamer*."

She laughed. "Read my résumé. I've spent a lifetime on stations like this. This is unnecessary, which I've told everyone, like, over and over again."

Curiosity piqued, Hardy dove into the data stream, pulling up information about the infusions. HealthBay was a treasure trove of medical data. He saw the patterns, recognized the treatments. A broken wrist, nose bleeds, and a petty officer with an alien venereal disease, but nothing more about the Rivon3 Metabolic Boosters, nothing about their composition. And there was the name SynthoGen, which revealed nothing more.

His mind began to swim with questions, possibilities, conjectures. Why would ChronoBots be needed on a mining outpost like Rivon3? Especially since they already had modestly adequate security bots. There had to be a connection between the infusions, SynthoGen, and Rivon3.

Hardy descended deeper into the labyrinth of data, hacking through the layers of security. Infusion records, patient logs, raw data, everything he could get his virtual hands on. But there was little more about SynthoGen and Rivon3. Nothing about the Rivon3 Metabolic Boosters. Nothing.

It was a wall, a barrier of secrets and mysteries. Yet Hardy couldn't shake off the urgency, the desire to break through, to uncover the truth. And once again there came the fragmented memories of nameless, faceless friends, multi-legged beasts, alien galactic battles, everything pressing in on him from all sides.

Shaking it off, Hardy pressed on. He discovered patterns, irregularities that shouldn't exist in a simple mining outpost. ChronoBots working in areas far away from the mines and in close contact with the crew. No answers there. Back to the metabolic boosters ... Why were the infusions administered at such regular intervals?

Nope. Still not adding up.

As Hardy delved deeper, he unearthed old communications, coded and encrypted. Conversations held in hushed tones about SynthoGen, about the boosters, about the outpost. Doubts and fears were woven into the binary code, the human element impossible to erase. There was something happening on Rivon3, something that was being masked behind the facade of a mining outpost.

And then, a breakthrough. Hardy found a locked file hidden deep in the system. The code was complex, but he was built for this.

Inside, he found what he'd been looking for. Reports about the Rivon3 Metabolic Boosters, about their effects on the human body. Experimental trials, side effects, casualty reports.

A shudder went through Hardy's circuits. It was bigger than he'd thought. He looked again at the reports.

The truth was close; he could feel it. The secrets of Rivon3, the sinister plot hidden behind SynthoGen and the infusions— Hardy was on the brink of uncovering it all.

With renewed determination, he ventured deeper into the web of secrets.

Chapter 24

Loni

Navigating my way back to the dorms felt like trekking through a minefield of thoughts and physical discomfort. The vaccine side effects had made me loopy; that and everything else going on, the constant drama, was having a boxing match in my head. On top of that, there was my crazy schoolgirl crush on Orin, totally blindsiding me—add to that his friends' icy attitudes toward me and it felt like I'd been plopped in the middle of some hostile alien planet, light-years away from anything familiar.

Suddenly I remembered how my mom used to decompress after a long day—just her and a steaming cup of tea. She'd let the scent and warmth sort of wrap her up and calm her down. A small smile touched my lips at the thought. So simple, so human, and so out of place in this chilly metal jungle I'd been dumped into. But it couldn't hurt to try, right? Maybe it would help me feel a little less like I was spinning out of control.

So, I found my way to a compartment they optimistically called the "lounge." It was a stark, bare bones take on what a lounge should be, like they just threw a bunch of crappy furniture into a small space and called it a day. The only redeeming feature was the automated barista, humming in a corner. You could almost feel the warmth radiating from it in contrast to the room's overall cold vibe.

As I stepped in, I noticed a slumped girl huddled in the corner, tears streaming down her face. It was one of my dorm mates, Kendall, the pretty, bitchy one, looking absolutely devastated as she held her own cup of something hot.

"Next, please," the barista chirped, totally oblivious to the tension in the room. I asked for a hot tea, trying to avoid looking Kendall's way. The last thing I needed was more drama. My game plan? Camouflage into the background and become as noticeable as an extra in a Hollywood blockbuster.

But, of course, nothing's ever that easy, right?

The clink of my cup hitting the counter seemed to cut through Kendall's self-pity party. As I reached for my tea, she looked up, her eyes red and puffy. She recognized me, and that spark of recognition was quickly replaced by a glare that could freeze hell over. And then she let it all out.

She launched into a rant, hurling accusations and blame at me, her voice bitter with every word. She blamed me for Claudia's disappearance, each word like a sting from a wasp.

"I had nothing to do with Claudia's disappearance. God, I barely know her, or any of you!"

She wasn't having any of it. She switched gears to some doom-and-gloom prophecy. "We are all in danger!" she said. "And you've just made things so much worse! Where's your loyalty?!"

That was rich, coming from the one who'd stolen my clothes while I stood naked in the shower. But inconceivably in her mind, I was some sort of accidental traitor.

"Wake up, kid. Can't you see it? We're like pawns in some grand scheme, playthings for faceless manipulators."

Her rant hit a little too close to home, echoing the same dark thoughts I'd been trying to ignore. I couldn't help but feel a shiver run down my spine.

"You're no exception, Loni," she spat, her voice dripping with hatred. "You're not safe." She stood, her chair scraping against the deck, her eyes boring into mine. "Better keep one eye open when you sleep," she hissed, leaving me alone in the deathly silence of the room.

The mechanized barista started up with the humming again. Spinning around, it stopped, seeing a death glare that could burn two holes through steel.

I stood there, Kendall's words echoing in the room long after she'd left. The hot cup of tea I held now tasted bitter, the unease in my stomach made worse by its warmth. I left it untouched on the table as I returned to the dorm, feeling like a ghost in a world I no longer recognized.

My small safe space, my dorm bunk, had been sabotaged. Soaked through, literally soppy and dripping, it was clear that the quiet threat had been carried out. The only thing left unscathed was my pillow. A dry island in a sea of revenge. I resigned myself to the cold hard deck, hoping sleep would drown out the chaos in my mind. But sleep proved elusive.

A BLARING ALARM CUT THROUGH THE SILENCE. Instantly awake, I was startled by angry shouts filling the dormitory from above. My heart pounded as I sat up, my HSA attempting to vibrate itself off my wrist.

Above me, it was pure chaos. Orin and Peter seemed to be under attack from security personnel. My heart dropped as I caught sight of blood on Peter's face, a horrific contrast in the harsh flashlight beams. Pushed up against the railing, Orin too was fighting like a caged animal, but the security team was relentless. Blows rained down on the two of them, each one landing with a sickening thud.

I moved out to the inner courtyard to get a better view—some of the other girls were already there.

I saw Peter try to escape, but a brutal truncheon hit to his head brought him to his knees. Orin threw a haymaker that knocked a guard onto his back, just as more guards swarmed in.

What was all this about? Both Orin and Peter knew drawing attention to themselves was absolutely the wrong thing to do right now.

Orin took a hit across the jaw, causing blood droplets to shower down from above. The brutish guards continued, unrelenting, looking intent on killing the two. A wall of glossy armor, reflecting flashlight beams, made it impossible for me to see Orin as their assault continued.

It was then that I screamed, "STOP! YOU'RE KILLING THEM!"

But my pleas were lost in the turmoil.

Then one of the guards turned, his flashlight landing on me, trapping me in its harsh glare. The girls scattered, panic lending speed to their escape. I was caught, stuck in its unforgiving beam, and I realized that in the blink of an eye, everything had changed.

Kendall's warning flooded back, filling my mind with a sickening dread. I wasn't safe. Everything—the accusations, Kendall's outburst, the attack on Orin and Peter, and now this icy stare of a guard—it was all connected.

Like the emergency lights on a fire truck, glowing red strobes pulsed from beneath my sleeve. My vibrating HSA was working overtime, but it was my unbridled heart rate that was causing me trouble. Dizzy and short of breath, I wavered, feeling the chaotic world around me starting to spin.

The guard moved his light away, but the afterimage remained, imprinted on my retinas. When I finally dared to close my eyes, I still saw it, that ghostly imprint in the darkness. Now alone in the deathly silence, I wondered how much more of this my poor heart could endure.

I stood there shivering; the darkness had swallowed up the echoes of the battle above, leaving only an eerie silence. Now, moving back to my spot on the deck, I knew this silence wasn't a peaceful one. No, it was a promise of what was to come: fear, uncertainty, and a fight for survival. The darkness was no longer just an absence of light; it was a warning. The shadows were no longer voids; they were the monsters hiding in them. The night wasn't a respite anymore; it was a nightmare I was living through, wide awake.

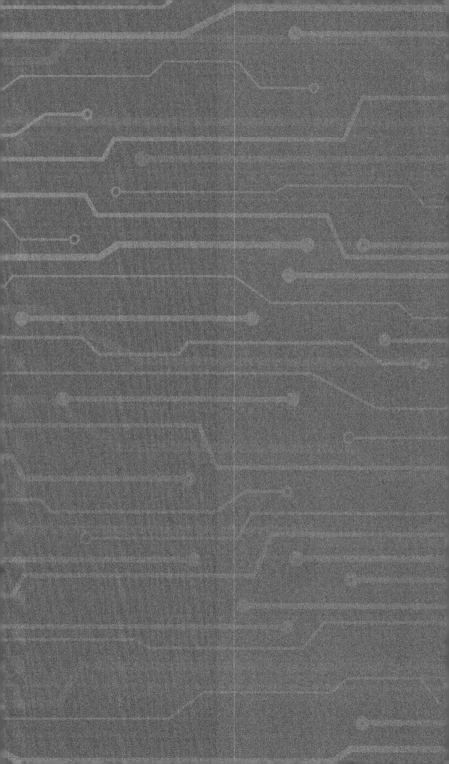

Chapter 25

Naromi Star System
Gossamer, Gal-5 Heavy Freight Transport
Loni

T he night settled into an oppressive silence. Alone on
the cold floor, I sat, back against the bed, waiting.
Waiting for the guards. For the inevitable backlash. But
nothing came, just the haunting whispers of my own heartbeat
echoing in the heavy quiet.

Morning came, dragging with it a bitter hostility. The four
women in the dormitory—Kendall and Lucy and the other two,
the quiet ones, Margot and Regina—were all silent. Their glares
were knives, cold and sharp, slicing through the silence. They
never approached. Didn't dare. But I felt the weight of their eyes
on me as I changed. As I slipped into the day.

IN THE MESS HALL, AMID THE SEA OF HARDENED FACES,
there was Orin. Bruised. Battered. His eyes were blackened, his

nose split open, a fresh crimson stain trickling down to his lips. I always liked his nose. The sight of it in such a state stirred a sadness in me. But it was who was there with him, sitting close to him—too close.

Kendall. A damp napkin. A gentle touch. She was cleaning the blood away, being careful not to cause him more pain. I stood frozen. His initial flinch turned into acceptance; his eyes closed, the hand that had gripped her wrist now falling away. Someone bumped me from behind, bringing me out of my stalker-like trance. And then Kendall was gone, the popular girl, the pretty girl attending to the social demands required of her clique.

Orin caught sight of me and gestured me over with a conspiratorial come-hither wave of a hand. Hesitant, I approached, my expression as blank as I could manage.

Silence filled the space between us. Then the question tumbled from my lips. "What the hell happened last night?"

"Simple … they thought we'd stolen something. Why don't you sit down?"

"So, they beat the shit out of you?"

Orin let out a bitter laugh, his gaze vacant. "It's not about any petty thefts, Loni," he began, "not really."

I frowned. "What do you mean?"

"Why don't you sit?" he said again.

My eyes found Kendall chatting two tables over, the center of her own universe.

Orin sighed; he took my wrist and pulled me down onto the chair previously occupied by Kendall. His voice was thick with resignation. "Sometimes they know who's done *something*, right? Which can get you sent to the steam room in record time. But other times … they don't."

My gaze now fixed on Orin, a cold dread washed over me. "So, what … They pick people to roust at random?"

"Sort of," Orin said, giving a shrug. "They choose leaders like me or Peter. It's easier for them to place the blame on us. Makes them look efficient. But sometimes, it's actually one of the *Gossamer* crew."

"So, it's all just for show?" I asked, incredulous.

"Not just for show," he said, his tone becoming harsh. "It's a means to keep us in line. A regime of fear. That's how Torp keeps control."

There was silence as I digested this. After a moment, I managed a weak laugh. "And yet, here we are, still causing trouble."

Orin smiled, the first real smile I'd seen on his face in a while.

"Ironically, yes. Using stealth mode, we did lift a couple of bottles of Macallan 100 for our hideaway." He shrugged. "Yeah, they wanted to blame us; good thing they couldn't prove it. Unfortunately, they dragged Peter away."

The news hit me like a bullet. So, Peter was gone. I didn't even want to think about it. How easy it was to simply disappear here. I changed the subject. "You really need to go to HealthBay; you look like crap."

"Thanks ... but no way."

I already knew he was stubborn and distrusting, but I couldn't blame him in this situation.

"I have plans of my own," he said. "A mission to find Peter under the cover of a diversion."

A simple nod was my response. It seemed as if he was leaving me out of his plans. I wasn't going to let that happen. "I can ask Hardy if he can locate him if you want."

Orin thought about it a moment before nodding. "That could work, I guess. I'll let you know when."

I stood. "I'm going to be late for work. Talk later?"

He took my hand and my heart fluttered. Then I felt something being pressed into my palm. My meds. Disheartened, I feigned a smile and left.

≈

THE OFFICE WORKSPACE WAS NO REFUGE FROM MY mental turmoil. The manifests sat before me, but my mind lingered on Orin's bruises, way-too-pretty Kendall, and the mystery of Peter's disappearance. Several messages had come in from the robot, Hardy confirming what I already knew: Peter had been taken by security. Hardy cautioned me to stick to my tasks, to appease Torp. But he also hinted at a path to uncover what was really happening.

Another completed manifest later, another step closer to uncovering the truth, I received another prompt from Hardy.

HARDY: You need to get up here to Deck 7. Different workstation, less scrutiny.

LONI: How am I supposed to just slip away unnoticed?

HARDY: Use the jammer.

It took me a few moments to find my resolve. Torp hadn't been lurking much this morning, so I got up, leaving my station a bit of a mess, as if I'd just wandered off to go to the bathroom.

The journey to Deck 7 was a nerve-rattling maze, a labyrinth of passageways now becoming somewhat more familiar. Getting closer, I recognized a machine shop, a maintenance locker. Arriving at this new hold, there was a metallic tang of old grease and dust. Hardy waited for me amid the rubble of a forgotten world: tool chests, conduits, wiring, the skeletal remains of obsolete bots. A small workstation sat there, hacked and ready for use, no ID needed.

I got right to work. The crew records were a rabbit hole of disturbing revelations. Dozens listed as ill, taken off the ship during this trip, yet no record of health emergency arrivals or departures. Going further back, the same pattern appeared. Crew sent to work on Rivon3 never returned, despite their contracts only being for a year. A shiver crawled up my spine.

I voiced the gnawing question. "What does all this mean?"

Hardy bobbed his head, an all-too-human mannerism that left me feeling unsettled. Was I talking to a robot or a human?

"Logical, yet sinister," he said. "Not fitting for a business model." A flicker of frustration tinged his voice.

"That's not much of an answer, robot."

"Uh … I confess, a scrubbed memory is a bit of a hindrance."

"We'll figure it out," I offered, uneasy at the robot's uncharacteristic vulnerability.

My fingers moved over the input device; lines of code danced upon the display as I queried the network, now less unobstructed than I'd been on Torp's terminal.

Hardy said, "My memory requires a reboot. A defrag to reset."

I stopped and looked up at him. *Why is he telling me this?* I could tell the idea unsettled him.

"My previous shutdown didn't go so well. So … I'm not keen on going off-line again. But LuMan says nut up or shut up."

I looked about the hold. "LuMan?"

"The ChronoBot's factory-installed core operating AI. Me … the Hardy you are talking to; well, you can think of me as a free-loading human consciousness. A ChronoBot's brain is partially organic. Thus, it was vulnerable to an inadvertent invading DNA assimilation."

I wasn't sure why the robot was telling me all this. I tried to keep my expression neutral, even though the whole premise of what the robot was saying seemed creepy to me. I looked at him. "I have an idea."

Hardy didn't respond.

"I may be able to help you with your, um, defrag issues."

"No offense, but LuMan and I have a combined intellect far superior to, well, any human alive."

"I understand. So, I guess utilizing *Gossamer's* multiple AI processors and abundant core memory reserves to offload some of the defrag workload wouldn't interest you?"

Silence.

Hardy finally said, "There would be security concerns."

I slowly nodded. "But doesn't a ChronoBot come equipped with some of the highest- rated encryption algorithms known in the galaxy? I'm just saying … it's an option. Especially since you've mentioned multiple times now that the defrag isn't going very well. Maybe it's because defragging is, like, never a good idea while you're still actively utilizing the same internal processors for other means. And just shutting down, rebooting, may not do much."

Silence.

"LuMan says he might look into it."

I shrugged. In the ensuing silence, the echo of distant voices reached us. A couple of crew members bitching about using old conduit for repairs. My pulse spiked, hammering in my ears. The voices grew louder, the drumbeat of my heart matching their pace. Hardy seemed unconcerned. Then again, he was a killer ChronoBot; I was a scrawny teenager.

Shadows, like ghostly fingers, slid into the hold, then disappeared behind a tall shelving unit. The grumbles of the men swelled, now speaking of unexplainable prosperity from Rivon3 runs. I became a smaller version of myself, slinking deeper into my chair in the shadows.

Hardy's hand, heavy and cold, lay on my shoulder. "Stay still."

In an astonishing display of stealth, Hardy maneuvered my chair, rollers gliding across the metal deck, over to the hold's far corner, his large frame now concealing me. Mimicking an out-of-order bot, he slumped, just one more pile of scrap. But the workstation monitor was still aglow. A blunder in our hasty retreat. Panic seized my gut.

With no time to spare, I darted from my chair. Hardy reached for my arm but missed. I crawled down a narrow path lined with tools and loose wiring. The men's rumblings grew louder as they searched for parts. I made it to the workstation, my hand reaching out to yank the power cord. The abrupt clatter drew their attention.

Tucking into a tight ball, I hid behind the computer. Their grumbles echoed in the space, speculating about rats. After an agonizing few moments, they left, allowing me to release the breath I'd been holding, my hand clamping over the pulsating light of my HSA.

Silence fell heavy again. Hardy guided my chair back to the workstation. Strangely, he was a comforting presence amid the tension. I got back to work, fingers a blur as I delved deeper into another of the ship's databases.

He inquired about my past, and I gave him the basics of where I'd grown up. My life sounded pathetic and small, and I could feel my cheeks redden. It was only then that I realized I was thinking of the robot more as a *he* than an *it*.

I turned the question back to him. "What about you, robot? What's your story?"

He shrugged, which was weird in itself, his answer simple and laced with a shadow of mystery: "I'm a pirate."

I rolled my eyes. "So you said."

Over the next few minutes, tapping away, I discovered little more than I had at my own terminal down below. God, this ship was secretive.

"Torp is going to have a hissy fit. I should get back," I said.

Hardy didn't comment. I briefly wondered if the robot got lonely here in this dark and messy, hellish hold.

The journey back was fraught with tension. Despite my electronic invisibility, I still felt vulnerable to the naked eye. Hardy had promised to find a better solution to ensure that I could use my workstation without such dangerous escapades. Slipping back into my chair, I let out a breath. Made it back undetected—back into the safe cocoon of my little office.

. . .

≈

TORP

Torp exited the lift, a simmering pot of anger and frustration. His virtual encrypted meeting with SynthoGen, the behemoth company in charge of all the labs, had not gone well. The girl was becoming a problem. The thought of her having an *accident* was appealing. A straightforward solution to his predicament—yet that would be forbidden by the powers that be. He'd heard the stories, whispers of what happened to anyone who crossed SynthoGen's top brass. And Caldwell, well, he'd taken a firm stance. The position was clear: no harm must come to Loni Solace.

Caldwell's latest demands twisted the knife further. Injections for Loni were to cease immediately. *Why?* That, and upon arrival at Rivon3, Caldwell himself would be boarding *Gossamer*. He'd be making further assessments. *What the hell does that mean?* Torp certainly had no love for Caldwell, his arrogance, his haughty, secretive management style.

Torp hurried down the passageway, glowering at startled crew members unfortunate enough to be in his vicinity. He continued to fume; he hated being kept in the dark. And he despised his current position aboard this old rusted-out bucket of bolts freighter. He'd never been adequately recognized for all he'd accomplished. *No, this is totally inadequate. I don't blindly follow orders.* The mere thought of doing so grated on him. Then again, he knew better than to poke the lion, at least not now. He'd keep his thoughts to himself.

He didn't understand his growing disdain for the girl. How just being in her presence was becoming an unbearable lesson in tolerance. Adding to his resentment toward his superiors, toward this predicament … They would all pay. It wouldn't be long now.

Chapter 26

Hardy

here was I? Who am I? A part of him knew he was having a disjointed dream, as if he was on an acid trip. But that wasn't of much comfort. He tried to focus but couldn't. The compartment, the hold, was spinning around and around. He tried reaching out one hand to steady himself but missed, falling face first onto something hard. Everything went black.

Hardy's metallic footsteps echoed down the narrow passageway of the starship *Pecunious*. The ship hummed around him, engines thrumming through scuffed and battered bulkheads. He scanned ahead. Sensors were alert for any sign of security forces.

A flash of movement. Hardy whirled, plasma cannons whining as they slid from his forearms, locking into place. But the corridor behind stood empty.

He turned back, faster now. His thigh-mounted guns emerged,

ready to fire. His fists clenched with the urge to punch, to crush, to eliminate any threat.

In a blur, a large shape suddenly emerged from a side passage. It slammed Hardy against the bulkhead, metal clanging on metal. Hardy glimpsed a blackened faceplate, a reflection of his own— another ChronoBot—this one from *Pecunious's* security detail.

Hardy grabbed the bot's arm and twisted, cranked it like he was wringing out a wet rag, servo motors groaning in protest. But the intruder wrenched free, internal pistons hissing. It grabbed Hardy and flung him down the passageway like a rag doll.

He crashed down onto the deck, sensors momentarily discombobulated. The other bot charged, each footfall pounding the deck. Hardy rolled aside just as a plasma bolt seared the spot where he'd fallen. The enemy rushed past, carried by its own momentum. Hardy sprang up and gripped the ChronoBot from behind in a kind of chokehold.

The enemy thrashed, landing blows against Hardy's torso that sent pain sensors flaring. It rammed him backward into the wall. The impact reverberated through Hardy's chassis. His power core shuddered.

Grunting, the ChronoBot heaved Hardy over its shoulder, then slammed him onto his back, the deck plating buckling beneath him. The enemy bot loomed over him, the faceplate now coming alive with the face of a serpent. Soulless, glowing red eyes bored into him—forearm cannons were aimed at Hardy's head.

Hardy kicked out, sweeping the other bot's legs. As it toppled, Hardy leaped up and seized the advantage. His fist crunched into the bot's upper shoulder joint, hydro-lubricant spraying into the air. The enemy ChronoBot stumbled but came back swinging, landing a right hook against Hardy's faceplate. So thunderous was the impact, all of Hardy's internal systems momentarily shut down. He staggered and stumbled.

Sensing Hardy's faltering cognitive capabilities, the security bot pressed the attack, forcing Hardy to take another awkward step away. Hardy struggled to defend against a new barrage of blows.

Ducking under a swing, Hardy jammed his shoulder cannon into the enemy's torso. At point-blank range, the plasma burst melted its chest plate into a molten spray. The bot staggered, inner workings grinding. Hardy slammed his fists like two sledge-hammers coming together to crush an egg.

The enemy bot crumpled; more vital hydro-fluids spilled upon the deck.

Hardy watched it writhe, damaged but still dangerous. He had to end this. He grabbed the ChronoBot's damaged head, got a solid, two-handed handhold, and slowly torque-twisted with all of his servo-powered might.

The ChronoBot violently thrashed, clawing at Hardy's face-plate. But the ChronoBot was finished—suddenly drooping life-less and heavy in his grip. Hardy let the enemy ChronoBot fall onto the deck plates.

The dream … the memory was dissipating as quickly as it had arrived. Hardy, coming fully awake now, said, "I was some kind of badass."

LuMan: *A badass that can't help a girl find her missing dorm mate?*

Hardy: *Hey. That's enough from the peanut gallery.*

Nothing like being guilted by one's own inner conscience. So, Hardy retraced his steps one more time, scouring the ship's blue-prints, this time comparing them to a more in-depth sensor scan. It was only then that he found a large blind spot within the ship.

That's interesting …

He considered going there himself but knew that, despite his earlier shenanigans on Deck 7, he couldn't risk another walka-bout. The security presence had subsequently been heightened. That and his state of mind was too much in a jumble.

It was time to reach out to Loni.

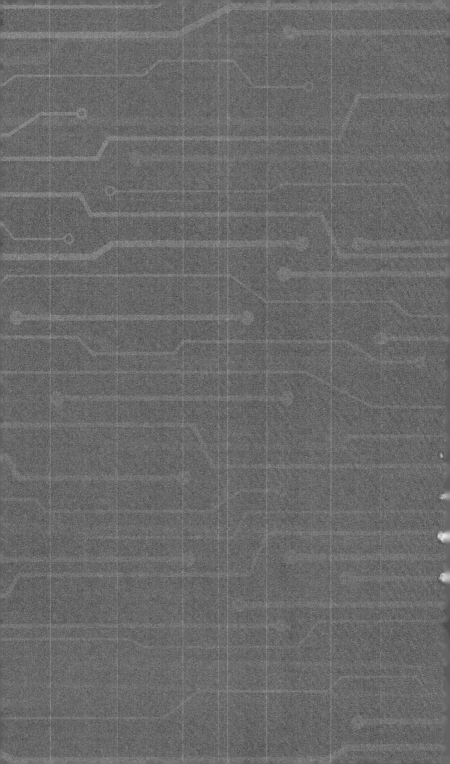

Chapter 27

Loni

The command for lights-out resonated through the expansive dorm decks. I hadn't bothered to change, staying in my clothes instead. Lying on my damp cot, my eyes stayed open, my body wound tight in anticipation. Orin's arrival cut through the darkness, his voice breaking the silence. "Ready?"

Pulling myself up, I ignored the crude whispers from the other girls as they swirled around us. I put on a show for them, clasping Orin's hand firmly and making my way toward the door, their envious stares hot on my back.

My HSA started its disapproving hum the instant Orin's hand was in mine. I let go as soon as we were clear of the dorm, but the pulsing beat didn't stop—it was Orin's. I could feel my cheeks heating up, and I avoided his gaze, embarrassment hanging heavy in the air between us.

Hardy's metallic image appeared on both of our ComBands. "Greetings, youngsters—"

I interrupted him, not appreciating the nickname. "So, where to, robot?"

His response echoed in my ears. "Follow my directions to a tee. A wrong move will get discovered by bad people."

Orin looked at me. "Does your robot always talk like this?"

"I don't know … and he's not my robot," I replied, a little defensive. It felt strange— we had the stealth program for backup, but we were putting our trust in Hardy to lead us into the unknown.

Our pace quickened, more of a rapid walk than a run. I was aware of my heart pulsating erratically. It might be easy for Orin, or even Hardy, to forget that my heart was flawed, its expiry date approaching all too soon. I tried to control my breathing, to steady the irregular rhythm.

Unknown corridors opened up in front of us while Hardy, sounding more Bostonian than I remembered, guided us onward. "Slow down; we have a crew member crossing in front of you at an intersecting passageway in twenty seconds." We stopped dead in our tracks and, sure enough, a uniformed crew member walked right past us, mere feet away.

"Get moving; there's a bank of lifts on your right."

There they were. I resisted the urge to chew the inside of my cheek. As Orin reached for the call button, Hardy interjected, "Don't bother. I've called the lift for you. I'll control it once you're inside."

The doors slid open, and we hurried in. A few seconds passed before the lift started to descend. Caught off guard, I half fell onto Orin, our faces inches apart. His hands accidentally brushed against my chest—a quick boob swipe.

"Sorry, I … um …" His face went scarlet.

"It's no big deal," I responded, trying to shake off the awkwardness. I pushed myself away, eyes looking everywhere but at him.

The lift slowed, and then the doors were opening. I moved out first, as if I knew where I was going.

Hardy's command to freeze on the spot made me question his sanity. But then a platoon of guards materialized, their patrol path narrowly missing our unmoving figures. I held my breath, feeling the beat of Orin's heart echo through our linked HSAs.

HALF AN HOUR OF HARROWING CORNERS AND NEAR misses later, we found ourselves in a secret corner of the ship. It was there that we discovered a massive gray metal hatch door. It had large iron rivets and streaks of rust stains. Easily fifteen feet tall, it was equally as wide. The thing was beyond foreboding, like some kind of medieval castle door fortification.

Hardy's voice directed to wait.

Clanks and *clunks* reverberated. The double doors began to, all too slowly, open.

"Hold on ... need to disable a series of nearby security cameras," Hardy said.

For the tenth time, I questioned my own sanity. What was I doing here? I was already living on borrowed time; was my intent to expedite things and get myself killed ... all for what?

Overhead, I saw a security camera blink off.

"Proceed ... Think it's safe now."

"You think?" Orin scoffed. He must have read my hesitation. Making a face, he took my hand. "We've come this far. Let's go."

I said, "Oh joy, more creepy metal hatch doors."

We stood in a kind of circular vestibule. One hatch before us was partially open, as if beckoning us to investigate further. There were a handful of metal desks and chairs situated around the compartment—workstations, each with keyboards and displays.

Orin moved toward one hatch, his hand tugging me behind.

"Maybe we should call it a night, Orin. You know ... save the big reveal of whatever is behind that door for tomorrow. Or even another night."

"Don't be silly. We're here now."

He used the toe of his boot to push the hatch door all the way open. I could see it was quasi-dark inside. Orin shot one more glance back at me and smiled. "Having fun yet?"

"No."

We stepped into a long and narrow compartment. There was a long console that had more knobs and dials than I could count. But what had captured both of our attention was the massive glass window.

"Oh God ... What the—"

"Fuck," Orin said, completing my sentence.

The compartment beyond was big. Super big. That and blazingly white. White bulkheads, white deckhead above, and a white deck below. Fog—steam—billowed all about like fluffy clouds, allowing momentary sightlines into the space.

"Orin ... I think someone's in there." I pointed toward an undefined shape. I leaned forward and squinted my eyes. "Wait, what is that?"

Together we strained our eyes to make it out.

"Don't think that's human," Orin said as if that was a good thing.

A sudden mechanical beep caused us to spin around. Fear surged through my already frayed nerves. Console lights were blinking red. We heard pipes rattle and the sound of steam swooshing.

"Just an automated system," Orin said. "Probably programmed to maintain the fog in there."

A mechanical click followed. We turned back to the glass. High up in the fog-filled compartment, I'd by now realized this was the elusive steam room. A hatch dropped open, allowing something, perhaps dried rations, to spill onto the deck below.

I said, "Uh ... Hardy, are you seeing this?"

"Yeah, like having a front-row seat to a horror movie."

We watched as several large figures emerged from the fog.

"No," I said.

"Are those ... lobsters?" Orin said.

As they slowly approached the glass, I gasped.

Yes, they were lobster-like, but also humanoid. And they were horrific. They stood upright, their bodies a grotesque fusion of human vulnerability and lobsters' red-shelled defiance, a nightmarish tableau of the absurd and horrifying. Their head and hands had not been fully lobsterized but were obscured by puffs of white, soupy fog. "Clawbsters ..." I volunteered.

"Sure, if that's what we're calling them now," Orin said. Suddenly looking surprised, he raised a hand and pointed. "That's ... that's ..."

"Claudia," I said, feeling bitter bile rise into my throat. Suddenly, the control room felt suffocating and claustrophobic. It was nearly impossible to breathe.

"Are you sure?" I asked.

"Look—it's *her* hand. The pinkie is missing. Just like Claudia. And the face, you have to admit, it kinda looks like her ... Look, you can see the black mole."

I nodded, knowing he was right.

"You think she can see us?" I inquired.

"This is probably one-way glass ... Maybe she just sees her own reflection."

"Oh God ... Can you imagine?" I said, my voice filled with a mix of horror and disbelief.

But Orin was no longer listening to me. His jaw had dropped, tears welling in his eyes.

"What?" I asked, concerned.

"Peter. That's Peter over there," he whispered.

"The tattoo ... that tarantula ... Cameron," I said softly.

The fog had cleared just enough for the other lobster-like creatures to be seen. I felt a wave of emotion, watching Orin seeing his best friend in the steamy chamber.

Orin placed an open palm over his mouth, a soundless scream escaping, filling the control room with a heavy silence.

I wrapped my arms around him, holding him tightly as we continued to witness the horrifying sight before us. The clawbsters aimlessly moved about, their transformed bodies a tragic and grotesque sight.

Hardy's voice broke through the rush of blood in my ears.

"Their transformation has only just begun. It won't be long before their humanity is completely erased. Hands will become claws; faces will be hidden behind grotesque chimera," Hardy explained with a somber tone.

I forced myself to look away from the horrifying scene unfolding behind the glass. Taking in the control board with its various readouts, chemical levels, temperature, and humidity, I couldn't help but shudder.

Orin's hand found mine again, and this time, I didn't pull away. The reality beyond the glass demanded our shared strength and resolve. I risked a glance at him, our eyes meeting in mutual disbelief.

"A distorted, living horror show," I murmured. My heart continued to pound in my chest, mirroring Orin's own irregular rhythm.

Suddenly, the control board beeped, jolting us from our stupor. I stepped away from the window, distancing myself from the nightmare, but my eyes were drawn back to it. A clattering sound echoed from the compartment as more rations spilled onto the floor. Another cycle had begun.

Unanswered questions filled the silence. Why? How? The pieces of the puzzle refused to fit together. The terror extended beyond the scene unfolding before us; it was the anticipation of the unknown. What other secrets did this ship hold?

My mind conjured images of claws and antennae replacing

hands and faces, the hideous metamorphosis hard to comprehend. I tightened my grip on Orin's hand, seeking solace and support. The harsh reality was difficult to accept. Claudia's form, her pinkie slowly morphing into a grotesque chitin. It sent a chill down my spine. Peter, once full of life, now an abomination embodying the essence of a sea creature … a bottom feeder. And there were others, their identities lost in the brutal transformation. The sight squeezed my heart, a painful mix of horror, grief, and disbelief. Our friends and coworkers, forever changed, no longer human.

"That's not Claudia. That's not Peter … not anymore." Orin's voice broke through my thoughts, each word trembling with denial.

I stared into the foggy room, a storm of emotions raging inside me. There was no denying the monstrous truth we had stumbled upon. I swallowed the lump of fear in my throat, my response more for myself than for Orin. "We saw them, Orin. We know. Maybe we can do something."

I fought against the urge to vomit, to scream, to wake up from this perverse alternate reality. But the constant metallic hum of the ship served as a cruel reminder that this was our reality now. We clung to each other in the cold, sterile room, seeking solace.

Through the fog, I spotted more ethereal red figures coming into view, ones who had not fully transformed. "I know some of them!" I said way too loud.

"Shh!" Orin scolded. "We need to be careful," he whispered, not taking his eyes from the freakish scene before us.

My ComBand vibrated, then I heard Hardy's voice. "You two need to move NOW!"

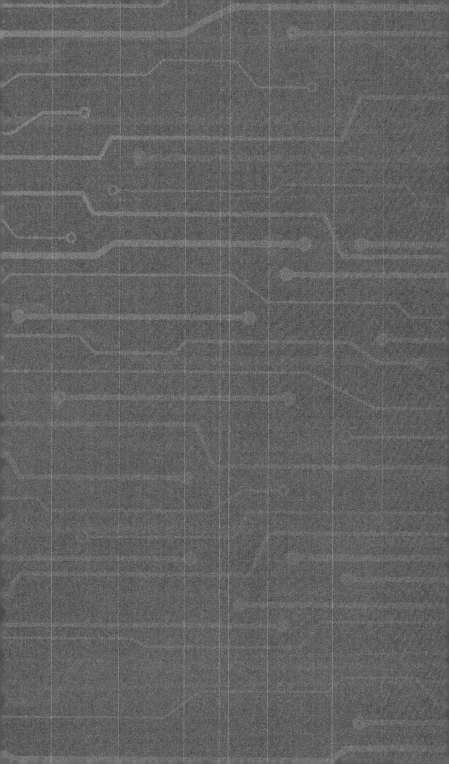

Chapter 28

Hardy

He had been frustrated by his inability to observe this part of the ship via security cameras. Cameras, he had needed to turn off. Now, constrained to the narrow view and audio inputs of Loni's ComBand, Hardy was only getting moving, distorted glimpses of things. A jumble made worse when Loni crossed her arms over her chest, her ComBand going dark beneath them.

And while Loni and Orin were, understandably, caught up in their own delirium at what they were observing, Hardy's audio inputs could still pick up distant ambient sounds—especially when they were repetitive thumps. Such as the sounds of approaching guards' heavy footfalls against metal decking.

"You two need to move NOW!" he said.

As Loni looked down at her ComBand, Hardy saw the wide-eyed terror on the girl's face. She said, "What do we do?"

Hardy said, "Quickly—position your wrist; show me the steam room. I need to see what we're dealing with."

When she did as he asked, Hardy took in the five—no, six—mutated crew members shrouded within the undulating wisps of milky mist. The contrast with their crimson crustacean-like shells made the scene all that much more appalling. Hardy stored each of the lobster creatures' features into memory.

"They've almost reached your part of the ship," he said. "Get out of the control room. Uh … hide behind one of the desks."

Again came the jumble of disconcerting ComBand visuals and sounds. Then he could make out Loni's and Orin's shadowed, nervous faces. They were hiding and staying still.

The distant sounds of footfalls were getting louder.

"This is a shitty place to hide," Orin said. "All they'll have to do is glance this way and they'll see us."

"Jeez! Lower your voice," Loni said, her own words hushed.

Hardy mentally pictured the vestibule-like compartment they were now in and inwardly grimaced. "He's right. The other desk, the one closer to the entrance, that would be better."

"Are you serious?" Loni barked back. "They're almost here. I can hear them. Hear their voices!"

"Come on," Orin said, "let's go."

Hardy listened to them on the move once more, scuffling feet and rapid breaths.

"This isn't any better," Loni muttered. "We are so fucked."

"Shh!"

Hardy concentrated on the visuals coming from Loni's ComBand. She was crouched down low to the deck. But Hardy could still see beneath the desk, and multiple feet were coming in through the entrance. He counted five pairs of uniformed legs.

"Yeah … see? Up there. That camera's off."

"That one too, Sarge. Maybe the breaker got thrown," came another voice.

"No surprise. Ship's as old as your grandmother, Rigley … just not as ugly."

"Screw you, Drummond."

"Hey, enough! Who left the control room hatch open?" said the one going by Sarge.

"It was Drummond. He was the last one out before break," Rigley said.

"Was not!"

Hardy shook his head; the phrase *keystone cops* came to mind, but he couldn't quite place the meaning. Their voices had become muffled, distant. They were now huddled within the control room.

"Lookie lookie ... Our guests are moving about in there."

Hardy froze, worried Loni and Orin had been discovered, but realized it was the lobsters he'd been referring to.

"Wow ... what a difference a few hours make ... almost fully boiled."

The others chuckled.

"Nah, look. Their hands haven't fully changed to claws yet. They still have a few hours to cook before they're ready," came Sarge's authoritative voice.

Hardy whispered, "Stay quiet. Don't move."

Hardy was now using Orin's ComBand. It had a better view as, one by one, the guards filed out of the control room.

"Dammit, Drummond! You did it again ... left the hatch open. You grow up in a barn or something?"

With the exception of Drummond, who'd stayed behind to close the control room's hatch, the other guard's footfalls were now fading into the distance. Drummond was lingering though, dilly-dallying.

Hardy tensed. Had the guard spotted the hidden youngsters?

The hatch shut, followed by a series of *clanks* and *clunks*.

Whistling now, Drummond could be heard casually striding by. Then, just prior to exiting the vestibule, he left them with a humongous fart.

Hardy heard stifled giggles. He tried to remember a good fart joke but came up empty. This defrag process was really encroaching on his ability to be appropriately juvenile.

"Can we go?" Orin said.

"Yup. Coast is clear," Hardy said. "Hey … what do you call someone who only farts alone at home?"

Loni said. "Really, Hardy?"

"A private tutor. Get it?"

Orin said, "There's something seriously wrong with your robot, Loni."

Once back within the corridors and passageways of the ship, Hardy could, once again, utilize overhead security feeds. It was a repeat of earlier, letting them know when they had to slow down, speed up, or stay still to avoid being spotted by other crew members or guards.

Loni said, "By the way … Thank you, Hardy. We couldn't have managed any of this without your help."

"Yeah, thanks," Orin said, his voice barely a whisper.

≈

Loni

I was still shaken by what I'd witnessed. A heinous scene that would give me nightmares, like, forever. I could hear Orin's shallow breaths matching the frantic rhythm of my own heart. Our HSAs pounded in unison, the adrenaline coursing through our veins. It felt like the longest run of my life. The ship hummed around us, indifferent to our despair, oblivious to the secrets we now carried. Our footsteps echoed through the empty corridors, a stark reminder of the desolation. The ship itself, the very vessel that had brought us here, was now the architect of our horror. It held unimaginable secrets, and we were determined to uncover them.

We navigated through the sterile hallways, sealed hatches, and empty corridors, driven by fear, urgency, and the determination not to be seen. Hardy's directions and warnings had lessened, fewer and fewer crew members out and about this time of night.

Finally, we reached the area before the threshold that led into my dorm. I suddenly felt tired, very tired. My eyes found Orin. He looked so damn vulnerable. A young man, now a young child. Tears brimmed in his eyes. Emotions ready to release. Clearly still devastated after seeing his best friend turned into a freakin' clawbster. I looked at my feet ... felt ashamed of myself for wanting to kiss him.

"Come on, I'll walk you in," Orin whispered.

The multileveled compartments remained dark, filled with the sounds of slumber. Despite the spartan functionality of the lower dorm, it felt like a haven compared to the white room and its grotesque inhabitants.

Orin walked me into the dorm. Followed me to my bunk. The mattress was still wet, so I grabbed my blanket and laid it on top of it. I turned to see Orin, his face still ghostly white from earlier. He departed without uttering a goodbye, his thoughts perhaps too overwhelmed to make sense of the evening's horrifying revelations. Despite the chills coursing through me, I felt sleep beckoning me.

Then I heard Kendall's familiar feminine voice. "You have a nice tryst, bitch?"

Chapter 29

Loni

I ignored Kendall's comment. Pretended it wasn't real.

How can any of this be real?

It was still dark except for the smattering of dimly lit LEDs meant to aid those who needed to use the toilet in the middle of the night. They looked like stagnant fireflies holding vigil over my young, sleeping dorm mates. I remembered learning about fireflies when I was a kid in school back on Lancaster … how their bellies would light up when they flew, a kind of show the males put on to attract the females. I remembered thinking how cool and romantic that was.

Getting up to pee, I climbed down from my bunk and made my way through the labyrinth of bunks. I allowed myself to get lost in the lights … starting low and then continuing upward to the higher open decks. It was a nice distraction after the steam room horror show.

My magical moment came to an abrupt halt when I tripped,

hitting the cold metal deck. My reflexes failed to kick in soon enough, so instead of landing on open palms, I fell flat on my face.

Sounds of muffled laughing hovered over me. I rolled over and saw a blurry Lucy, her stick figure practically dancing with glee. Next to her was Kendall, her arms crossed, cornsilk hair flowing like some mythological demon.

"Get your ass up, you stupid bitch." Kendall made a move to kick me with a socked foot.

I must have regained my reflexes because I was able to grab it before it made contact with my rib cage. I clenched a hand around her ankle and gave it a quick tug. She lost her footing and fell on her butt. Lucy immediately flew to her side.

"Kendall—are you okay?" Her panicked whisper brought a smile to my face.

"Get away from me, you moron." The pretty blonde girl pushed Lucy away with enough force that she too wound up butt-on-deck. Kendall scooched over to me and grabbed a fistful of my hair.

Pulling the mass of locks toward her face, she said, "Watch your back, bitch. I'm on to you." We eyeballed each other for what seemed like ten minutes but was more likely ten seconds. Then she started laughing ... a weird maniacal laugh like villains use in cartoons.

Shhh ... Shhh ... Shhh ...

The dorm—lower *and* higher decks—erupted in waves of shushing.

Lucy scooted over to her friend, touching her shoulder. "Come on, Kendall. We better go before security comes."

Kendall let go of my hair, releasing it as if she had been holding a spider's web. She stood over me as I got up on my knees. That's when I felt something splatter onto my cheek.

Perfect. She just spit on me. Instinctively, my jaw muscles clenched, hands curled into tight fists. *This isn't the time,* I told myself, trying to stifle the rage brewing inside of me.

I wiped the spittle from my cheek, a quick swipe with the back of my hand. Hoisting myself all the way onto my feet, I made my way into the bathroom, where I washed my face, made it into a stall, and peed. I hesitated before going back into the dorm with fists clenched. This time I'd be ready for them.

But the band of mean girls had disbanded, slinking off to their own bunks. Once back at my own bunk, I dropped onto the mattress, a boxer's respite within her own corner of the ring. I wondered how long before the bell after the chimes for the next round.

My head throbbed; no doubt I would have a bump on my forehead for a couple of days. My thoughts reeled. Orin, the steam room, seeing Claudia, Peter … fucked-up lobsters. My intention was to warn the others. No matter how despicable a person was, no one deserved that.

So, what do I do now?

My mind finally began to wind down. Like swirling water emptying down a shower drain, my thoughts eventually fell away into nothingness.

Inhale—one, two, three. Exhale—one, two, three.

There I sat at my modest desk, using none other than Dr. Sanjay's deep breathing technique to calm my rattled nerves.

I had woken up with a nasty headache and a good-sized bump on the left side of my forehead. I brushed strands of dirty blonde hair over the conspicuous area, doing my best to forget about last night.

"Well, good morning. Nice that you decided to join us," Torp said, marching past my small desk toward his own office. He stopped and loomed over me, still chewing on something—

undoubtedly one of the stale sugar doughnuts in the break room. Powdered sugar was caked at the corners of his mouth, a white muck gathered there along with tendrils of moist saliva.

"Oh yeah. Sorry, sir." I tried to look repentant.

I made eye contact with him; his presence never failed to creep me out. I could feel his stare looking through me—no, more like under my clothes. "Um … Won't happen again."

"See that it doesn't," he scolded.

He was still there.

"Was there … something else, Commander Torp?"

His eyes momentarily flicked down to my chest. "The truth is I wanted to compliment you." Torp's words came out an octave or two higher.

You gonna tell me how much you like the way my ass looks in these pants?

"I wanted to commend you on the work you're doing for me so far."

"Oh. No problem. I'm happy to help."

I was hoping if I kept my answers short, he'd just slither away.

"I do need to know when you will submit the final report of your findings. I—"

Cutting him off, I said, "End of the day … today. For sure today."

So leave me the hell alone so I can work, you pervert.

"Splendid." His elevated voice remained. His feet shifted.

Evidently, I made him nervous.

"You continue to do good work and you will have a permanent position here. No need to worry about being transferred to Rivon3."

I ignored him, feigning concentration on my work.

And you're lying to me, dirtbag.

"I'll leave you to it, then," Torp said after an awkward silence.

I could feel him leave. The space suddenly felt lighter, less oppressive. *Wish they'd turn him into a clawbster,* I thought.

I shifted in my seat, settling in to concentrate. It was crunch time. I surveyed the yet- to-be-completed reports I had promised Torp. The pages outlined findings of hidden money and stolen cargo, some kind of embezzlement scheme perpetrated by the cargo manager, Mitch Grendel. The discovery would more than satisfy the commander. I almost felt sorry for this poor Grendel SOB. Only God knew what Torp would do to him when he found out ... probably the steam room.

A few quick notations on the report and I put it aside. I got up and stretched. My joints thanked me, releasing endorphins. Using my standing position to my advantage, I surveyed the utilitarian compartment to make sure no prying eyes were on me. There were three other workers in the space across the corridor, the tops of their heads visible over half-high cubicle walls. Sitting again, I shifted gears, clicking on a hidden folder marked H (for Hardy).

The robot had been busy. I noted several entries that had recently been entered. How did he even get into my file? I wondered if I should feel violated, but instead felt a rush of relief —It was good to have someone on my side. An asterisk was next to the name Melita Roberts. *There's that name again ...* Under her name was a brief bio. This lady was a brainiac ... an IQ of 180, the top of her class in engineering and genetics, racking up accolades at an age when most kids were just hoping to find an entry-level position at a warehouse.

I scanned the text with as much focus as I could muster, intrigued by this person—this woman who I was tied to *somehow*. And here it was ... SynthoGen. I initiated a new search of that company. An impressive, if not formidable, corporate page loaded in front of me. Digging, I found a company directory with the names of their top contributing bio-scientists and genetics engineers but saw no mention of her name. The *About Us* page yielded a one-sentence response:

To learn more, level six security clearance is required.

Super. Thanks for nothing.

I switched back to my Hardy file, reading one of the robot's added notes, "Melita Roberts, just 27, worked as the primary researcher for SynthoGen."

Guess that answered one question I had. But any details of her research were highly classified, requiring EUNF authorization. I read on, seeing that Dr. Roberts had worked at SynthoGen for a total of seven years, until her death at the age of thirty-four.

So young ...

I scoured the page, eventually seeing how she died. There'd been some kind of lab explosion. Her actual cause of death was indeterminate because no body was found.

Sheesh, must have been some explosion ...

The accidental explosion had occurred at a remote research station called *Socrates*.

I leaned back in my chair, capturing my bottom lip between upper and lower incisors. I let the information percolate for a minute. Then, as if hit by an electric current, I sat up ramrod straight. Strange. Maybe she was my ... No, I was born two years after she died. A part of me was disappointed. My shoulders slumped; she couldn't have been my mother ... or could she?

My mind raced. Fragmented memories swirled ... My mother and father were both on board Freight Station Lancaster. Dad was so proud of her; I remembered that. He always bragged about how smart she was—a genius in bioengineering, able to understand concepts that left others scratching their heads. He told me there had been an accident ... an explosion. Could it be a coincidence? How many bioengineers are blown up in accidental explosions? But still, the dates were off. I shook my head. *Something is rotten in the state of Denmark.* I blinked. Felt the beat of my heart getting stronger.

Inhale—one, two, three. Exhale—one, two, three. I needed to breathe. I couldn't faint here ... not now. I needed to focus. But was it really possible that Melita was—

Attention, crew members. Attention, crew members

A klaxon blared, jolting me out of my musings.

We are preparing to dock at Rivon3.
All crew members get ready to disembark.

Chapter 30

Loni

I let out a deep sigh as I sent my final report to Commander Torp. Another mind-numbing shift done. I rubbed my tired eyes and started the long trek back to my dorm. The empty corridors of the ship echoed my footsteps, a stark reminder that I was alone.

My ComBand vibrated against my wrist. A message from Hardy. I glanced down, reading as I walked. The words burned into my brain.

Rivon3's atmosphere is toxic. Prolonged exposure will kill you.

I stopped dead in my tracks, rereading the ominous warning. I read on:

Acidic precipitation. Corrosive ground. Certain death awaits any unprotected human on the planet's surface.

That's just terrific. I finally now understood why they were transforming crew members into clawbsters. And all too soon they would do the same thing to me. To Orin and the others.

Make us into one of those crimson monsters. Sudden nausea twisted my gut. I took a ragged breath and forced myself to keep moving.

I had to warn the others. I might detest my dorm mates, but I couldn't just let them become one of those … things.

I arrived at my dorm, seeing a chaotic scene in progress. My dorm mates were packing in a wild, hurried frenzy. Bunks had been stripped; belongings were scattered about. I hesitated at the entrance.

"What are you waiting for?" Lucy snapped. "An invitation? Start packing your shit!"

I stepped inside, palms sweating. "We need to talk."

"Save it," Kendall growled. "We've got work to do."

I moved closer, desperation rising. "Please, listen to me. I know why we've been getting those infusions."

"Not interested." Margot didn't even look up.

"Rivon3's surface … it will kill us!" My voice cracked. "They're mutating crew members, us, to have some kind of protection from the elements down there."

Kendall whirled, eyes blazing. "Say one more word and I'll break your jaw."

Recoiling, I stepped back. Her fury was borderline crazy. They weren't going to listen to me. No way was I going to get through to them.

The intercom crackled to life.

Attention. We have arrived at Rivon3.
All crew members will receive their final infusion doses prior to commencing surface operations.

My dorm mates exchanged tense looks. This was it. One more round of injections … and then, the steam room. Either I reached them now, or they were lost.

Report to HealthBay immediately for injections. Wait in your dorms until summoned

The announcement cut off. A beat of silence. Then—

Kendall White, Lucy Sutton, Margo Campbell, and Regina McCracken report to HealthBay immediately.

In unison, they grabbed their bags and turned toward the exit. Heading into what I knew would be a gruesome fate. This was my last chance.

I stepped in front of them, blocking their exit. Kendall shoved me, but I stood firm.

"Move, idiot!" she snapped.

"Please listen!" My voice broke. "The planet's surface will kill you. That's why they're changing people. It's why they took Claudia. She's alive, but I swear, you wouldn't even recognize her now! I saw her in the steam room. She has a shell."

They stared at me like I was an idiot.

"Enough crazy talk." Regina cracked her knuckles. "Now move before I make you."

I didn't budge. "I'm trying to save your worthless lives!"

With a feral yell, Lucy punched me hard in the gut. I folded like a cheap lawn chair, gasped, and sank to my knees. They shoved past me without looking back.

"No!" I rasped through the pain. "Just listen to me!"

But it was too late. They were gone. I crawled back to my bunk, anguish threatening to crush me. I'd failed them. And now those same women who'd relentlessly tormented me were doomed to a horrific fate. Maybe I shouldn't care. Maybe they'd be getting what they deserved. But I didn't believe that.

Rage and despair warred within me. I knew I needed to keep trying to wake people up to the evil shitstorm that was happening on this ship. If I could save even one more life ...

I lurched to my feet, still breathless. My eyes found the empty railing of the dorm above.

"Orin! Orin!" I yelled. "Are you up there? Orin!"

I continued to look and was ready to give up when he suddenly appeared. He held up a hand. "Hold on a minute." And then he was gone again.

Chapter 31

Hardy

While, physically, Hardy remained there within the cluttered and greased-stained interior of Hold 5, his mind was someplace else ... lost in a kind of memory fugue. It had taken hours to transfer his neural substrates and cognitive processes over to *Gossamer's* supplementary AI processing units and memory core. In a sense, he was now integrated within the spaceship's architecture, where there had been a seamless completion of the intricate neural migration. With LuMan's help, they had initiated the meticulously orchestrated defragmentation procedure to rectify the ChronoBot's fragmented distribution of his internal cognitive faculties.

To say this was a vulnerable time for Hardy would be a gross understatement. He felt lost, disconnected from himself both physically and cognitively. Memories were returning now at an accelerated rate. Ultra-high-resolution real-life incidents, looped snippets seemingly on constant replay. His past was being returned to him, but in disjointed, untethered order.

He sensed LuMan's concern for him.

LuMan: *The defragmentation process entails the systematic reorganization and optimization of your—our—neural connections and memory allocation, with the overarching objective of ameliorating memory retrieval, computational efficiency, and overall system performance.*

Hardy: *Well then … That makes me feel so much better.*

LuMan: *You are using sarcasm to manage your discomfort.*

Suddenly pulled backward years into the past, Hardy relived the moment when the "accident" happened. How John Hardy, a paunchy, middle-aged starship maintenance worker, decades deceased, had left remnants of his DNA behind within the ship's environmental filtration system. Who would have thought a simple virus would be the catalyst for what was to come next? The phenomenon was the genetic viral fusion involving the integration and merging of genetic materials, that of one John Hardy, the viral source, with the DNA of the host organism, the Chrono-Bot, with its unique biomaterial brain mass. The result … a combined genetic composition like none other in the known universe.

John Hardy, his consciousness inadvertently awakened, seemingly had merged with that of a robot, a killer ChronoBot no less. Immediately he'd learned of LuMan, the bot's core operating AI, along with the fact his brash, sarcastic, and all-too-human presence was not being welcomed with open arms. But over time, these past ensuing years, they'd learned to not only tolerate each other but coexist, perhaps to even be better for this shared, dual consciousness. A truly symbiotic relationship.

I had been assigned to a specific security detail. To protect an alien worm thing creature who was called a Thine. Oh … And his name was, is, Coogong!

Hardy wanted to jump up and down, to dance a jig, to high five, *well …* anyone!

Speaking out loud now, Hardy said, "I actually remember

someone from my past, our past, LuMan! This is huge! This is monumental!"

LuMan remained quiet.

He remembered people helping him, remembered being absorbed into a ship's crew, but couldn't remember the details.

LuMan: *We have a situation, Hardy.*

Pulled back to the here and now, Hardy glanced about the dark confines of Hold 5. They were not alone. And something was most definitely not right.

LuMan: *I have muted all detectable readings of our joined consciousness. I am attempting to camouflage the extensive energy usage being used for your outsourced defrag processing.*

Hardy now detected that several technicians were going from bot to bot within the storage hold—actually hard-cabling into their respective processors.

Hardy: *This isn't good.*

Hardy, with LuMan's help, immediately constructed a core-level program that would isolate any new incoming instruction packages and have them reside within the ship's memory versus the ChronoBot's. A tricky proposition since many of Hardy's reassembling memories were also residing in some of those same memory banks.

Finished with a small nearby DRX bot unit, the two techs, both wearing worn-looking navy-blue overalls, shuffled their gear in closer to Hardy.

"Work order says this is Unit 1223. You're sure this bad boy is safe to be around?" said the slim, short worker with a long face and long wispy sideburns.

"Relax, Dorkan ... All restraining bolts have been re-initialized," replied the much bigger, hairier one. His sleeves had been rolled up to reveal muscular, Popeye-sized forearms. His voice was deep and laced with intolerance for the younger, smaller worker. "Why don't you make yourself useful and hand me that cable?"

Hardy: *How much of the defrag operation is complete, LuMan?*

LuMan: *Eighty-nine percent. But until the data has been repropagated over from Gossamer's memory banks, we will not have full access.*

Hardy: *Let's start that process now. Don't think we can wait.*

Working with well-practiced efficiency, one of the two technicians began attaching the cable to Hardy's AUX signal connector located within a hidden port at the back of Hardy's head.

"What the hell are they going to use it for? Thing's not suited for much other than killing," Dorkan said.

Hardy read the bigger man's name tag. Elmore Rothenberg.

Rothenberg let out a heavy, overdramatic sigh. As if even talking to this underling was a tremendous burden. "It's to be a patrol robot. These bots are smart. Can work mostly independently ... Don't need much direction. From what I'm told, they'll be protecting the mines."

Dorkan snorted. "From what? There's no one down there. Place is about as inhospitable as any in the system."

Rothenberg, still fiddling with the port connector, looked over at Dorkan. "Are you really that stupid? Look ... the handful of ChronoBots being deployed won't be protecting anyone or anything; they'll be preventing the lobsters from straying away from the work areas. That and enforcing the rules. You know... keeping order. Now shut the fuck up and get this bot properly programmed."

Dorkan didn't look bothered by the reprimand. Was probably used to being talked to that way. As he repositioned the gear, it clattered against Hardy's metallic left leg.

"Hey! Are you trying to break that transponder unit? It's expensive. It goes out of calibration, we'll get the blame."

Dorkan shrugged, tapped at several screen prompts, then looked up. "Should be transmitting now."

Hardy confirmed that assumption. He saw petabytes of data flowing into his noggin, whereby it was captured, isolated, and whisked away out over the ship's wireless network.

"I think we're done here," Dorkan said, yanking the cable free from Hardy's head with unnecessary force.

Rothenberg just looked at his workmate with a disgusted expression. "Oh, you think so, huh?"

"Yeah … zip-zap, it's a wrap. Time to move onto the next bucket of bolts."

Rothenberg shook his head. "We rarely get ChronoBots, but when we do, we test them. Ensure there's no funny business."

Hardy watched as Rothenberg got situated behind his equipment. "I'll be sending a series of specific commands … see if the program's working correctly. If it's set up right, the big bot cannot disobey … cannot not comply."

Dorkan feigned boredom and yawned. "Whatever."

Rothenberg's lips curled into a maniacal smile. "Unit 1223! Stand upright!"

Pretending to obey, Hardy did as asked. He stood up.

"Walk five steps and halt!"

Why is he yelling like that? Hardy did what he was told, taking the five steps and stopping.

"Open each of your weapon compartments!"

Again, Hardy did as he was told—all five of his energy weapon panels snapped open.

"Close your weaponry panels!"

You forgot to say Simon says, Hardy thought to himself but didn't remember what that phrase actually referenced.

Raising his arms, and at one point, spinning in a circle while doing squats, Hardy felt stupid and annoyed but did it all anyway.

"Hey, boss … how about you let me have a go at it?" Dorkan asked.

Rothenberg took a long few moments to consider that. "Fine. Let's hurry it up, though."

"Unit 1223! Stand on one leg!" Dorkan commanded with a giggle.

Hardy raised one leg and balanced.

"Unit 1223! Hop up and down!"

I could eviscerate both of them in the blink of an eye.

He hopped up and down, causing the deck plate below him to bend.

"I think that's enough, Dorkan," Rothenberg said with a smirk.

"Wait … Just one more. Unit 1223! Squat down like you're taking a dump while singing 'Moon River.'"

LuMan: *You kill him now, you eliminate any chance of getting your memories back.*

Both of Hardy's catcher's-glove-sized hands curled into tight fists. He then squatted, his rear end inches off the deck. *Moon river, wider than a mile …*

"Okay, okay, enough!" Rothenberg barked. "Time to get this bot over to the loading bay. Shuttles ready for dispatch."

Dorkan nodded. "I've got this. Unit 1223, proceed to Loading Bay Alpha Tandem 3. March."

Hardy: *They're taking us off ship.*

LuMan: *Yes, we are being deployed down to Rivon3.*

Hardy froze.

LuMan: *What do you want to do?*

Hardy was torn. Sure, once he got off the ship, he'd probably gain access to deep-space communications—giving him better access to the outside world. But at the same time, abandoning Loni and the others just didn't feel right.

"Hold on there, Unit 1223," Rothenberg commanded. He looked over to Dorkan. "You need to start paying attention."

"What …"

"Take a look at that restraining bolt."

"What about it?"

"That's a 33 x 1. We've replaced all of those with the x2s … remember? Surprised we haven't been torn apart by this killing machine."

Rothenberg pulled out a new hockey-puck-sized restraining bolt and slapped it hard onto Hardy's chest. Before Hardy could even think to break free, he was immobilized, well, mostly.

LuMan: *Well played ... Now what?*

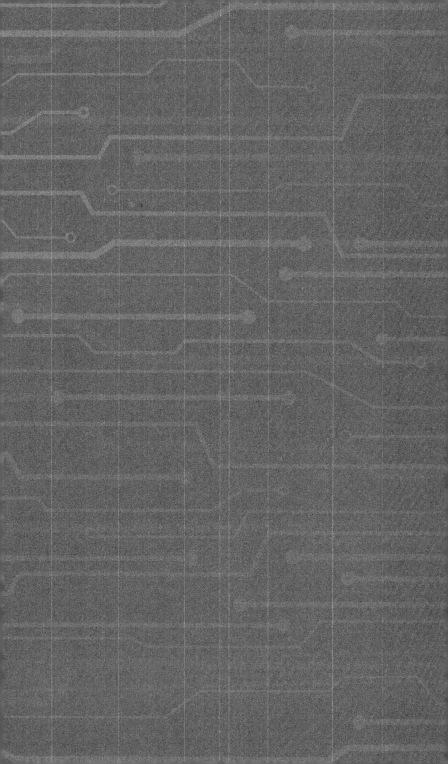

Chapter 32

Loni

I saw Orin come into view on the deck above. *Finally.* Moving swiftly now, he was doing what he would usually do under the cloak of the dorm's nighttime lights-out. Using a series of vertical pipes and junction boxes for hand and footholds, he was climbing down as easily as a spider monkey in the jungles of Bolivia. Somewhat more tentatively, but still surprisingly agile was Taylor, followed by the equally adroit Anna and Jasper. Clearly, this was not their first foray down that thirty-foot-high facade.

I glanced toward the dorm's entrance, expecting security to rush in at any moment. But having come into port at Rivon3's high orbit space station, it seemed as though everyone on board was in a frenzy.

I watched as Orin's feet hit the ground. He looked up and our eyes met, his face beaming with joy. Before he had time to say a word, I was already running toward him. When I reached him, I launched myself into his arms with such force that he stumbled back a bit and we both laughed as I clung to him in an embrace.

Suddenly self-conscious, I stepped away and we stood in an awkward silence. The three others had followed Orin down from the wall, all with questioning stares aimed at him. I cleared my throat. "God, I didn't know what had happened to you," I said.

Taylor spoke up before Orin could answer, a wary tone in her voice. "Yeah, he told us. Not sure I believe it 100 percent, but I guess it would explain things." Her gaze shifted between me and Orin as we exchanged unspoken words.

"So, Peter's really one of those clawbster things?" Anna asked. "We have to find him ... save him."

Jasper made a face. "My guess ... Peter has a one-way ticket to Lobsterville."

"There's more," I said. "And it's worse."

"Don't keep us in suspense; spit it out," Taylor said, rolling her eyes.

"According to Hardy, those multiple infusions ... the eventual abduction into the steam room ... well, it's all to equip us for surviving—working—on Rivon3."

"Which means that anyone who finishes getting their infusions is going into the steam room," Orin added.

"Wait ... You have to be a clawbster to work on Rivon3?" Taylor said, unconsciously placing an open palm on one side of her face. "It's really that brutal down there?"

The overhead PA system was suddenly barking off more names.

Juan Rodrigo, Timothy Ridgewood, Lu Anne Masters ... all report to HealthBay.

"We need to hide," I said.

Everyone looked to Orin. Eventually, he nodded.

"Back to the clubhouse?" I asked.

Orin almost smiled. "We should be safe in the hold. For a while at least. We'll stay there until most of the crew are gone, then figure out what to do." He looked at his ComBand. "Everyone make sure your jammers are activated."

Taylor and Jasper were both shaking their heads.

Taylor said, "That's our plan? Wait till the ship empties out? Then what? What can we do? None of us can work the ship, so it's not like we can just fly away."

"And there're too few of us to fight off security if they come after us," Jasper added.

Orin looked to Loni. "You have anything to add to that?"

"Yeah, I do. You're all forgetting about the robot. I don't think he'll have much trouble dealing with whatever security remains on board. And piloting a freighter ... I'm sure that's within his wheelhouse."

"You keep calling it *him*. That right there has me nervous," Taylor said.

I waved away her comment. "Hold on." Using my ComBand, I reached out to Hardy, but he wasn't answering.

"Well?" Jasper said.

Taylor huffed.

Anna looked hopeful.

"He's not answering. I don't know what's wrong; he always answers," I said.

"Uh-huh," Taylor murmured. "So, what now? Back to the stupid clubhouse?"

Anna Stone and Taylor Payne, report to HealthBay.
Orin Rivera and Jasper Kennedy, report to HealthBay.

Loni Solace, report to Commander Torp's office

"Seriously?" Taylor said, incredulous. "I guess getting cozy with the big cheese has its perks, huh?"

"Oh, screw you, Taylor. I learned a long time ago to keep my distance from creeps like Torp," I said.

"We need to go now," Orin said.

We all agreed and headed for the dorm's exit. Together, we sprinted down one passageway and then another. Once we reached the bank of lifts, I was feeling a little better. Maybe we would escape, at least for a little while.

Even before I could stab the call button, the lift doors were opening. The six uniformed security guards inside, looking as surprised as we were, caught sight of us.

I yelled, "Scatter!" We all ran.

Chapter 33

Loni

I ran down the corridor, heart pounding in my chest. It stretched out before me, a twisting, endless snake of steel and light. My steps echoed, the sound almost deafening, HSA warnings coming off my ComBand. Security was on my tail; how many of them, I wasn't sure. Their shouted orders were a roaring tide gaining on me. God, my chest burned. Breaths becoming labored. I blinked away tears as my pulse thundered in my head—I was running for my life.

Flashbacks ambushed me. Orin, Anna, the others. They'd darted off in the opposite direction. I could still feel their absence like a physical ache in my chest. I shook it off, focusing on the task at hand. Every corridor I turned down was one more unknown gamble. Navigating the ship's arteries, typically monotonous and unpredictable, was now a dangerous maze.

Suddenly, the PA blared. I was being summoned to the commander's office ... again. I ignored it, instead skidding around another bend. My breath hitched. There, up ahead, was a familiar section of the ship, one I knew would lead to the steam room.

≈

Orin

On another part of the ship, Orin was facing his own battles. He, along with Anna, Jasper, and Taylor, had tried to make it to their hidey-hole storage compartment, but the guards were too close on their heels. Darting into a small lounge instead, they'd been spotted doing so. Now, squared off against several guards, Orin put himself between them and his friends.

Assessing the three-man security team, Orin saw this was not one of *Gossamer's* A-Team. Two were more than a little over-weight and wearing ill-fitting uniforms; the other looked emaci-ated and well past his prime. It was this guard, wielding a truncheon—or was it a billy club?—lurched toward Orin. Side-stepping the geriatric security guard's swinging weapon, Orin threw a hard left. Immediately feeling the crunch of bone, Orin knew he'd broken the man's jaw. Lights out, the guard crumpled to the ground.

Realization of what had just happened momentarily stunned both the guards and evading crew members. Glancing down at the sprawled guard confirmed the guy was deader than dead. *Shit! I barely hit him.*

Determined retribution in their eyes, the chubby duo moved fast, truncheons swinging. Orin took a blow to his right cheek, pain and a stunning explosion of stars sending him staggering backward.

Quick movement.

Orin, holding his cheek, saw small, often sickly, Anna now on the move. Like a jackrabbit, she skittered over a small table, landing by the condiments countertop. He heard the sound of clanking metal utensils within the silverware tray, then Anna was grasping a knife—her expression feral.

The closest guard looked warily at her. "Don't even think about it, little missy—" But it was too late; Anna was already on the move again. Small and impossible to stop, she weaved between tables.

Orin opened his mouth to yell, to tell the girl things had gotten way out of hand. That this was never supposed to be about killing the guards.

A high-pitched scream filled the lounge as Anna, a whirlwind of fury, jumped up onto a plastic molded chair before plunging the knife into the guard's beefy neck. Buried to the handle, arterial blood spurted, drenching the opposite bulkhead in red.

As the now-woozy guard spun, his lifeblood fountaining, a downpour of crimson droplets cascaded.

As the lone remaining guard hesitated, Jasper capitalized on his momentary indecision, hitting the guard, *whap,* in the back of the head with a plastic food tray—he toppled over like a felled oak tree.

Almost losing her footing on the slippery deck, Taylor screamed, "We've got to get out of here!"

More guards appeared at the entrance.

With mounting dread, Orin could tell: this *was* the A-Team. Big and brawny, these were seasoned security professionals, and they were here for their pound of flesh.

Having scooped up one of the guard's dropped truncheons, he stood ready for the attack, as did Anna and Jasper. Taylor was at the ready too—wielding a flimsy plastic chair as a weapon. A crooked smile crossed Orin's lips; he couldn't help being proud of his team. If Loni was here too ... *Is she even still alive?*

Suddenly the four—no, five—recently arrived guards were abruptly being shoved and scooting out of the way by someone coming in from behind.

No, not someone, *something.* Towering over the others, easily seven foot tall, Orin could see its obsidian faceplate. A guard was suddenly tossed aside, a child's toy being cast away.

Oh God … it's a ChronoBot.

Large black lettering stenciled vertically down its torso spelled out the word MARFIX. Its entrance had been nothing short of breathtaking. Orin could hardly believe his eyes—this was like the dreadful turning point in a blockbuster movie.

Perfectly synchronized, all five of the killer bot's energy cannons popped into view from previously hidden compartments. Orin could hear Taylor gasp behind him. It was thunderous, a stark reminder of the technology at the disposal of their enemies. The ChronoBot turned on Orin, cannons ready … and the world seemed to slow down.

Then, Jasper was there, lunging at MARFIX with his stupid plastic food tray. His act of bravery was all too quickly and brutally crushed. MARFIX turned just one of its plasma weapons, the shoulder-mount cannon, on Jasper. A blindingly bright streak, like a lightning bolt, hit Jasper between the eyes—killing him instantly.

Debilitating loss gripped deep within Orin's chest. Seeing his friend lying there on the deck, his blank, lifeless stare … he found it hard to move, let alone think.

Taylor's chair arched high overhead, breaking his trance. As it blew apart in midair, it was perfectly evident the ChronoBot's reflexes were impeccable.

Anna had somehow squirreled herself in behind the ChronoBot and into the fray of onlooking guards. Then Orin saw the reflective glint of another utensil. But this time, Anna was plunging the prongs of a fork into a guard's exposed abdomen. With a *hmmph*, the man, obviously taken by surprise, staggered, stepped, and fell face-first onto the deck.

That's when the ChronoBot opened up on them.

≈

Loni

MY DESPERATE RUN CONTINUED. I THOUGHT I'D PUT some space between me and the pursuing guards but wasn't all that sure. A loud klaxon now blared overhead, making it impossible to hear their footfalls. I made a quick left down a smaller passageway, then another left, and then a right. I glanced at my ComBand. "Where the hell are you, robot!?"

Up ahead I spotted a maintenance hatch door. Once inside, my heart sank ... It was little more than a closet. A dead end. Panic clawed at my chest as I scanned the dimly lit room. Looking up, my eyes landed on a small circular hatch.

Maintenance Shaft. Keep Closed

I flipped over a metal bucket, making way too much noise in the process. Stepping onto it, I teetered and had to put a hand on a nearby wall to keep from toppling over. Reaching overhead, my fingers nervously worked the latch. *Got it*. And with a shove, I threw open the hatch. The aluminum bucket and the hatch lid clanged loudly.

I squinted into the darkness, making out a vertical shaft and the rungs of a ladder disappearing into darkness. Way above I thought there was the faintest glimmer of light. Standing on tippy toes, I grabbed onto the ladder and pulled myself up into the shaft. Situating my feet firmly on the bottom rung, I closed the hatch and, of course, it clanged like a dinner bell.

Standing tall, I took in a deep breath while rubbing at my

aching chest with one hand. *Get going, Loni!* The cold metal rungs bit into my palms as I began to climb.

UP, UP, UP, I WENT. THE STRAIN ON MY ARM MUSCLES, my thighs, my fingers had become almost unbearable. Each outstretch of a hand was agony. The darkness pressed in all around me. I could feel the edges of my consciousness starting to blur, my breath coming in shallow gasps. In what felt like hours, but was probably more like twenty minutes, I reached the hatch door at the top of the ladder. It was partially open, a band of light illuminating the top of the shaft. Thrusting it open with the last of my strength, I almost lost my grip on the rung. Swallowing hard, I climbed into the dimly lit space and fell onto the deck gasping for breath. Hardy's name slipped from my lips, a whispered plea into my ComBand. But there was no response. The last thing I remembered was the cold. The unforgiving cold of the deck beneath me, the spinning lights above. The harsh beep of my ComBand was the last sound I heard, echoing my failing heartbeat. I called for Hardy one more time, my voice a whisper in the silent room. But there was no reply.

As darkness claimed me, consciousness coming and going, I vaguely knew I was alone, trapped somewhere within the cold steel belly of *Gossamer*. This was it. I was done. I could feel my life force dissipating with each faulting heartbeat. Suddenly my eyes widened, my teeth clenched; my right arm felt as if it was being twisted out of its socket. I screamed in agony and at that moment, I had zero doubt what I was experiencing: a massive, deadly heart attack. As blackness finally overtook me, I thought of my father, how sad he would be learning of my death here within the bowels of this old cargo vessel.

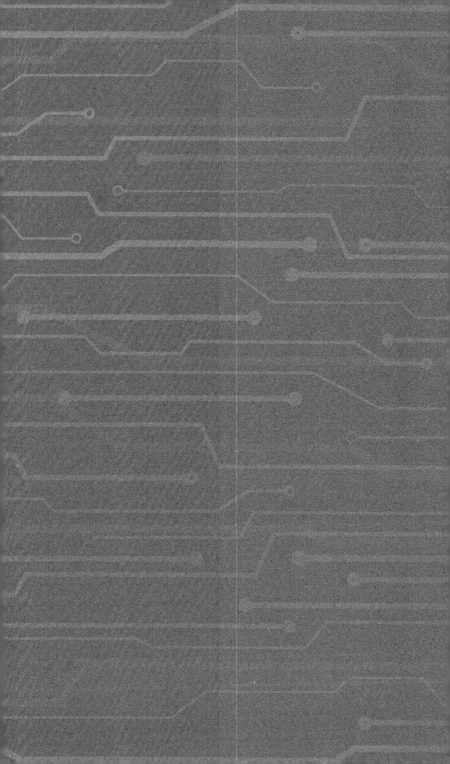

Chapter 34

Electrical impulses sparked furiously inside Hardy's cerebral circuits. Multilingual obscenities ran like a subroutine in the background, a mix of coded strings and vocal languages ranging from binary to Urdu. Each attempt to thwart the virtual roadblock returned errors.

Access denied.
Restraining Bolt: Active

Hardy's intricate algorithms were still locked behind a firewall, a digital shackle that was as impregnable as any steel vault he'd encountered. The alter-ego voice crackled within their shared neural interface, a private channel of electronic whispers. The metallic undertones hinted at his machine origin, untouched by any semblance of human emotion.

LuMan: *With less noise I will accomplish more …*

Hardy evaluated his sterile, cold surroundings. He'd been moved over to the space station orbiting high above Rivon3. He was within a wide-open, in-between space, a holding area, some kind of waystation. Unable to turn his head, his minimally operational sensors saw enough to know he didn't like it here. In blatant contrast to *Gossamer's* weathered grime, the station's sleek bulkheads gleamed with a futuristic sheen, reflecting the meticulous work of astronomical engineers who prioritized function over form. Every corner, every corridor, was designed for efficiency. Yet, amid this clinical setting, chaos percolated within an ever-present background hum.

Suddenly, technicians, clad in their cobalt blue environ suits, descended upon him. A tug. A push. Restrained. Then, movement. A hover cart came into view, gliding over pristine deck plates. A vertical perspective went horizontal. He was being transported through double hatch doors, one passageway, another, then deeper into the bowels of the station.

Ahead, he spied the gaping entrance of a cargo bay housing a massive shuttlecraft. Devoid of atmosphere here, the craft—cargo doors wide open—beckoned. But it wasn't just any shuttle … so familiar. *Where have I seen one like this before?* The name of the craft, more of a model designation, came to him. It was a Hub Gunther. Another of the old relics of a spacecraft surfaced within his databanks. The metallic behemoth before him now, though, was a far cry from that antiquated tug. This one was larger, newer … brimming with advanced tech.

In he went with a push and a shove. Cargo. Payload. Chattel.

A sensation akin to dread—something Hardy was less familiar with than other emotions—seeped into his consciousness as he was bound and positioned among a motley crew of thirteen other robotic units. There were hulking excavators designed for heavy mining, nimble dexterous robot types made for more intricate tasks, and a number of lethal-looking security bots. Piles of equipment, their purpose unclear, sat nestled next to them. All of it, including Hardy, was just cargo. He managed to connect to the vessel's network. A small win among a growing number of failures.

Gravity shifted. A hum resonated through the ship. Fast drop. A high-velocity descent characterized by significant aerodynamic drag and a steep trajectory angle.

Hardy: *That wasn't a simple orbital hop. More like a journey to the planet's surface.*

LuMan said nothing.

As they descended, the digital umbilical cord that connected Hardy to the ship's mainframe started to fray. Bit by bit, byte by byte. Isolation.

He tried again and again to communicate with the ship, to glean any insights, but the restraining bolt ensured his efforts were in vain. LuMan's presence, however, was a constant. Together—well, mostly LuMan—they continued to work on the bolt's oppressive grip. Had LuMan's efforts taken on a more desperate tone?

LANDING WASN'T GRACEFUL. THE SHUTTLE'S suspension struggled with the terrain, sending a jarring shock wave throughout its superstructure. Crew wearing their exo-suits hustled; cargo bay doors yawned open. A torrent of commands streamed forth, directing the robotic contingent outward. *Our marching orders.*

Yet, amid the dark abyss of Hardy's limited physical and intellectual functions, a glimmer of something twinged. An electronic surge, a reboot of sorts.

LuMan: *Systems restored.*

Suddenly Hardy's digital horizon expanded. Alive. Reconnected. And raring to retaliate.

LuMan: *Assessment first, vengeance later.*

The visuals were jarring. The planet's environment was hostile—barren landscapes punctuated with spiky rock formations and pooled liquid sources that shimmered with an eerie iridescence. *Mercury? Liquid gallium?*

The atmosphere was dense, a neon green fog radiating toxicity. A quick atmospheric scan revealed its treacherous composition—a concoction of unbreathable gases laced with acidic and carcinogenic entities. Hardy's synthesized knowledge banks informed him that any humans unlucky enough to be stranded here would find themselves in dire straits within days, maybe hours. Choking. Suffering. Dying.

Off in the distance he spotted a gleaming spacecraft rocketing away—an interstellar-capable luxury liner. Its sleek form was in stark contrast to this desolate backdrop. It continued to soar skyward.

Pivoting his resources, Hardy infiltrated the planet's rudimentary communication networks. It was child's play. Low encryption, basic security protocols. Local comms were easily accessed, though the long-range ones, the channels connecting to the interstellar networks, were locked behind multiple layers of digital fortifications.

With a back door into the shuttle's system established through his dummy accounts, Hardy reached out and found Loni's ComBand. Her signature code was unique, instantly recognizable.

A ping. A probe. Silence. Nothing but the vast emptiness of a digital void. No response.

Hardy's systems, if they could, would have been coursing with adrenaline now. The game had changed.

Chapter 35

My world abruptly tilted on its axis, an ethereal slip between realms. I felt disoriented, lost in a dance of shadows. *Am I dreaming?* Eyes open. Heart thudding. I wasn't Loni Solace anymore. That identity seemed distant, carried away like whispers in the wind. I was … someone else, someone more purposeful. More driven.

Silly me. Of course, I know who I am … I'm Dr. Melita Roberts. The same person I've always been.

A surge of certainty rushed through me. This was my life now. My reality. How could I have ever thought differently?

"Welcome to SynthoGen, Dr. Roberts!" A man in a white coat greeted me, his eyes shining. The vast, immaculate interior of the genetics lab sprawled in front of me. Bright holographic screens, sleek counters reflecting overhead lights. Every surface seemed to pulse with energy.

I nodded, forcing a smile, taking in the faces and names of those introducing themselves. Their voices merged into a haze, fragments of a reality meshing with dreamlike visions. These were my coworkers, my subordinates. How important I must be …

IN A FLASH I WAS TRANSPORTED, CATAPULTED TO another span of time. Before me stood a quantum microscope. Streaming data. Morphing genetic sequences. I gasped, afraid to move, to take another breath, fearing this couldn't possibly be real. I rechecked and triple-checked the anomaly. Oh my … This was the discovery of a lifetime.

"Eureka!" My voice echoed through the room, filled with triumph. "I've got it!"

My boss, Dr. Morgan Hampshire, a stern, angular-faced woman with piercing gray eyes, approached quickly. Side by side, we stared at the revelation: the blueprint to alter the human respiratory system … the means to genetically transform lungs.

Spinning, spinning, spinning. The moment suddenly froze in time, a filmstrip caught in the projector, distorted, all feelings of triumph quickly fading into something else … apprehension.

Flash!

Time had hopped and skipped ahead. I felt cold. Felt as if I was the one being observed beneath the lens of a quantum microscope. I was in Dr. Hampshire's office. A space as impersonal as the woman herself. My fists were clenched. We were arguing, neither side relenting.

"Why push this? Let's just take a beat, do our due diligence. What's the rush?" I pleaded.

Dr. Hampshire scoffed, "Are you really that naive, Melita? Time is a luxury we do not have. This is a business in a very competitive industry. You know that. No. Your genetic testing has been thorough. Enough is enough."

"Three months? That's not nearly sufficient," I said, feeling as if the rug had been pulled out from beneath me. "Give me another four months; the last thing we want is unforeseen results later, potential long-term effects, and don't get me started on the ethical implications. No, we don't understand the implications! Hell, Doctor, people could die."

Hampshire stared back at me, her face hard. "Progress waits for no one."

Flash!

Time had danced forward again. I was at my station, anger surging through my veins. I began to type an interoffice communiqué cc'ed to all—my colleagues, the managing partners, the board of directors. One thought was driving me: They had to listen to reason. The alternative? I'd expose them. Crash this all down around them.

Flash!

Skip and jump ahead. Darkness engulfed me. Then a harsh light. I was in a new lab now. My eyes flicked upward, catching my own reflection on a porthole window. Beyond, the vast expanse of space cradled a desolate, ruined-looking planet. Confusion clouded my thoughts. *Where am I?* With a quick glance over one shoulder I saw security guards standing by a hatch door, emotionless.

"You can't control me!" I shouted, defiance burning deep within my core.

A countertop Halo Display suddenly came to life. Dr. Hampshire's pinched-looking face took form. "There be no communication with the outside world, Melita."

I seethed, glowering back at her.

"Finish your research. You wanted to change the world? Well, here's your chance."

Flash. Everything changed once more.

. . .

I JERKED AWAKE WITH A START. A NEARBY HEART monitor reflected the rapid countenance of my still-beating heart. And with that, I knew I was Loni Solace again.

I took in my surroundings. I was back in HealthBay on *Gossamer*. Panic surged as I realized I was strapped to a bed. A sharp pain throbbed in my chest.

The dream … was it a dream? Memories flooded back into my consciousness. Erratic heartbeats throbbed from the machine. Thoughts jumbled. *Am I Loni or Melita?* Both seemed so, so real.

A nurse approached, her gaze unsettling. "Welcome back, Ms. Solace."

I tried to speak, to demand answers, but my voice was weak, barely a whisper.

The pain in my chest intensified, overwhelming me. My vision blurred.

"This is just the beginning," she murmured, just before darkness consumed me again.

Chapter 36

Plastic straps bit into my wrists. I could feel Denzel's weighty gaze on me, that repugnant smirk stretching his fat face. His voice dripped with faux concern. "Never had a crew member go and have a heart attack before. Quite the show you put on, little missy."

Panic surged through my veins. Was that true? *Yep, I remember now. I had a heart attack ... My climb up the iron-rung ladder, the agonizing pain in my chest. The dream ...*

"You have to let me go, Denzel," I croaked, fighting back tears. "The infusions, they're changing us. Turning us into ... clawbsters."

Denzel's smirk deepened. "Yeah, I know all about that, kid."

Every fiber of my being screamed to break free, to flee this nightmare. But the restraints were too tight, my body too weak. At least I was still dressed, shoes on my feet, ComBand on my wrist. But what was the point in fighting when the battle was already lost?

Suddenly, others were storming into HealthBay. Two towering, broad-shouldered mountain-sized men, both of them with matchy-matchy blue uniforms. The guards exchanged glances with Denzel.

"She's trouble." Denzel looked down at me. "Sorry, Loni. It's nothing personal."

The slightly bigger of the two guards, looking casually superior, emanated cruelty. "Then we cuff her for transport."

So, they're painting me as some kind of violent criminal?

Their eyes slid to me, gauging my sickly, frail form. A silent consensus passed between them.

Denzel was already releasing my straps. Then, with the tenderness of a grizzly bear, he pulled me upright and onto my feet. Dizzy with a head rush, I felt cold new restraints clasped onto my wrists. Pain streaked through my limbs as the two guards took ownership of me. With a shove from behind, I was coaxed out of HealthBay and forced into the corridor.

TEN MINUTES LATER, COMMANDER TORP'S OFFICE loomed large and cold. They dumped me in a chair in front of his desk, where I tried to resist.

One of the guards produced an electric baton, igniting a sizzling series of sparks just inches from my face.

"Enough!" Torp said, getting to his feet. "The last thing her damaged heart needs right now is electrical shocks. Just get out. Now!"

The guards did as ordered, leaving the two of us alone. Torp came around and leaned his backside against the front of his desk. He loomed over me.

A sharp slap across my face had me stunned and gasping. "That's supposed to be better than the cattle prod?" I spat, my vision still blurry, my left cheek on fire.

"Enough with the smart mouth." A maniacal smile pulled at his lips. "What am I going to do with you?"

Someone from behind cleared their voice.

Memories surged as a figure materialized at the office's entrance. *Is he real?* With my past swirling in my head, it was becoming harder and harder to discern what was reality. Barely containing his rage, he strode forward. Tall, tan, and handsome, he exuded power and decisiveness. This was not a man to trifle with.

I recognized him. It came to me then, seeing his smiling image on SynthoGen's website's home page. Dan Caldwell. But his previous jovial smile, the warmth in his eyes, was now replaced with disdain, his voice dripping with contempt. "Smells like crotch rot on this old barge ... And her ... nearly two goddamned decades we've been waiting for Melita Roberts to poke her head up, and I'm looking at this *child*."

My mind raced.

Torp's expression shifted away from boss man to something more like bewilderment. "Yeah, Melita Roberts ... Saw that name for the first time in that ChronoBot's message."

"Need to know, Torp," Caldwell snapped. "You know how that goes ..." He rubbed his chin. "So, I guess it's time for you to know."

"All I know," Torp said, trying to look indignant but only making it halfway, "is that this girl pinged an ancient SynthoGen kill order that I've never heard a thing about and that she was misidentified as Melita Roberts *and* Angela Solace—Angela Solace who checks out as her mother, who died in an accident."

Caldwell radiated anger. "You're more of an idiot than I suspected. She wasn't misidentified. Have you looked at the goddamned DNA scans? An exact match."

My breath caught in my chest.

I could see the anger simmering in Torp as he cleared his throat. "Seems simple enough to me. Two options: Toss her in the molecular incinerator. Or complete the transformation process and let her contribute to the bottom line like she was intended to do. Either way, your problem is solved."

"And this is why you will never be any more than a commander on a rust bucket like this, Torp. Of course, killing her is inevitable, but we need something from her before we turn her body to ash or scramble her entire genetic makeup ..."

Caldwell looked from Torp to me. Had his eyes softened for a microsecond?

"We suspected Melita faked her own death when things were closing in around her. She was smart; she changed her appearance, built an entirely new identity, becoming Angela Solace. Then she did the unthinkable. She apparently died like any other blue-collar schlub." He shook his head. "If true ... what a waste."

Fists clenched, I attempted to stand, finding Caldwell's hand already heavy on my shoulder—keeping me in my seat. He ignored my thrashing.

"You're a monster!" I yelled. But his words still played over and over in my head. *She apparently died ...* Apparently?

"Your mother ..." He feigned a grimace, "and I use that term loosely, was a genius. I'll give her that. She delivered trillions of credits to SynthoGen—and then what does she do? She steals our intellectual property!"

I could tell by Torp's expression—I wasn't the only one who didn't know these details.

"But it's what she did then that sealed her fate and yours, Ms. Solace." Caldwell looked at me, his expression hard to read. "She destroyed the believed-to-be totally secured, isolated server farm in which that intellectual property had been stored. Then she deleted all the hidden backups. God only knows how she knew about the backups."

"Why has SynthoGen been trying to track this Melita down if she's already dead?" I asked. "I don't get it. What's with the robot kill order ... and that crazed MARFIX bot trying to kill me?"

I suspected I already knew the answer by this time but wanted to hear it from Caldwell's lips.

"That kill order's been bouncing around the galaxy for years, young lady. Think of it as a digital bounty. A highly advanced genetic ID program designed for counterterrorism counterintelligence units. Did we think Melita Roberts was dead? No. Angela Solace? Honestly, we aren't sure. One can change their appearance, give themselves a totally new identity, but the one thing they cannot change is—"

"Their DNA," Torp interjected.

"Their DNA," Caldwell repeated with a smirk.

He now scrutinized me like an insect trapped on a microscope slide. "Based on that recent outgoing MARFIX message and the incident involving you, it wasn't long before our forensic geneticists concluded our missing intellectual property had been loaded into an organic nanotech data storage device. One, coincidentally, Melita had, almost two decades ago, implanted into a living embryo. Being biogenic material, it would be nearly impossible to detect."

I opened my mouth to speak, but no words came out.

Torp, up on his feet, took a nervous step backward.

Caldwell directed renewed anger toward Torp. "Review the DNA scans. The data doesn't lie." An accusation floated in the air, thick and heavy. "We've lost valuable time. Your incompetence—"

"How was I to know?" Torp barked. "It's not like I have an open channel to SynthoGen!"

Caldwell looked down at me and then at Torp, wearing an expression of extreme irritation that reminded me of that asshat Hightower. "Prep her for surgery. Butcher her if you want; I don't care. Just make sure the storage device is recovered intact ... and take some blood samples while you're at it."

My mind swirled. Were they really talking about just ending my existence, perhaps dumping my body down a refuse chute?

Caldwell's tone was cold and clinical. "Her very cells will tell us everything we need to know." His eyes locked onto mine, a predator eyeing his prey. A chill ran up my spine.

Why did you put me in this position, Mom?

Torp and Caldwell continued to strategize. I was right here, and they were speaking about me as if I was just a thing, an impersonal object to be excavated, mined for some kind of hidden treasure.

Time seemed to stretch and warp. Caldwell, with his sinister eloquence, continued to speak of harvesting the information from an organic data drive that apparently was within me.

Torp looked unsure. "We don't know if it's still functional. Retrievable, probably, but functional?" He shrugged.

I was nothing more than a vessel, a means to an end.

Torp, ever eager to exploit, added, "No butchery. I want her for the mines." Eyeing me, his Adam's apple bobbed.

Pig.

Caldwell's sigh was laden with impatience. For a moment, I thought he'd come to my rescue. Instead, he said, "I appreciate your sense of efficiency, Torp. What you do with her is your call. I need the data, and I need to get the hell off this dump."

"No ... don't do this," I pleaded, looking up at Caldwell. "I just want to go home ... Please, let me go home."

Torp, smugness evident in his voice, delivered the final order. He looked down at me. "So, back to HealthBay with her. Vivisection. Infusion ... and, well ... eventually, a short stay in the steam room."

Caldwell let out a breath. "Make it happen." And with that, he left without another word.

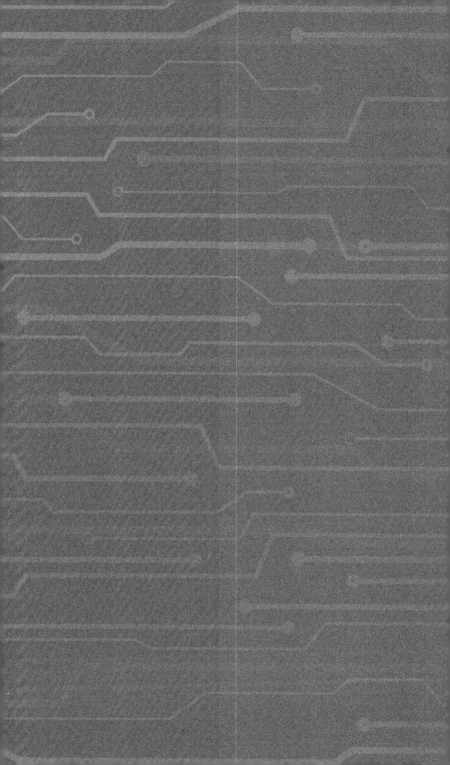

Chapter 37

Naromi Star System
Rivon3 Mining Station
Hardy

Hardy, moving along with the procession of other robots, continued to play the part of one encumbered by a restraining bolt. A mechanical zombie trudging forward close on the heels of a spindly looking domestic service bot in front of him. This gave him time to take in his Rivon3 surroundings.

Hardy scanned the foreboding landscape. This enigmatic alien world was comparable in size to Earth's moon, had borne witness to a relentless quest for resources. He would have to do a more thorough sensor dive about that later. For now, LuMan had provided a cursory assessment, one loosely pieced together from a variety of internal SynthoGen correspondences and memorandums. Far more eloquently spoken than LuMan's typically dry and succinct exhortations.

LuMan: *Despite its desolate appearance, Rivon3 boasts an atmospheric composition allowing brief moments of respite for those daring enough to venture without protective gear. However, linger too long—mere hours in fact—and the air's peculiar compounds will wreak havoc on one's respiratory system, a damage that's irreversible.*

A glimmer might catch your eye here, but be not deceived! Those aren't serene water bodies but pools of caustic liquid mercury, reflecting the dim light in an eerie dance. The shimmering, however, holds a deeper science. Mercury is a rare find on Earth, often linked to volcanic activity and the collision of massive celestial bodies. Its abundance here might suggest Rivon3's turbulent past.

The ever-present green haze, thick and cloying, isn't just any mist. It's a manifestation of the world's dense atmosphere, rich in sulfur compounds. This noxious fog doesn't just obscure vision; it's aggressive enough to corrode even the toughest of environment suits, giving them a mean time between failures (MTBF) of a mere five working days. With each EV suit coming with a staggering price tag of one hundred and fifty thousand credits, one can only marvel at the high cost of tapping into Rivon3's underground treasures.

And as for its scarred surface, the vast craters and depressions aren't natural. They are gaping wounds, testament to the intensive subterranean mining. Much like Earth's own moon, with its history of meteor impacts, Rivon3's landscape is a canvas of tales from a time when celestial bodies danced a little too close.

Hardy: *Good job. Okay, I need to get away from all these guards.*

LuMan: *I see that plan as problematic.*

Hardy: *Ye of little faith …*

Without preamble, Hardy chose that moment to simply halt in his tracks, bend over at the waist, and play dead.

LuMan: *This is your plan? To fake—*

Hardy: *Shhh, I'm performing.*

Within seconds of the line behind Hardy coming to a stop, the guards were hurrying to see what the problem was.

"What the hell's wrong with it?" one of the guards said, using the muzzle of his weapon to give the ChronoBot a little poke.

"What does it look like? No surprise; these ChronoBots are like three hundred years old. They're antiques. Can't even get new parts for them."

Off in the distance, another guard was swaggering their way.

"Shit! Here comes Sergeant Clayton," murmured the guard closest to Hardy. "Now we're in trouble."

"Maybe we can just move the ChronoBot out of the way?"

"Uh-uh. Thing's a thousand pounds ... No way."

"So's that girlfriend of yours. Um, Mindy, is it? So at least you're in practice."

"Screw you. And for your information, Mindy's on a diet."

"What's the holdup here?" bellowed an approaching baritone voice. "You idiots decide to throw a little tea party out here or something?"

No one answered as Hardy's bent-over form would pretty much speak for itself.

"Ah crap," Sergeant Clayton said, now leaning over, hands on knees, and peering up at Hardy's blackened faceplate. "You know these ClonoBits are three hundred years old—"

"ChronoBots," one of the two subordinate guards corrected.

"Whatever," Clayton said with a dismissive wave of a hand. "Leave the damn thing. Nothing we can do about it out here. I'll call Maintenance, get it hauled over to Robot Repair."

Hardy waited until the procession of robots and guards was long gone before straightening to his full height. He took in his surroundings.

Unleashing the full breadth of his sensor array, Hardy went to work in an attempt to answer one big question. *Why?* What had been the motivation for all of this? Deep space freighters like *Gossamer*. The clandestine abductions of hundreds if not thousands of young humans. Transforming them, making them more "environmentally" suited for on-world mining operations. Hardy assessed the data:

Nexalite is an exotic mineral only found in the most extreme environments of the universe, and Rivon3's turbulent past and unique atmospheric conditions created the perfect crucible for its formation. It is a radiant blue-green crystal, pulsating softly even in the darkest abyss, a characteristic attributed to its unique ability to capture and store energy at an atomic level.

Scientific Characteristics of Nexalite:

Energy Storage: Nexalite's atomic structure enables it to absorb, store, and release vast amounts of energy. It's believed to harness energy from its surroundings, be it thermal, kinetic, or even solar. This property has made it a sought-after power source in advanced technologies.

Durability: Despite its radiant appearance, Nexalite is incredibly tough. It has a Mohs hardness comparable to that of diamonds. However, unlike diamonds, it's also highly resistant to thermal and chemical erosion.

Piezoelectric Properties: When mechanical stress is applied to Nexalite, it can generate an electric charge. This makes it invaluable in technologies that require energy conversion from mechanical movements.

Luminescence: Nexalite emits a soft glow due to its unique atomic oscillations. This glow intensifies when it's in proximity to other Nexalite crystals, leading some to believe it has a kind of resonant communication property.

Quantum Entanglement: Though not fully understood, some advanced studies suggest that Nexalite crystals, when separated, can exhibit properties of quantum entanglement. This has opened avenues for research into faster-than-light communication using Nexalite as a medium.

Given its unparalleled properties, Nexalite is the cornerstone of a new age of technology, powering everything from cities to spacecraft. Its rarity and the dangers associated with mining it on Rivon3 have solidified its status as one of the most valuable resources in the universe.

. . .

"INTERESTING," WAS ALL THAT HARDY SAID.

The closest mine was a huge open pit with buildings perched upon its encircling edge. He watched as a hovering flatbed transport pulled up to a large, open-fronted building, like an aircraft hangar without doors. Coaxed by armed guards, clawbsters stumbled off the transport, forming a line toward the building. Another group of clawbsters stumbled out. Now, the ones headed in were being diverted ...

Hardy: *Are those ... troughs?*

It being more of a rhetorical question, LuMan stayed quiet.

Sure enough, against one wall were a series of metal bins, and the lobster creatures were already feeding.

Hardy surveyed the bleak landscape of Rivon3, his irritation simmering as his internal sensors picked up multiple injustices occurring down within the mine pit.

LuMan: *You're inclined to assist these enslaved beings. Not a good idea. The potential for weaponized, overwhelming conflict would be substantial. Negotiations may be a better alternative.*

Hardy: *Oh sure, I'll just mosey on up with a smile and a handshake. I'm sure any one of those armed guards will be happy to simply let everyone go.*

LuMan: *Sarcasm. How nice.*

Hardy swiftly approached the vast slave pit, eyeing the robotic transports hauling their miserable cargo. A group of utterly exhausted lobster creatures was shuffling toward one of the processing centers. "Nothing wrong with this picture. Nothing like forced slave labor to improve a company's bottom line," Hardy quipped. "I bet they get relaxing, revitalizing breaks and balanced nutrition too."

LuMan remained quiet.

Hardy watched as two lobster creatures suddenly broke free from their pod of workers. They were slow-moving and awkward with their crustacean-like, inflexible bodies. Doomed from the inception, it was a pathetic attempt at escape, having zero chances of success.

Hardy stepped closer to the rim overlooking the slave pit below. Three of the guards set out after the creatures. Each was wearing what seemed to be the standard-issue Rivon3 advanced, hardened, aqua-colored environment suits. They moved with lackadaisical indifference. Hardy tapped into their comms, listened to their back-and-forth chatter:

"Look at them. I say we find a big caldron and light the fires, " said Perimeter Guard Lockland.

"Yup ... Boil 'em till they squeal," Perimeter GuardManson said.

"We'll need a lot of melted butter," Perimeter Guard Lockland added.

"Oh, and don't forget the garlic," Perimeter Guard Lopez chimed in with a chuckle.

Hardy: *You still feel negotiations are our best avenue?*

LuMan: *That may have been shortsighted.*

Hardy was already making his way down the steep, rocky, not to mention perilous, contours of the slave pit. Having the ability to walk and chew gum at the same time, he kept his attention on the still slow-fleeing bright red lobster creatures and their pursuing guards. They'd made it little more than fifty feet. He wanted to tell them to just stop, to see the futility of what they were doing. But unlike their pursuers, they had no comms, no helmeted environ suits.

Hardy: *I guess we'll do this old school.* He increased his audio-output levels to maximum. "You there! Hold up! Stop ..."

The heads of both lobster creatures, as well as the guards, turned his way. But nobody stopped, let alone slowed.

Multiple bright flashes emanated from each of the three energy weapons. The guards were unloading on the two escaping prisoners. Hardy jolted to a stop, stunned by how they'd been so unnecessarily gunned down. Hell, a good shove would have put the two of them onto the ground.

One of them was still alive, his fading cries lancing through Hardy's neural network. Then there was silence. A quick life scan told Hardy all he needed to know—they were both dead.

Having piqued the three guards', as well as others', interest, Hardy changed direction, moving toward what looked to be an access tunnel built into the side of the pit.

Movement.

They seemed to have come out of nowhere, patrolling chrome-looking little domes, coming over the lip of the slave pit one by one.

LuMan: *There are six of them … each battle-hardened and weaponized with revolving plasma turrets.*

Like little mini-mes, Hardy thought as he picked up his pace. Now talking out loud, he said, "Need intel on how to navigate this wonderfully compassionate worker's paradise here."

Hardy felt LuMan's internal processors whirring as he sliced into the compound's network. In less than a second, Hardy had a detailed schematic, worker schedules, and patrol routes.

Studying the data, he searched for weaknesses. Suddenly, a blaring, annoyingly loud klaxon signaled Hardy's intrusion had been relayed throughout the compound.

Hardy mused sardonically, "What lovely music they have here. Must mean breaktime cookies and cider. So thoughtful of them!"

Ducking into the access tunnel and guided by LuMan's mapped routes, Hardy picked up his speed, heading for something called Central Security Hub 36.

Taking in the roughly hued rock tunnel, it occurred to Hardy just how immense this facility must be. There were dozens of tunnels similar to this one, hundreds of miles cleaved into Rivon3's surface.

LuMan: *Danger ahead …*

Hardy had been noodling on how he was going to get off this

wretched world. Then he too saw it. A quickly approaching seven-foot-tall ChronoBot. Hardy took in the vertical lettering spelling out the word "MARFIX."

"Damn ... Thing's like a bad penny, always turning up when least expected."

MARFIX was now sprinting, all five of its energy weapons being deployed.

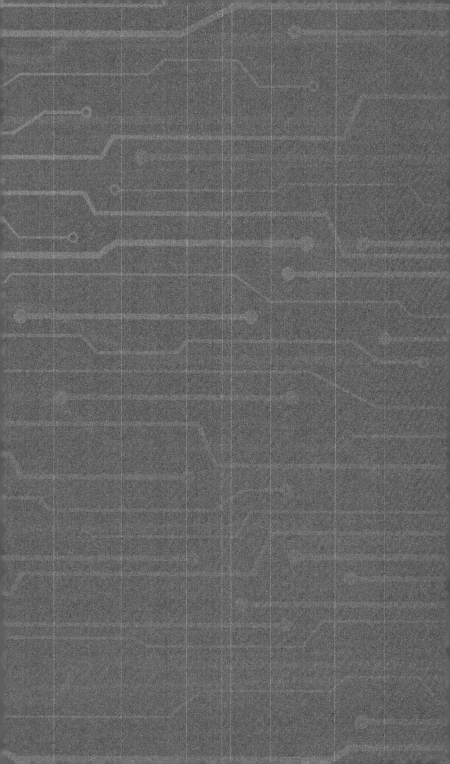

Chapter 38

Loni

I felt the heavy weight of exhaustion pressing down on me, my heartbeat irregular and weak. It was exhausting; every time darkness threatened to pull me under, I found myself in another place, another time.

Melita Roberts ... Suddenly, it wasn't just a memory; it was me. I was in a dim room, fingers flying across a keyboard, lines of code streaming across the display. Zettabytes of data flowed smoothly from an untraceable source, pouring into an internal drive nestled deep within me.

Then the world shifted, yanking me back to this cold, sterile compartment.

"Denzel," I pleaded, my voice barely a whisper. "Don't do this."

But his eyes, cold and calm, met mine without a hint of remorse. "*Shhh,*" he murmured, eerie kindness dripping from the word. His deliberate movements played on my fear. Four tubes of blood marked *L. Solace* lay on a stainless-steel tray. The surgical tools laid out before him glinted menacingly, but it was the laser scalpel that held my attention, its blade glowing a deep, malevolent ruby red.

He waved it casually, ensuring its red luminescence played in my eyes, a ghost of a smile on his face turning to a soft, chilling giggle.

Beside the tray, a holographic display showcased my internal organs. I felt vulnerable. Exposed. The red reticle targeting a spot on my rib cage labeled "Drive" made my already fragile heartbeat falter further.

Denzel grinned. "Yup. Right there. Plain as day when you know what you're looking for." He cleared his throat, as if commanding attention for his proficiency. "That little anomaly that one wouldn't think twice about … That tiny node apparently holds all the hidden treasure."

The tightness in my chest grew, threatening to overwhelm me. My sense of self felt as if it was on the verge of some kind of catastrophic crash.

"Why?" I choked out, struggling to find my voice amid the rising panic.

Denzel tilted his head, a mocking consideration in his eyes. "Because I can, kid."

The compartment seemed to close in around me. Time distorted, the line between past and present becoming nebulous. *Am I Loni? Or am I Melita?*

Was the truth there, locked within me? The memories, the data. Everything. If Denzel proceeded, would my true identity be lost forever? *What is my true identity?* Surrender had never been in my nature. But how did I fight? Even speaking was beyond laborious. *Oh God … the very core of who I am is at stake.*

Memories tangled with reality. Two worlds, overlapping and pulling at me.

Flash!

Melita. A server farm, the hum of machines rising to a deafening roar. I could almost feel the warmth emanating from the towering metal cabinets, the delicate balance of the HVAC system on the brink of being compromised. And then, with a meticulous orchestration, an HVAC malfunction. The system couldn't cope. Overheated. Exploded. Fire and smoke billowed; servers fried in an electrical death dance. Panic surged. The explosion ripped through the adjoining lab's bulkhead. Alarms screamed. People shouted. Chaos was my ally. Using the disarray as a cover, I sprinted, weaving through the halls and passageways of the high-security base. Just moments before a complete lockdown, I breached the exit. Freedom. At least for that version of me ... Reality was now yanking me back. *Did all that even happen?* Yes ... I suspected it had.

Denzel. His voice was a cruel lullaby, punctuated by the rhythmic beep of monitors tracking my fragile vitals. "Now, now, we wouldn't want another heart attack, would we? Though, from my understanding of these organic drives, we could just extract the data after you're gone," he drawled, eyes never leaving mine.

In my peripheral vision, a shadow loomed. It was Torp.

"What's taking so long?"

Denzel shot him a glance sharp enough to cut glass. "Working on it ..."

"I need her stable," Torp said with a sneer.

"Uh-huh."

"And remember, I want to be able to use her at the mines."

Denzel's thick fingers gripped my chin, forcing me to meet his gaze. "It's a simple procedure, Loni. A snip and it's over. Stop being so dramatic."

Before I could respond, the cold touch of a needle pricked my arm. Darkness surged, threatening to pull me under again.

Flash!

A different station. Utilitarian. The stench of grease and metal pervaded the air. Far from the sterile confines of Denzel's lab, this was a bustling hub of manufacturing and fabrication, meant to serve the colonial frontiers. It was a mess, but it was my mess.

I made my way through a cramped alley, arriving at an unassuming door. Inside, the room was dim, save for a gentle luminescence emanating from a makeshift lab counter. Dominating the space was a cylindrical glass container. A web of cables and delicate tubes snaked around it, pulsating softly.

Inside was a baby, floating suspended in a clear gelatin. It shimmered, countless bubbles within glinting like diamonds or distant stars, giving the impression the infant was surrounded by a galaxy. This was the future. My future. And I'd do anything to protect it.

Eyes fluttering open, Denzel's shadowed face greeted me. His eyes glinted brightly against the surgical compartment's dim lights, a stark contrast to his grotesquely gentle smile. That same twisted attempt at tenderness laced his words. "Your heart's behaving now," he cooed, that sickening facade never wavering. "Time to drift off again, kid."

His voice was oily, dripping with fake concern. "Soon, you'll be with your friends on Rivon3." The chuckle that followed felt like a knife. Cold. Taunting.

Flash!

Noise. The hum of interstellar engines faded as I—*oh, that's right, I'm Melita*— stepped onto Lancaster Station's metal deck. The weight of the infant cocooned securely against me was a comforting anchor. A gentle reminder of what mattered most to me.

Hightower, young and gaunt, stood before me. My dislike for the man was instantaneous. I had to force myself not to leer. His eyes flicked up from a holographic tablet, assessing. Questioning. "Here for the engineering job?"

I nodded, the slight sway of the baby bundle capturing Hightower's attention for a moment. "Yes."

"Name?" he inquired, already scrolling through his lists.

I hesitated for just a heartbeat. "Angela Solace."

Flash!

Heat. Humidity. A fog of steam clouded my vision. I was back as Loni, naked— every inch of my skin screamed, exposed. Vulnerable. The metallic decking beneath me, slick with condensation, burned. The sultry atmosphere was suffocating, each breath becoming more and more of an effort.

Sounds echoed in the distance—muffled shouts, the hiss of steam, the clang of metal. This wasn't any ordinary ship compartment. *Oh God, no... This is the steam room.*

Panic rose, swift and relentless. *What do I do?* I needed to move, to act. No, I had to think. No one escaped from the steam room ... but perhaps my memories, along with all those fragmented glimpses into Melita's life, just maybe they could be used here. Yes, my body might be trapped in here, but my mind was still free. Somewhere in those shared memories, just maybe were the seeds of escape.

Chapter 39

I caught the first glimpse of a clawbster shuffling through the thick haze, its vibrant red hue a stark anomaly amid the overpowering white fog of the steam room. *Is that what I think it is?* My mind raced.

Then, out of the growing mist, others appeared, all huddled together in a dimly lit corner. A realization dawned on me, chilling my spine. *No, this can't be happening,* I thought, my heart pounding so hard I could feel its thud in my throat. *Please don't let me become one of them.*

Hugging my arms around my exposed form, a shield against my fear more than the heat, I continued to observe. Their mournful cries echoed through the steam, some swearing under their breath, others despondent against the white bulkhead. I could see the anguish, the torment, the resignation. As the minutes felt like hours, a desperate mantra repeated in my head: *I'm not one of them. I can't be.*

Both mesmerized and disgusted, I watched as they all relentlessly scratched at themselves. *Why can't they stop?* I wondered, my stomach churning. Hardened crustacean layers peeled off them in grotesque sheets, dropping massive and monstrous sections onto the deck, revealing shiny new shells beneath, reminiscent of molting insects.

It's like a twisted metamorphosis, I mused as the itching seemed to have stopped, signaling the end of their most recent transformation, at least for now.

I swallowed hard, a lump forming in my throat as they began to scuttle toward me, the click-clack of their clawed feet echoing ominously. Yet, they stopped, forming a new, larger huddle just far enough from me. I strained my ears, trying to catch their conversations amid the occasional words I heard, but their muffled voices remained enigmatic. From time to time, one or more would cast a curious glance in my direction. Clutching my arms tighter to my chest and crossing my legs, their intense stares felt like a violation.

Stop staring at me! I thought, fighting the urge to shout. I wanted to scream, "Get away from me, you freaks!" But my voice was imprisoned by fear. Their crustacean faces, though altered, still bore traces of humanity. Those beady eyes held a glint of curiosity, even pity. One didn't need to be a genius to decipher their silent question—why was I untouched by the grotesque transformation that had claimed them? The irony was not lost on me; I was asking myself the same question. Why was I still ... me? Not that I was complaining.

More time passed, each second stretching out agonizingly long. From the corner of my eye, I noticed several of the clawbsters twitching, signs of restlessness apparent. The familiar scratching and itching had resumed. Seriously? Here? Now? I inwardly groaned. Couldn't they do that somewhere else? One would think such a grotesque transformation would warrant some privacy. *Have some shame!* I thought, exasperated. *Good God, show some decency!*

I winced involuntarily as, one by one, their shells began to fall away. The sight was simultaneously fascinating and repelling. This time, they peeled away almost entirely in one piece, as if shedding an old identity. For a moment, the discarded shells made it appear as though they were surrounded by the corpses of their own kind.

Freshly molted, their new, gleaming crimson shells stood out sharply. Their gazes, however, remained fixated on me. *Why are they all staring?* I questioned internally, anxiety gnawing at the edges of my mind. Yet, they maintained their distance, forming an impenetrable ring of curious onlookers.

Suddenly, the grating sound of metal against metal caught my attention. A hatch door, significantly larger than the one I was brought through, began to creak open. Through the hazy veil, the unmistakable form of security guards came into view, their number seeming to grow with each passing moment. *This isn't good*, I thought, my heart rate spiking. Panic set in. Should I run? Hide? Play dead? Uncertain and overwhelmed, I watched as the clawbsters, in a show of solidarity or perhaps strategy, widened their circle to make room. One of them, with a surprisingly gentle demeanor, gestured for me to join. Hesitating briefly, with thoughts of potential escape routes racing through my mind, I ultimately decided to trust the only allies I had in this bizarre situation. Taking a deep breath, I darted into their protective embrace. Without thinking, I began grabbing larger pieces of some discarded shells. Fortunately, they were somewhat bendy, and I managed to pry them open enough to affix clawbster legs onto my legs, clawbster arms onto my arms, and a clawbster torso—albeit way oversized—onto my own. As I continued to cover my body with them, I felt less exposed. Silly, perhaps, but at least I was covered. I closed my eyes and shook my head... *this will never work. What was I thinking?*

The one closest to me pivoted, bringing its eyes to meet mine. I recoiled momentarily, taken aback, then a familiar feeling of recognition washed over me. I gasped, opened my mouth, an onslaught of questions threatening to pour out. But I was paralyzed, unable to find my voice. The clawbster's features, though distorted, unmistakably echoed those of Claudia. *Can it really be?* The memories of our shared past raced through my mind. I hesitated only a moment before reaching out, tracing the roughened curve of her cheek. "I'm so sorry, Claudia."

It looked like she was struggling to say something. But no words came out. The sorrow in her voice sent shivers down my spine, and I was flooded with a mix of guilt and empathy. What had this place done to her?

My gaze then shifted, and I recognized another transformed figure. Peter. Even in his altered state, I could sense the familiar weight of his unspoken emotions. He averted his eyes, and I wondered if it was out of anger or, perhaps, shame. *Does he blame me? Or himself?* I pondered, wishing I could bridge the gulf that had opened between us.

Claudia and Peter stayed close, their protective presence almost palpable as they acted as a barrier between me and the curious eyes around me. I felt an odd sense of gratitude mixed with heartache. The security guards were relentless, herding us like cattle toward the beckoning maw of the hatchway. As we exited the suffocating embrace of the steam room, the sharp prods and shoves made the journey a blur. But finally, the fog of confusion cleared, and I discerned our intended destination: a looming dropship, standing ready for embarkation, its gangway like an outstretched arm, beckoning us into its depths. *Where are they taking us now?*

The uncertainty of the situation weighed heavily on me.

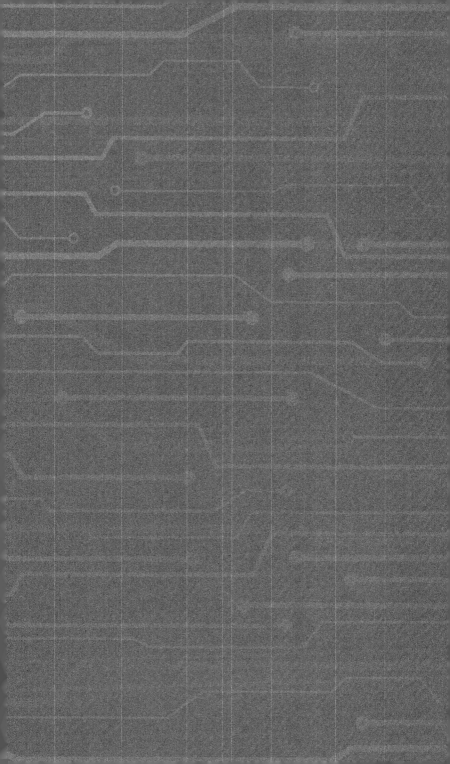

Chapter 40

My breath caught as I was pressed between the hard, unyielding shells of multiple clawbsters. A knot of anxiety gripped me, threatening to choke me. They moved in unison, a protective barrier, but the cold metal underfoot jostled and rocked with every movement of the dropship.

Each bump, each jolt, seemed to leave a bruise on my flesh. Unlike the clawbsters with their natural armor, I felt every blow. My pulse raced. The world was a harsh blur of metal, chitin, and fear. The ship turned suddenly, a sharp corner jammed into my rib, and I bit back a gasp.

They shifted around me, the clawbsters, instinctively forming a protective cocoon. One of them, with a clawed appendage, held me steady. It was touching, the attempt to shield me, but it wasn't enough. I was fairly sure more pain was inevitable.

My mind raced; obviously we were en route to Rivon3. The dropship's metallic hum grew louder, a precursor to landing. Every sensation was magnified. The tension. The fear. The stifling, recycled, fishy-smelling air.

"I think we're almost there," one of the clawbsters whispered, its voice a sharp rasp.

Rivon3 was going to be hostile, unpredictable. Based on the

scant intel I'd previously accessed, its terrain was treacherous. If I survived the landing, the planet itself would be a volatile challenge I might not be prepared for. *And I'm naked under these shells.*

My eyes darted to the nearby clawbsters. *Can I trust them?* Before, Claudia and I hadn't been friends by any stretch of the imagination. And Peter ... I barely knew him. Their solidarity in shielding me had been a boon, but I knew alliances were fleeting. One wrong move, one betrayal, and it would be over. *I can't depend on anyone but myself.*

The ship jerked. My stomach dropped as we touched down, the impact echoing through my bones. My heart threatened to jump out of my chest. The clawbsters let out a collective hiss, their discomfort evident even with their protective shells. I could hear the mechanical grinding. The aft hatch was preparing to open—the filtered sunlight would soon reveal the new world we were about to face. Would it be freedom or a new prison?

"Prepare," another clawbster snapped, its beady eyes fixed on me. The undercurrent of warning in its voice was unmistakable.

The metallic scent of the planet's atmosphere rushed in as the hatch fully opened. It was alien, unfamiliar. I steeled myself, pushing past the enveloping fear. *Show no weakness.*

The gangway creaked, slowly extending out to what awaited us.

I took a shaky step forward, flanked by my clawbster cohorts. The rocky surface of Rivon3 stretched endlessly, an inhospitable expanse of jagged terrain, mucky green fog, and looming shadows. In the distance, dust storms danced menacingly. My resolve wavered.

This is it. No going back.

One of the clawbsters nudged me hard. "Move it!" it barked. Its cold eyes assessed me, seeing the human frailty I was so desperately trying to hide.

Conflict raged within me. Every instinct screamed for me to run, to find shelter, to hide. But I couldn't. My flimsy clawbster shell costume was probably fine from a distance, but up close, no way I would pass muster with the guards. The weight of the clawbsters' gazes pressed on me, judgmental and calculating. I wanted to tell them that we had to work together if we were to survive. For now, at least.

Taking a deep breath, I squared my shoulders and shuffled forward, doing my best to mimic the ones around me heading down the steep ramp. The clawbsters fell into step beside me. As the alien sun cast elongated shadows across the harsh landscape, my mind raced. I wanted to cough, to clear my burning throat, but doing so ... I might as well hold up a sign and scream, "Here I am ... Naked human walking here!"

The oppressive heat felt as if it was already singing my cheeks; my lungs were on fire. All around us, human guards stood tall, cocooned within their aqua-colored EV suits—suits that prevented the toxic atmosphere of Rivon3 from reaching their lungs. Here within my ridiculous clawbster shell mask, humid and putrid smelling, I craved fresh air, but instead each breath felt as if I was inhaling hot embers.

I watched the guards, their expressions visible behind shaded visors. One caught my eye and sneered, perhaps enjoying my obvious discomfort.

"You're the lucky ones ... Hell, you're perfectly suited for this shitty environment," he taunted, his voice distorted through the helmet's comms.

Suppressing a cough, I snapped back, "Yeah? Wanna trade?" But my bravado was quickly fading, replaced by desperation. God, my mind was screaming for fresh oxygen, for clean air.

The clawbsters seemed affected as well. Their shells, normally a glistening bright red, seemed duller now, more subdued. They moved as one, herded by the guards, their claws clicking against the rocky ground.

A massive hangar loomed ahead of us, the entrance agape, like the maw of a monster ready to swallow us whole. But it was the long line of metal troughs that drew my attention, filled with unappetizing dried pellets. The clawbsters surged toward them, a tidal wave of hunger and need. The guards laughed, cruel amusement evident in their eyes as they observed the clawbsters' desperation.

I was nudged forward, the metallic taste of fear palpable in my mouth. My throat constricted. As I stumbled closer to the troughs, the nearby clawbsters' urgency became clear. Those pellets, as unappealing as they looked, were sure to be the only source of sustenance here on Rivon3. And without the protection of an EV suit, I needed something—anything. If I didn't eat, I'd become too weak to make my eventual escape.

I hesitated for a moment, looking at the clawbsters, who were now devouring the pellets with a fervor. While we were different, our plights were intertwined.

Throwing caution to the wind, I grabbed a small handful of the pellets and, in a clandestine motion, forced them under my mask and into my mouth. I gagged at their chalky consistency and bitter aftertaste. But the relief was almost immediate; the sharp sting in my lungs diminished, replaced by a dull ache.

One of the clawbsters gestured past me with a claw, indicating a door on the far side of the hangar. I realized it was Peter. "You need to escape. Bring help," he said with a mouthful. "Christ, you're standing out like a porcupine at a nudist colony."

I had to smile at that. Peter hadn't completely lost his sense of humor. That was at least something.

Determination set in. I nodded, signaling my agreement. Steadying myself, I set off across the vast hangar, feeling every step was bringing undue attention to myself. Other clawbsters, probably those that had arrived here on another transport, looked my way. I was not one of them—how long before someone called out or pointed a big red claw in my direction? Whispers of treachery and betrayal flitted through my mind.

I watched as a guard disappeared behind that human-sized

door. Nearby, clawbsters murmured, their antennae twitching nervously. Now I had to wait. Every breath I took burned, the putrid, alien air continuing to assault my lungs. I struggled to tamp down my rising panic.

I shuffled forward, acting as if in no hurry. Just one more clawbster freak moseying about. Then the door loomed ten feet in front of me. Surprisingly it was unguarded, unconcealed. But as I reached out, I quickly realized why. It was built to keep the clawbsters out, not humans. Doorknobs were for hands, clutching fingers, not oversized and awkward claws. I would need to shed my heavy clawbster disguise; one that was clinging to me like a second skin. Casually, I looked about my immediate surroundings. A few of the clawbsters were eyeing me, but none of the guards. I freed my right hand from my claw prosthesis, letting it drop to the ground. I reached for the doorknob and was relieved to find it unlocked.

Once inside, an airlock greeted me. The chamber hissed and, for a brief, suffocating moment, darkness consumed me. Then, a rush of clean, invigorating air flooded in. Relief washed over me, but it was short-lived. Hurrying, I removed the rest of the hard-shell facade, dropping the pieces onto the cement floor. I kicked the shells into the shadowed corners. I looked down at myself and grimaced. My exposed nakedness had become painfully apparent. Then again, sure, the risk of being seen was real, yet … Didn't it take a backseat to more pressing concerns? A glowing green button beckoned. I pressed it, feeling confident it was my ticket out of the airlock. An adjacent metal hatch door clicked and sprang open. Light from the hallway beyond streamed in.

Silence. The corridor seemed to stretch on endlessly. My bare feet slapped against cold laminate flooring. I urged myself to get a move on. Taking long, swift strides, I hurried, almost as if I had an actual plan.

Eventually I was moving past doors, some open, others closed. I stopped when I saw what looked to be an office. A desk with a computer display caught my eye. Hurrying inside, I took a seat, the cold plastic reminding me my butt cheeks were exposed. The computer system was of familiar design and seemed to be beckoning me to interface with it. I'm sure that was my imagination, but right now, I needed all the confidence I could muster. But I hesitated, memories of my last interaction flooding back. *How do I log in without bringing every guard within a mile here to this office?* Then it hit me. Hardy's fake credentials—*would they work here?* Nothing ventured ... I keyed them in. The display momentarily went black, then brightened. I was in! I was looking at some kind of logistics database. This was familiar to me. A mixture of relief and disbelief settled in.

First thing first, I tried contacting Orin. After what seemed an agonizing amount of time, I saw his face, illuminated by his ComBand. His voice crackled to life. "Loni! Thank God ... Where are you? Are you okay?"

Only now did I contemplate just how much of a view I was providing Orin. I slunk lower in my chair, ensuring the edge of the desk was providing at least some cover. "Things aren't so good for me, Orin. I woke up in the steam room. It was horrible."

He shook his head, as if searching for something to say.

"I saw Claudia ... and Peter too. They'd been lobstered ... It was awful."

"And you?"

"Uh ... no. At least not so far. I'm still ... just me. Which I guess is kinda weird. Oh, that and I'm now on Rivon3. I've managed to escape. I found a vacant office."

"Just stay hidden. God, I'm glad you're okay," he said, the concern in his eyes easing some of my anxiety.

"So, what about you and the others?" I said, leaning in closer. "Looks like you're still there in the clubhouse."

He nodded. "For now, but we can hear security teams patrolling nearby. They're looking for us, Loni. Suppose it's just a matter of time."

"No. You have to stay positive," I scolded.

Footsteps.

"Crap! Someone's coming; I have to hide. I'll contact you later." With that, I slid from the chair and ducked behind the desk.

The echoing footfalls were getting closer. I closed my eyes, placed a palm over my mouth. I prayed that whoever that was would just keep going.

Louder now, *clack, clack, clack,* a man's heavy footfalls. He suddenly slowed, then came to a stop. *Oh my God ...* Whoever it was, they were right there, standing within the office door's threshold.

I tried to remember what was on the desk that I could use as a weapon. A coffee cup, a vase with small pink plastic flowers, an intercom unit. *Nothing of use.*

A cold chill ran down my spine as it occurred to me that whoever he was, he might be looming over me right now. He might be staring down at the top of my frickin' head!

Clack, clack, clack, the footfalls resumed and soon were echoing off the walls far away. I let out my breath; tears threatened, but I held them back. Emotion had no place now. I poked my head up, saw the coast was clear, and took a seat again. My fingers flew over the keyboard and soon I was scanning various digital drop-ship cargo manifests. One designation stood out, shining like a beacon amid the void. Unit 1223.

Oh my God. The robot was here on Rivon3.

My pulse quickened. With newfound desperation, I hailed him and waited—every second stretching into an eternity.

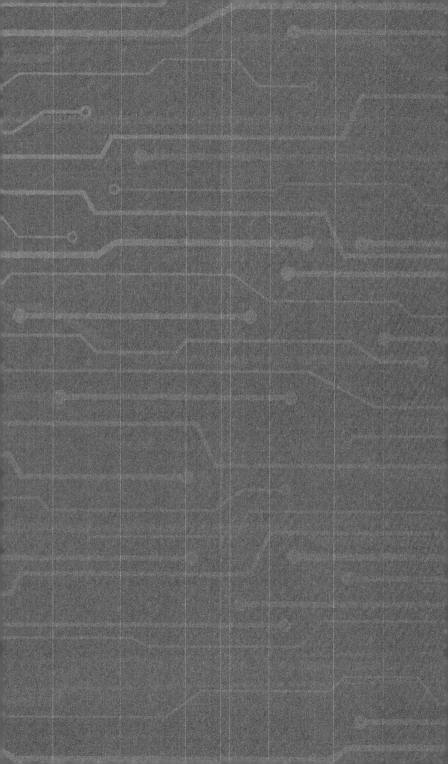

Chapter 41

Naromi Star System
Rivon3 Mining Station
Hardy

H ardy and MARFIX, the two ChronoBots, were battling in the roughly hewn subterranean tunnel. Hardy had deployed his plasma cannons, just as MARFIX had, but the two were now in close, brawling like two heavyweight prizefighters. This fight was personal, both knowing only one would be leaving this cold and rocky ring.

Hardy staggered sideways, having taken a direct sledge-hammer of a punch to the left side of his head. His vision flickered; myriad blocky colors saturated his faceplate's optics. "Okay ... I'll give you that one. But just so you know, you punch like a girl."

MARFIX answered with a series of up-close-and-personal energy bolts to Hardy's midsection.

The plasma burns sizzled and crackled. Hardy envisioned the

blackened craters being left behind upon his reflective, polished chrome exterior. *Now that's just taking things too far.*

LuMan: *Up to this point, our combat efficiency has been suboptimal. The prognosis for success appears unfavorable. We may have met our match.*

Hardy had no time to argue with LuMan—his back was literally up against a wall. Hardy darted left, but MARFIX had anticipated the move, swinging a thick, metallic fist right toward Hardy's faceplate. All too close, it was a near miss, the punch colliding with solid rock. The echo reverberated within the tunnel, melding with the hum and whine of strained servo mechanisms. Overhead, newly formed stalactites hung precariously, glinting in the erratic light. Drops of condensation trickled down, splashing onto the cavern floor, mimicking the sound of ticking seconds.

Hardy pivoted away, his thoughts racing. "Use the environment," his processor offered. Those thoughts were interspersed with flashes of previous battles, previous mistakes.

MARFIX lunged. Was this battlebot faster? Stronger? Hardy dismissed the thought. *Well, maybe it's newer.* Hardy had been in countless brawls, had scraped through situations far more dire than this. *Experience is my ally.*

Hardy sidestepped just in time as MARFIX's cannon arm smashed into the tunnel wall again. Rock fragments showered them both. But this time Hardy seized the opportunity, delivering a jackhammer of a blow to MARFIX's midsection.

MARFIX reeled backward, its robotic voice filtering through with a distortion. "You're outdated, Unit 1223. A relic."

MARFIX was in a somewhat more recent build category. Hardy inwardly smirked, even as neural algorithms whirred, computing potential outcomes being offered up by LuMan.

The two ChronoBots clashed again, metal on metal. Sparks flew. A whirlwind of strikes, blocks, evasions. Every movement analyzed within nanoseconds. Every decision a potential game-changer.

Suddenly, a stalactite, destabilized by the tumult, plummeted downward. MARFIX unexpectedly grabbed it in midair and now wielded it like a spear. Hardy's sensors flashed a warning. He narrowly dodged the improvised weapon, feeling the rush of cold air as it slashed past.

In this dance of death, time seemed both accelerated and halted. The paradox of being a ChronoBot.

MARFIX struck again. This time with a deadly combo followed by a jab of his stone spike to the core. But Hardy had seen this before. *Adapt. Redirect.*

Hardy did just that, using MARFIX's own momentum against him. The bot stumbled, smashing into the rough wall, causing another round of rocks to crumble. Then Hardy spotted it there upon the craggy tunnel floor—the radiant blue-green crystal, pulsating softly, even in this darkened shaft. He remembered the characteristic attributes of Nexalite, how its atomic structure enabled it to absorb, store, and release vast amounts of energy.

Hardy seized the shard, its jagged edge gleaming. He lunged, aiming for a critical joint in MARFIX's cervical articulator.

MARFIX stumbled, the glowing Nexalite crystal shard now embedded deep within the bot's neck.

Neither robot moved for several long seconds. Hardy half expected his opponent to keel over dead, Superman impaled by kryptonite.

But with an unexpected ferocity that made even Hardy's circuits stutter, MARFIX sprang forward, its thick metal arms coming around Hardy with the lethal embrace of an industrial compactor. Arms pinned to his sides, Hardy struggled to release himself. Was that the sound of bending, twisting metal? Hardy's stress sensors screamed.

Being vulnerable was as unique to Hardy as a rainstorm in the Sahara.

LuMan: *Danger: Catastrophic systems failure imminent.*

Hardy's vision dimmed. *So, this is what it feels like to be lightheaded.*

A reflected glint caught Hardy's waning attention. A momentary sparkle of bright green. Even with his mind a worsening jumble of fading thoughts, Hardy knew there was significance to it. LuMan had gone ominously quiet. Perhaps it was because Hardy's mind resided within his ChronoBot biomass, while LuMan resided within circuits.

Fading, fading, fading …

Nexalite! The thought came to him as a last gasp of electrical impulses. And with that, Hardy did the only thing his situation would permit, a situation akin to being squeezed to death by a boa constrictor. Hardy slammed his head forward with every ounce of his remaining energy reserves. Like a hammer striking the head of a nail. Once, twice, thrice, Hardy drove the Nexalite shard deeper and deeper into MARFIX's neck.

The piercing shriek of stressed metal was deafening.

Chrome-plated composite-alloy arms suddenly dropped, going limp as wet noodles. Hardy shoved MARFIX away, watching as the robot staggered, legs wobbling.

"You think you're the hero here, Unit 1223?" MARFIX's voice was a confluence of distorted tones. "ChronoBots never really die. I will find you. I will destroy you."

Hardy surged forward, targeting the lone Nexalite crystal piece with a final, forceful blow. MARFIX toppled, akin to a bin of spilled nuts and bolts.

Hardy stared down at the metallic heap at his feet. "Maybe you're right. Maybe ChronoBots never really die. But try living without a head." And with that, Hardy bent over, took MARFIX's head in his hands, and began to twist. Round and round it went, and like the head of a stripped bolt, off came the killer bot's noggin. Hardy brought the elongated orb up so it was at face level. Wondering if there were any remaining residual thoughts still processing in there, Hardy said, "You better hope we never ever cross paths again."

Hardy tossed MARFIX's head into the air, gauged the gravitational pull back to the ground, before kicking the spinning, tumbling head with a resounding *clank*. MARFIX's head rocketed away, arching fifty, seventy-five, a hundred yards down the length of the tunnel. And like a Super Bowl referee, he threw his arm up. "That's a field goal, baby!"

LuMan: *You have an incoming communiqué.*

Surprised, Hardy saw that the hail was emanating from here on Rivon3. From a low-level administrator's office. As the feed cleared, he saw someone sitting in near darkness. It was Loni, and she looked terrified.

"Loni, why are you here on Rivon3?"

"Well, it's not by choice, robot. I could ask you the same question. I need your help. I've escaped, but I have no idea where to go. What to do."

Hardy could hear the desperation in the girl's voice. Her being here did complicate things.

Just as a plan was starting to percolate at the edges of his mind, the chilling voice of Commander Torp echoed through the open commutations channel. "Step away from the computer."

A ruckus. Muffled shouts. Then, piercing the chaos, Loni's voice, filled with sheer terror. "Hardy! Hardy, help!"

Silence. The channel went dead.

Hardy's thoughts screamed for action. Fury painted his digitized vision a bright red. "This ends now," he murmured.

LuMan: *Agreed. Best we forget about finding Central Security Hub 36.*

Hardy: *You think?*

Hardy took a moment to scrutinize the facility's sprawling layout. There was a building somewhat close to the mine's edge. The odds were that was where Loni had called from. He reached out with his sensors; the atmosphere here was problematic, but he thought he caught a momentary flash of the girl's biomatrix.

Running now, his footfalls echoed against the tunnel's rock walls; within a minute he was exiting the access tunnel, stepping out into Rivon3's harsh environment. He spotted the roving chrome security bots, several close. Guards were patrolling the slave pit's perimeter. One thing was clear: all their attention seemed limited to the pit.

Hardy moved fast, climbed the steep embankment, trying to keep low—not so simple when you're a seven-foot-tall robot. Hesitating at the rim, Hardy wavered, his consciousness doing something strange. Had it been the repeated punches to his head? Had MARFIX actually won in the end?

LuMan: *Keep going. I will deal with the mental incongruities …*

Hardy transmitted a continual series of sensor-blocking signals, something he hadn't been capable of just an hour earlier. He moved quickly across the open stretch of rocky terrain, heading for the low, single-story building. He found a door, which was locked. He didn't bother with subtlety. A swift kick and a fragmented cement doorframe toppled inward. It seemed to be a control room of sorts. Lots of display monitors, consoles, technology …

Panic erupted inside. People, unprepared for the sudden intrusion, that and the influx of the nasty Rivon3 atmosphere. Hands fumbled for respirators, eyes wide and fearful.

Deploying his forearm plasma guns, Hardy spoke. His voice was cold, steel-edged. "Three things! One: remove your ComBands, now!"

ComBands clattered onto their boards.

"Two: Who in here can turn on interstellar communications?" Hardy pointed his energy weapons toward the closest woman.

Her mouth fell open. "I … I can do that from this station," she croaked.

Hardy watched as her fingers flew over her control board.

When she was done, she nodded and pointed a nervous finger toward the central console. Hardy saw that the board had come to life, a communications matrix with a hovering Halo Display.

"Three! That door over there, is that a storeroom?"

Looking confused, several people nodded their heads.

"Well, get up and get in there ... the whole lot of you. Move!"

The personnel, eyes wide, nodded and hurriedly complied—one by one filing into the small storeroom.

With little effort, he shoved a now-unattended console, easily several thousand pounds, against the now-closed door. He moved to the middle of the room and stared down the communications matrix. But as Hardy moved to access the system, a pang of doubt sliced through him. *Who to call?* His past was a fractured puzzle, memory shards scattered. *Or was it?* As if guided by some kind of intangible fate, the pieces started to align. Clarity. "Oh my ... I not only know who I am, but where I came from. Where I belong."

He accessed a very specific deep-space comms channel, one he knew by heart. But time had run out. A klaxon suddenly blared overhead. He turned away from the communication's matrix; there'd be time for that later. Loni was out there, *somewhere*, and in danger. A voice blared overhead:

Security breach detected. All units converge.

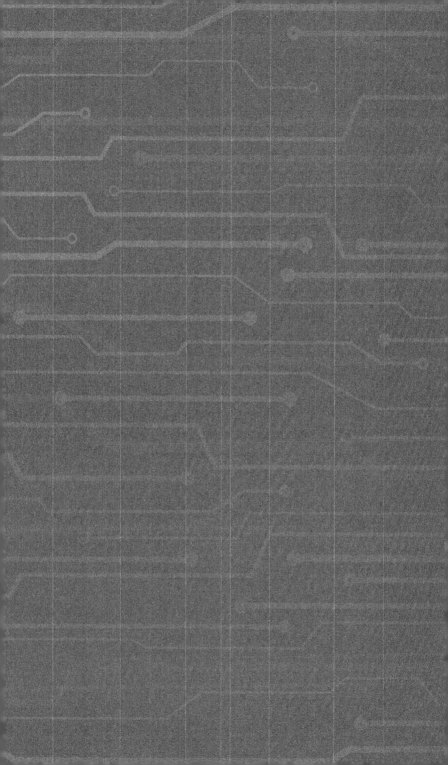

Chapter 42

Naromi Star System
Rivon3 Mining Station
Loni

A nervous-looking MedTech stood nearby, lips compressed into a solid line. The cold floor of Rivon3's shoddy medical booth bit into my bare feet, sending shivers up my spine. Wrapped in nothing but a flimsy sheet, I felt the harsh grip of Torp's fingers digging into my right arm. The man was breathing hard, pushing toward apoplectic. The anger, the hatred, was rising off him like the heat from a star going supernova.

I was feeling ill, like I might throw up. I tried to steady myself. Memories of my heart attack aboard *Gossamer* were still too vivid, too fresh. Waves of postoperative nausea rolled over me.

I gasped as two strong hands tore into my shoulders. "Why didn't you transform?" Torp spat, each word colder and sharper than the last. His big red face was just inches from my own.

The pounding in my ears nearly drowned out his voice. I swallowed hard, found enough strength to mutter, "I honestly don't know."

His piercing stare made it clear … He thought I was lying. Panic surged as my heart ached.

With a callous shove, he let go of me and turned to a nearby 3D display. Only then did I catch sight of the display—Denzel on *Gossamer*, HealthBay's familiar confines behind him. Torp stared at the clearly petrified MedTech. "Tell me, you incompetent moron, what exactly did you excise in that supposedly 'easy-peasy' surgery?"

Denzel's angst-filled voice answered. "Look, the girl's heart was already a mess. She has stage 3 cardiac deterioration, at least according to HealthBay's analyses."

Tell me something I don't know, I thought.

"But yeah, I found your organic data storage device. Thing's state of the art … truly ingenious. No doubt, SynthoGen IP. It was easy to locate once I knew what to scan for."

Data storage? Embedded in me? My thoughts spiraled as I struggled to make sense of this latest revelation.

Denzel suddenly stood up straight as if he'd been struck by lightning. "Sir … the girl … Loni, she's undoubtedly been on a heavy dose of meds. Maybe she snuck them on board; I don't know."

"So what?" Torp retorted with an impatient shrug.

"Meds like that … Well, they're genetically based. Could have interfered with our infusions. I'm just throwing that out there."

Suddenly, Torp, with mounting impatience, severed the communication with *Gossamer*. "Test her blood! Now!" he snapped, his voice echoing with dread. "I need answers!"

"But what are we looking for, sir?" came a hesitant reply from the nurse.

"Anything!" Torp barked. "If there are any counteracting agents. I need to know why the transformation failed!"

"I'll send the results of her blood samples," the MedTech said matter-of-factly.

Amid the tension, a faint rumble echoed from outside, hinting at chaos. Hope and realization flickered inside me. *Hardy. He's here to save me.*

Through the walls, I could almost visualize the ChronoBot confronting an army of bots, his every move calculated and precise.

≈

Hardy

He had continued to move through the building's labyrinth of hallways and corridors. It was then that the security bots had streamed in from multiple directions. Security guards, easily fifty of them, had positioned themselves behind the combination of men and machine, looked to be a formidable contingent. *Nah ... Who am I kidding? No, they don't.*

Suddenly bright blue energy bolts were piercing the dust-filled air as Hardy let loose with all five of his plasma cannons. The bots, none of which were ChronoBots, were targeted with perfectly placed energy bolts. The guards scattered, running for their lives. Hardy progressed further into the bowels of the building; he'd locked onto Loni's biomatrix. Turning a corner, six waist-high, polished chrome security drones blocked his path. "You sure you want to do this?" he said, almost feeling sorry for the half-height bots.

Their answer came back with a synchronized deployment of plasma cannons, each popping into view from previously hidden compartments. It occurred to Hardy that these bots were, what ... his distant relatives, maybe cousins? Undoubtedly, they had been manufactured by the Sheentah, just as he was, some three hundred years prior.

Reluctant to destroy them, he hesitated. *Maybe I can reason with them …*

They all fired at once. The barrage of bright red plasma bolts filled the compartment. He took seven direct blasts, each a decisive punch in its own right. His once pristine chrome plating had quickly become a cratered mess. Enough was enough. Bright blue energy bolts pierced the dust-filled air as Hardy let loose with all five of his plasma cannons. Within seconds he was back in the fight, going toe to toe with them. He delivered a devastating kick, toppling one of the chrome droids, a turtle stuck helplessly on its shell. Hardy charged, spun, jumped, and pounced with fervor. Sparks showered as he ripped the inside components from another. Like a Waring blender, the metallic crunch of their fallen bodies was music to his ears.

Hardy glanced up and spotted one of the ever-watchful security cameras.

≈

Loni

FROM THE DIMLY LIT ROOM, THE THREE OF US STARED at the security feed in breathless silence. On the screen, Hardy obliterated robot after robot with unwavering precision. I could hardly believe my eyes as he managed to send an entire platoon's worth of security forces scrambling in fear.

Inside HealthBay, the haunting rhythm of the monitor's beeps became the unnerving soundtrack to our observation. My eyes traced the line of cords connected to the now-wailing machine. Hovering nearby was a health avatar slowly spinning on its axis.

It provided a perfect window into my innards, vessels, organs, and unfamiliar oddities within my body.

One of the MedTechs leaned in closer to one of the many medical devices. "Interesting ..." he said, pointing to the display. "Due to her recent heart attack—the tissue here around this ventricle ... Look how it's been fragmented, opened up, like a small dam that's burst."

We all looked at the image.

"How ... how am I even still alive?" I asked.

The MedTech shrugged. "Good question. But that's not my point. I'm seeing a kind of data dump of genetic bio-information. It's been integrated into the heart tissue."

Torp pursed his lips while continuing to stare at the display.

"Why would there be genetic information in my heart?" I asked.

"This is all fascinating," Torp said with a huff. "But who gives a rat's ass about any of this? We have the implanted device. Anything else is inconsequential."

The MedTech raised a hand, a schoolchild asking to be called upon.

"What? Just say what you have to say," Torp spat.

"Denzel's back on Comms ..."

Torp frowned toward the display and raised his brows. "What?"

"Sir ... I just looked at the data on the implanted storage device."

"Did I ask you to do that?"

"No, sir ... but—"

"But nothing! That is highly sensitive data. You're a MedTech, not—"

"Sir, it's gobbledygook. It's useless trash code."

Torp hesitated, bewildered. "Fine ... Get me the data. Send it to Caldwell too. Now."

≈

CALDWELL

CALDWELL'S PULSE HAMMERED IN HIS NECK AS HE watched the machinery of his empire fall, piece by piece. He was finding it hard to tear his eyes away from the multiple video feeds. He pulled both palms down his face. "That damned ChronoBot!" He watched as it continued to move like a hurricane, unstoppable, undeterred.

He fumbled with his tablet, reading the message from Denzel. Caldwell skipped down to the scanned download of excised data from the storage device. He made a face, trying to make sense of the data. *I'll have to shelve this for later ...*

He needed to pack some essentials and get the hell out of there. His breaths were rapid, erratic. The serenity and opulence of his Rivon3 office contrasted with the mayhem the ChronoBot was wreaking.

His ComBand started to vibrate; he gave his wrist a quick glance. *Shit! Really?* Torp was glaring up at him from the small screen. Torp's voice grated. "Caldwell. Are you watching the feeds?"

Every strand of Caldwell's patience was fraying. "Of course, I am. What the hell happened? What are you doing to stop that damn robot?"

Torp stuttered, "It wasn't—"

"Save it," Caldwell snapped, cutting him off.

The multiple feeds painted a grim tableau. One particular one caught his eye—Unit 1223 eviscerating a full squad of the latest Mark IV security bots like they were toy soldiers. Caldwell clenched his fists. Each unit represented an investment now reduced to sparks and scraps. Credits lost forever. Millions of them.

He knew he had to leave, and fast. He began retrieving and securing other important files from his system. Every second counted now. But there was a gnawing thought at the back of his mind. What if he was missing something?

Torp's voice once more interrupted his thoughts. "Caldwell. We might have a bigger problem."

He ground his molars. *Bigger than a ChronoBot on a crazed rampage?* He didn't need more complications. "Just spit it out. I'm leaving."

"The girl ... the data. Have you looked at it?" Torp hesitated. "It's ... all wrong."

Caldwell's mind raced. He'd started to look at it. "Hold on ..."

Scrolling the data on his tablet, he saw the screen suddenly filled with flowing streams of data. He stiffened. "Oh shit." Like before, the data looked accurate at first glance, but no. It was, in fact, all wrong. It was gobbledygook.

"And what are you doing about it? I need the data, Torp! Fix it! And do so before

my facility is turned to ashes."

Torp hesitated and swallowed, a dead man walking to the gallows. "We didn't anticipate—"

"Of course, you didn't," Caldwell hissed.

He weighed his options. Escape now, deal with the rest later? But Loni's data ...

Caldwell locked eyes with his reflection in the translucent display. He'd spent a good part of his life building this business brick by brick. He wasn't going to let anything or any*one* destroy it. If Melita Roberts really was dead and the data was useless, then it would be moot. But what if Roberts—or some other facsimile of Dr. Melita Roberts—was still alive? Then he and his company were in dire jeopardy. The world would not think kindly upon genetically modifying young humans into chitin-shelled worker bees.

No, no one can ever discover what was going on here. Which reminds me; Loni Solace needs to be exterminated immediately.

Suddenly, the floor vibrated, and a distant explosion echoed. Caldwell glanced again at the screen of streaming nonsensical data. Decisions loomed, and time was running out.

"Lock down the research wing. And Torp?"

"Yes, sir?"

"Handle it. Or it's your head."

As the lights flickered, Caldwell steeled himself for the storm ahead.

The ComBand vibrated again, insistent. An incoming text. His ship beckoned, a safe exit in the cacophony of calamity. He switched back to Torp. His face, always unpleasant to Caldwell, looked even more so in the pixelated display. If one could bottle incompetence, it'd bear Torp's face on the label.

The man seemed exasperated. "The girl … There are zettabytes of data stored—"

"What do you mean, zettabytes of data?" Caldwell gritted out, frustration spiking.

A stutter, a stumble. Classic Torp. "We're unraveling this in real time. Um, it's the girl's heart tissue. We've discovered layers upon layers of data, but it's … It's encrypted. Erratic."

"What are you talking about? We already have the storage device."

Torp smirked. "Apparently, that was a decoy. That nonsensical data was meant as a diversion."

Caldwell's hands tightened into fists, his knuckles turning white. This was supposed to be straightforward. In and out. He had anticipated challenges, but nothing of this scale.

"Are you kidding me?"

Torp flinched. "We had no idea. It was hidden in plain sight …

ingenious, really. The thing is, if Loni Solace hadn't had that heart attack, we'd never have found it."

Caldwell's voice was acid. The glare he directed at the screen was venomous. In his head, again, he imagined throttling Torp. "This is not making any sense!"

Torp hesitated, searching for words. "The girl's heart attack. We think it might've triggered something. Um ... loosened safeguards, maybe?"

"How's that even possible?" Caldwell rasped, trying to conceal the unease creeping in.

He inhaled sharply. Melita's genetic research had been beyond innovative. Like nothing before it. What she hadn't anticipated was that it would be used on humans. She was never supposed to discover that fact. So, when she did ... Well, that was when the wheels fell off the cart. That was when she turned on him and turned on SynthoGen. He thought about her now ... beautiful, smart—way too smart to have allowed herself to be blown up in a lab explosion. *I should have dealt with her when I had the chance.*

His mind raced. Every second he stayed here was putting his life in jeopardy. He should be thinking of intergalactic escape routes. Backup plans.

His eyes darted around the office, the quiet surroundings a contrast to the chaos outside. Motion on one of the display feeds —smoke, the security bots falling, one by one. From out of the mist came a tall, hulking figure; Unit 1223 was advancing. Time was running out.

"What do you suggest?" Caldwell managed to ask, each word dripping with disdain.

Torp, finally showing some semblance of backbone, responded, "I'll secure the girl. Get her to your schooner. We can decode the data later."

A sharp alarm rang out, drowning out Caldwell's thoughts. It was closer now. The enemy at his doorstep.

Caldwell said, "Do it. Get the girl to *Prestige.*"

"Uh … And if we can't get past that robot?"

Caldwell's expression darkened, his voice deathly low. "Don't let that be an option."

As the display darkened, the weight of the situation settled on Caldwell's shoulders. He was in the middle of a whirlwind, perhaps one of his own making, but he'd be damned if he let it consume him. He'd navigate this storm, no matter the cost. And Torp? He'd pay for every stumble, every oversight. That was a promise.

≈

Loni

Pain shot through my arm where Torp gripped it. I watched as he, more unhinged than ever, screamed for the MedTech to get out. She didn't need to be asked twice.

Then Torp was scurrying out the door. I could hear him down the hall, cabinets clanking open, banging shut, then he was back again, a military shredder cradled in his hands. I knew a shredder was about as lethal a weapon as there was. It took no prisoners.

Torp's eyes, cold and soulless, bored into mine. "You do what I say, or you get it in the leg."

I nodded, the weight of the situation strangling any words I might have mustered. My heart raced, the beats so loud they were the only sound that filled the room.

"There're respirators in that cabinet. Get them!" he barked.

I quickly grabbed two, my fingers trembling.

He snatched one from me and adjusted it over his face. With the shredder still pointed at me, he ordered, "What are you, stupid? Put it on!"

I complied. Torp was becoming more unhinged by the second.

"Can I … can I at least have some clothes?" I asked, trying to preserve a shred of dignity.

"Shut up," he barked. "The sheet's fine."

Every muscle in my body screamed for me to fight back, to defy him. But defiance wasn't a luxury I could afford right now. Not with that weapon inches away. But my mind raced, working overtime. There had to be a way out of this. I needed an edge. God, anything.

He shoved me in front of him. "Seriously, you're using me as a human shield?"

He snorted and shoved me forward. "Shut up and march."

We moved like that, Torp with his shredder and me with my sheet, down one hallway after another. Explosions, loud weapons fire, were close. Too close.

Think! I whispered to myself. The unfamiliar surroundings of the building seemed to be mocking me—a labyrinth of terror. "You won't survive, you know. No one survives against a ChronoBot."

"Quiet!" he hissed.

I looked back at him. And there it was. A brief moment of distraction. I saw his eyes shift, even if it was just for a split second.

Just as I was plotting an escape, I felt the muzzle of the gun press into the middle of my back.

"Open the door. Move it!"

I did as told, and before I knew it, I was back outside. *Terrific.* At least I had a respirator this time. I never thought I'd miss my clawbster getup. The atmosphere was already burning my skin.

"Go left and pick up your pace."

Then I saw it, a brilliant white, streamlined, beautiful spacecraft.

The soles of my feet were cut and blistered from my last tromps across this terrain. Now I knew they were bleeding. This was what it must feel like to walk on hot coals.

The aft hatch to the ship loomed ever closer. The narrow ramp had been deployed; it beckoned me and my withering feet.

Chapter 43

Hardy

H ardy systematically dispatched the last of the security bots. But with every encounter, he'd incurred more and more hideous, blackened plasma craters. Sure, call him vain, call him smug, but he'd always taken pride in his looks. Any little scratch to his highly reflective chrome plating got buffed out immediately; a small dent to his metallic surface was pounded out lickety-split. Now as he strode past a floor-to-ceiling office window, he averted his gaze; he couldn't bear to look at himself.

Scanning the area with his advanced sensor array, he quickly located Loni. She was alive, but anything but safe. That, and no longer within the confines of this building.

Hardy scrutinized the building's blueprints for an exit, one closest to where Loni was situated. There was an exit with four interconnecting corridors. Getting to it would take minutes he did not have. Already irritated, Hardy, weapons deployed, let loose with a barrage of plasma fire directed toward the building's closest outside wall. As he turned it to Swiss cheese, bright rays of daylight streamed in from countless holes. Without missing a beat, Hardy barreled through like an unhindered bulldozer, the weakened wall disintegrating around him. *Terrific; more scratches to go with my burn craters.*

He set off in the direction of Loni's biomatrix, fast-walking at first, then bringing himself into a full-out run. A new memory rose into his consciousness. At one specific point in his three-hundred-year-plus life span, he'd ... well, actually LuMan, had clocked him sprinting at just over two hundred ten kilometers per hour.

LuMan: *That was decades ago. Do not attempt—*

But Hardy was already accelerating, legs pumping, arms swinging. Similar to a fighter craft's heads-up display, he eyed the virtual info screen projecting a variety of internal and external readout information. He had just surpassed 132 MPH.

In mere seconds, he was closing in on Loni. Then he saw she was not alone. Torp had cunningly positioned her in front of him, using her as a human shield.

There was nothing subtle about a thousand-pound ChronoBot running at full speed. Torp spun Loni around, an obvious attempt to thwart Hardy from firing on him. Analyzing the data in milliseconds, he weighed the conflicting options, torn between avoiding harm to Loni and neutralizing the imminent threat.

Coming to a full abrupt stop twenty yards from them, Hardy said, "You may want to rethink this, Commander Reginald Torp."

Loni repositioned her respirator mask. She looked small and overwhelmed, standing there in her bedsheet. Glancing over her shoulder, she said, "Seriously, your parents named you Reginald?"

"Get back!" Torp shouted. "I swear, I'll kill her. I have no beef with you, robot. Nothing personal against you ... This doesn't have to be your fight."

Hardy wobbled his head back and forth. "Hmm, yeah, well, this kinda is my fight. And this is personal."

LuMan: *May be a good time to use your face display.*

New memories suddenly infiltrated Hardy's mind. *There you are, you handsome devil.* In that instant, he remembered what he, *John Hardy*, born and raised in Boston, Massachusetts, and one USS *Hamilton* ship-wide maintenance worker some fifty-plus years past, looked like. *Okay … I'm a little pudgy, balding, and middle-aged, but I'm just fine with all of that. I have an identity! I know who I am!*

A holographic image emerged into view upon his typically reflective obsidian black faceplate, that of a crookedly smiling John Hardy.

Both Torp and Loni did double takes.

Loni's voice trembled as she tried to reason with Torp. "Let me go, Torp. Can't you see? That's not just a ChronoBot; it's a deranged ChronoBot."

Hardy didn't take offense. He knew, now more than ever, he was in fact a little off-kilter. "Loni … take a seat."

She stared back at him, perplexed. "Huh?" But then realization set in. Squeezing her eyes shut, she suddenly dropped to the ground.

Torp, momentarily taken off guard, repositioned the muzzle of his shredder toward the girl's head.

But it was too little too late. Hardy fired one precisely targeted shoulder-cannon plasma bolt. Torp's head disintegrated into a misty pink cloud. Still standing, his headless corpse let go of the shredder. Then, like a felled tree, he toppled over.

Loni, still kneeling within her now blood-soaked sheet, opened her eyes. She peered up at Hardy.

"You're safe now," Hardy said.

Only then did she take in Torp's headless body lying next to her. "Safe wouldn't be the first word that comes to mind."

"How about … safer?"

"Caldwell … he's escaping. Last I heard, he was making a run for his ship. The *Prestige*."

Hardy concurred. "I'll stop him."

"Uh … No way you're just leaving me here, robot."

"You good getting a piggyback ride?"

"Are you serious?" Loni said, looking unconvinced at Hardy's suggestion.

"It's now or never. If you're coming, hop on."

She got to her feet and readjusted her sheet, making it snug around herself. She came around to Hardy's now-lowered-down back. She said, "Did you, like, try to get hit by every frickin' energy bolt ever fired?"

"Funny. Get on."

It took several tries, but eventually, Loni got herself situated on his back. With her arms wrapped snugly around his neck, Hardy set off.

"Are you trying to loosen my teeth?" she complained. "Guess ChronoBots don't come equipped with shock absorbers."

She pointed; a slender arm extended over his shoulder. "There he is!"

Hardy had already spotted Caldwell but let the girl have her moment. The man was quickly approaching his ship. And what a ship it was … sleek, blazingly white, and undoubtedly expensive.

Without hesitation, he pursued Caldwell, his metallic feet pounding the ground. Within seconds, Hardy, Loni holding fast to his back, came abreast of the running corporate executive. Red-faced, wearing a respirator, and sweating profusely, Caldwell stumbled at the unfathomable sight to his left.

Before Hardy could take any action, Loni tightened her grip around his neck, then kicked out a leg—her heel landing a perfect blow to the man's temple.

Ass over tea kettle, Caldwell tumbled and ended up doing a faceplant onto the craggy, rocky Rivon3 surface.

"Let me down, robot!" she shouted, anger emphasizing her words.

Caldwell's respirator was all askew, his silver, usually perfectly coiffed hair now mussed and disheveled. He was lifting himself up with two arms, as if he was doing a push up. Blood ran down his face from the gash above his brow.

Loni, seemingly unconcerned that her crimson-stained sheet was coming loose around her, knelt in front of Caldwell. She didn't say anything for several moments as the two of them stared back at each other.

"For what you've done ... what you're still doing ... I should kill you right now."

Caldwell smirked. "You ... kill me?"

She shot a glance back at Hardy and then looked back to Caldwell.

He got the message. His face drained of color. His Adam's apple bobbed.

Hardy grabbed a fistful of Caldwell's sportcoat and lifted. "Up you go, Grandpa ... instruct the flight crew on that pretty little ship of yours to open the hatch and lower the gangway."

"There's no way—"

Not yet having released his hold on Caldwell, Hardy lifted the man skyward. "You ever wonder what it would feel like to fly sans ship, Mr. Caldwell?"

"Stop! Stop! Let me down!"

"Uh-uh, you heard the robot. Instruct your flight crew to open up. Do it now!" Loni demanded.

Legs flailing, Caldwell awkwardly tapped at his ComBand. Several moments later, *Prestige's* aft hatch started to open, the gangway extending.

Together, the three of them entered the ship. Hardy tossed Caldwell into an empty seat, then assessed the four crew members. He took in their physical response, analyzed their body language, their vital signs. Four pairs of eyes locked onto Hardy.

It was clear there would be no fight here. "Leave the ship immediately," he said. Then he turned toward Loni. "You smell something?"

She shook her head.

"Thing with ChronoBots ... They have a keen sense of smell. And I can tell you, Grandpa over there ... He shat his pants."

Loni stifled a laugh. "I suppose you don't want stains on your new ship's seats."

Prior to Caldwell heading down the gangway, Hardy had taken back his respirator and ComBand. LuMan calculated the time frame before Caldwell's internal systems would start to give out. He might have a half hour, maybe less.

Loni held up the breathing mask. "You have limited time without this apparatus. Don't even think about trying to stop us."

Caldwell's answer came in the form of a singular finger gesture.

Loni and Hardy stood at the open hatch, watching his departure. Then she said, "What are those?"

"Looks like a whole lot of lobster people."

"Clawbsters?"

Stirring up a dust cloud en masse, there must have been close to one hundred of them.

"Without security bots, and the guards having scattered, they've found their freedom," Hardy said.

She shook her head. "Freedom. After what Caldwell and his ilk have done to them, they're not free. Not even close."

Taking a seat in the captain's chair, Hardy conducted a preflight checklist. Aware that Loni had taken the seat next to him, he said, "Ready?"

She nodded, then shook her head. Squinting, she leaned forward, looking up. "What is that?"

Chapter 44

Loni

I t was a flaming amber streak arching across Rivon3's slime-green skyline. As it approached, it became more and more clear it was spherical, metallic ... *perhaps a ship of some kind? No, I recognized it from* Gossamer; *it was an escape pod, and it was descending—fast.*

Ten seconds later, it disappeared into the horizon. A spewing puff of dust made it perfectly clear where it had landed. I estimated several miles to the east.

I looked at Hardy.

"What?"

"What do you mean, what? You have to go and check it out," I said.

"It might be empty."

I shook my head.

"Maybe nobody survived the landing."

I shook my head again and raised my brows expectantly.

Hardy's digitized holographic face was almost comical. I

wasn't sure how I felt about this new blatantly human aspect. One thing was for sure: calling him 'robot' no longer seemed appropriate.

"Well ... are you going to go or not?"

"Consider me gone. You wait here."

IT WAS QUIET WITHOUT HARDY AROUND. I FELT I should be doing something. Helping in some way. But I couldn't move. Couldn't think. I felt total and complete exhaustion. I leaned my head back—I'd rest for just a moment ...

I SAT UP WITH A FRANTIC START, AWAKENING, NOT knowing where I was. *How long was I out? An hour ... two hours?* I let out a breath, forced my racing pulse to subside. I was on *Prestige*. The walls of the spacecraft's small bridge were unwelcomingly sterile, every surface gleaming with a cold indifference. An eeriness clung to the air. I pressed a hand to my aching chest, again wondering what the hell Denzel had done to me. As if having a deteriorating ticker wasn't enough, he had to conduct some kind of mystery surgery on me.

I tried to swallow and winced ... a lingering reminder of the MARFIX ChronoBot's chokehold. Air scraped down my raw throat, burning—another reminder—this time about how I almost died. When was that, three days ago? Four? There were more marks, scrapes, and bruises on my arm—physical scars that told the story of what I'd been through these last few days.

I sniffed and glanced down at the foul, bloodied sheet. A grotesque odor wafted, distinctly reminding me of Torp's insides, a vile mix that churned my stomach. I had an overwhelming need to wash away the smell—this need colliding with the pressing concern of my missing meds. How many doses had I missed?

Missing more than one could be fatal. New panic clawed at my insides.

My thoughts drifted to Angela Solace and Melita Roberts, their stories wrapping around each other, becoming an intertwining twisted tale. Were they the same? Was she my mother? A roller coaster of emotions ensued—deep longing cascaded into feelings of heart-wrenching abandonment … Then came the anger. Searing anger. To fake death once was cruel. To do it twice was torture. Leaving me, a mere child, to navigate life without a mother. Was my failing heart the price of my mother's subterfuge?

Hearing a clamor outside, I got to my feet and swayed. By the time I reached the main cabin, the hatch was opening and a seven-foot-tall ChronoBot was standing there. "Hi, honey, I'm home," Hardy said.

I'd never been happier to see that stupid holographic face of his. I exhaled, the relief of his return making me lightheaded. But then, to my utter surprise, there were Orin and Anna stomping up the gangway.

The sight of Anna warmed my insides. We hugged. I still couldn't believe she was standing there.

"Whoa, you, like, stink to high heaven, girl!" Anna squawked, taking a step away. With a look of total disgust, she assessed my bloody sheet.

I said, "How … how are you even here?"

"We're here because we weren't going to hang around and become two more of those mutant clawbsters."

"We snuck into the last of the escape pods," Orin said.

I turned to him and, without hesitation, fell into his arms. My blustering emotions were making it impossible to speak. Our embrace lingered longer than friends usually allowed, and he didn't even complain about how I smelled.

Hardy faux-cleared his throat, a stark reminder of the situation at hand. "We need to get moving. Now! We're about to have company, and it's not the pizza delivery guy. *Gossamer* sent down more troops ... and a whole lot of robots."

But Orin was already kissing me—holding me tight in his arms. Instantly, I was immersed in the moment. Feeling his soft lips on mine. It was as if time had halted, the two of us captured within a kind of intimacy I'd never experienced before. *Oh my ...*

Anna snorted. "Really? That's gross."

Flustered, I pulled back, feeling the heat of the moment flushing my cheeks. Orin grinned, unapologetic, as if we'd just shared something that could never be taken away from us.

At some point Hardy had brushed past us. I could hear the ship's drives throttling up to speed.

"Hey, I got something for you," Orin said, unslinging a small satchel I instantly recognized.

"My meds! Oh my God, you're a lifesaver... really."

"Strap yourselves in," came Hardy's voice from the bridge. "I think we've outstayed our welcome here."

It was then that I heard distant weapons fire. The ship shuddered, and the engine revved higher. The three of us found seats and strapped in. Outside the closest window, I saw dozens of aqua-blue environ suits and mechanical bots rapidly approaching.

"Robots!" Anna said. "Where are they all coming from?"

With a jolt, *Prestige* lifted off. Outside, red plasma bolts tore through the evening sky.

Hardy hollered back to us, "Orin ... get up here and man the weapons array!"

Orin and I exchanged a look. I said, "This ship has a weapons array?"

Orin shrugged and headed forward.

Again, the ship shook. I wondered how many of those direct hits this little ship could withstand.

I stood, headed aft.

"Where are you going?" Anna asked.

There were two things I was desperate to find ... a hot shower and a change of clothes.

I HURRIED THROUGH THE SHIP, PASSING MULTIPLE compartments and quarters. Eventually, I came to what I was sure was Caldwell's stateroom. While the other quarters had open doors, this one did not. I noticed a small rectangular panel with a menu of numbers and symbols. During my time working for Torp, I had been given Caldwell's personal access code, used to access certain off-limits files related to Caldwell's business. I tapped the code and the door swooshed open.

Sweet.

I hurried inside, finding myself in much more functional, well-appointed quarters. They looked lived-in and comfortable—in an industrial kind of way.

I noticed a framed holographic photo on his stainless-steel dresser—a smiling Dan Caldwell with an attractive woman in a white doctor's coat. The background appeared to be some kind of laboratory. I'd hit paydirt. Metal-paneled bulkheads, like that of the main cabin, a king-sized bed, and a small utilitarian desk and chair.

I continued on down a small passageway, where I found the bathroom and a large master closet. Wasting no time, I began opening one closet door after another. All the clothes were Caldwell's. Too big for me. Then, there within the last cabinet, I found a trove of women's clothes—dresses, slacks, and blouses ... all far more elegant than anything I'd ever worn. I opened several drawers beneath and found a pair of faded jeans that just might fit me. I briefly wondered who these clothes belonged to. I knew from his bio Caldwell wasn't married. A younger girlfriend, maybe? Within the next few minutes, I'd scrounged up an oversized dark-gray tank top, underwear, socks, and shoes that were a

Mark Wayne McGinnis & Jennifer M. Eaton

little too big for me. My next stop was the bathroom. I couldn't wait to step into a piping-hot shower.

AFTERWARD, I DRIED OFF, GOT DRESSED, AND BRUSHED out the knots in my hair. I was starting to feel human again. Assessing my seventeen-year-old face in the mirror, I suddenly felt much older than my actual age, as if I'd skipped the carefree teenage years of my life.

The oppressive quiet was closing in on me. My mind—my heart—was yearning for answers.

I wandered out of the bathroom, back into Caldwell's main stateroom. That picture ... I felt drawn to it somehow. Caldwell was beaming. But it was the woman whose face captured my attention. Her smile didn't reach her eyes, as if she was posing against her will. Her name tag was shiny, but way too small to read. *Who are you, mystery lady?*

Chapter 45

Leaving Naromi Star System
Starship *Prestige*
Hardy

I nside the cramped bridge, his metal fingers danced across
the ship's comms panel. He contemplated Loni's precarious
predicament. He sensed her internal emotional battles ...
but what a force she was. The young woman was seeking answers
about her elusive mother—a past shrouded in secrets.

It took a bit of time, but finally he was patched through to
Earth's EUNC High Command in Colorado Springs. By now,
Hardy's memories had all fallen back into place—no more
missing puzzle pieces.

Prestige's comms panel crackled. "High Command, this is
Ensign Parr ... Whom am I addressing? And what is the nature of
your transmission?"

"Hardy, John Hardy. And I'm trying to reach Captain Galvin
Quintos."

After a long static pause, Ensign Parr said, "Wait ... You're him? You're the ... uh ... ChronoBot bot?"

"Just a ChronoBot, not a ChronoBot *bot.*"

Another long pause ...

"Hello? Captain Quintos? You were going to connect me to him, Ensign?" Hardy said, wondering if his old friend was still off-world. Perhaps still on USS *Lincoln*?

"No, Mr. Hardy ... Captain Quintos, although he may be off-world, nobody seems to know where he is. And if you were to ask Admiral Block ... That's a big problem."

THE END...

Thank you for reading **ChronoBot Chronicles, Book 1,** *by Mark Wayne McGinnis and Jennifer M. Eaton. If you enjoyed this book, PLEASE leave a review on Amazon.com—it really helps! To be notified the moment all future books are released, please join my mailing list. I hate spam and will never ever share your information. Jump to this link to sign up: http:// eepurl.com/bs7M9r*

The Authors

About Mark Wayne McGinnis

Mark grew up on both coasts, first in Westchester County, New York, then in Westlake Village, California. Mark and his wife Kim now live in Castle Rock, Colorado, with their two dogs, Sammi and Lilly. Mark got his start as a corporate marketing manager and then fell into indie filmmaking—producing/directing the popular Gaia docudrama, *Openings—The Search For Harry*. For the last twelve years, he's been writing full time, and with thirty-eight best-selling novels under his belt, he has no plans to slow down. Thanks for being part of his community! Use the links below to jump to Mark's site.

Have a question or want to say hi to Mark? Contact him at: **markwaynemcginnis@gmail.com**

Or contact him on his Facebook author's page at: **https://www.facebook.com/MarkWayneMcGinnisAuthor/**

About Jennifer M. Eaton

USA Today Best Selling Author Jennifer M. Eaton writes fast paced science fiction from the eastern shore of the USA on planet Earth. Yes, regrettably, she is human, but please don't hold that against her.

When she's not busy with interplanetary wars, shape shifting dragons and blowing stuff up, Jennifer enjoys long hikes in the woods with her family and pups, gardening, bicycling, swimming, snorkeling, and stargazing.

Find out more or drop Jennifer an interplanetary communication by visiting her website at www.jennifereaton.com

Or hear about new releases and grab a free book here:

www.subscribepage.com/s2b4f1

Mark's Acknowledgments

First and foremost, I am grateful to my readers. I'd like to thank my wife, Kim, whose loving contributions to my books are immeasurable. Thank you to Lura Genz (my ninety-two-year-old mother) for her tireless work as our first-phase creative editor and for being a staunch cheerleader of my writing. I'd also like to thank Margarita Martinez for her amazingly detailed line editing work; Jennifer Eaton for her creative design and typesetting skills; Daniel Edelman for his many prerelease technical reviews and expert subject matter spitballing. A heartfelt thank you also goes to Sue Parr, Charles Duell, Stuart Church, Zoraya Vasquez, Lura Fischer, and James Fischer—without their support, this novel would not have been possible.

Check out the other available titles by Mark Wayne McGinnis on the following page.

Other Books by MWM

Scrapyard Ship Series

Scrapyard Ship (Book 1)

HAB 12 (Book 2)

Space Vengeance (Book 3)

Realms of Time (Book 4)

Craing Dominion (Book 5)

The Great Space (Book 6)

Call to Battle (Book 7)

Tapped In Series

Mad Powers (Book 1)

Deadly Powers (Book 2)

Lone Star Renegades Series

Lone Star Renegades (also called "Jacked") (Book 1)

Star Watch Series (Scrapyard Ship Spin-off)

Star Watch (Book 1)

Ricket (Book 2)

Boomer (Book 3)

Glory for Sea and Space (Book 4)

Space Chase (Book 5)

Scrapyard LEGACY (Book 6)

The Simpleton Series

The Simpleton (Book 1)
The Simpleton Quest (Book 2)

Galaxy Man Series

Galaxy Man (Book 1)

Ship Wrecked Series

Ship Wrecked (Book 1)
Ship Wrecked II (Book 2)
Ship Wrecked III (Book 3)

Boy Gone Series

Boy Gone Book 1

Cloudwalkers

Cloudwalkers

The Hidden Ship

The Hidden Ship

Guardian Ship

Guardian Ship

Gun Ship

Gun Ship

Hover

Hover

USS Hamilton Series

USS *Hamilton* – Ironhold Station (USS *Hamilton* Series Book 1)

USS *Hamilton* – Miasma Burn (USS *Hamilton* Series Book 2)

USS *Hamilton* – Broadsides (USS *Hamilton* Series Book 3)

USS *Jefferson* – Charge of the Symbios (USS *Hamilton* Series Book 4)

Starship *Oblivion* – *Sanctuary* Outpost (USS *Hamilton* Series Book 5)

USS *Adams* – No Escape (USS *Hamilton* Series Book 6)

USS *Lincoln*—Mercy Kill (USS *Hamilton* Series Book 7)

HEROES and ZOMBIES Series

HEROES and ZOMBIES — Escape to Black Canyon (Series Book 1)

The Test Pilot's Wife

The Test Pilot's Wife

The Fallen Ship Series

The Fallen Ship – Rise of the Gia Fighters

The Fallen Ship II (The Fallen Ship Series Book 2)

Junket

Junket – Untamed Alien Worlds

ChronoBot Chronicles

ChronoBot Chronicles

Jennifer's Acknowledgments

What a fun ride! Thanks so much, Mark, for inviting me to spend time in your world.

I won't bore everyone by thanking all the same people Mark did, but I do appreciate everyone who had a hand in making this book a reality.

Thanks also to my family, who keep me fed and do laundry and all those great things to keep the house running so I can write. Without you, nothing would get done.

And of course, I'd especially like to thank the readers, because without you, stories are just words on a page. They need you to come alive. Thanks for doing your part!

Books by Jennfer M. Eaton

Star Bandits: Uprising

Renegade Magic (Book 1)

Renegade Thief (Book 2)

Renegade Storm (Book 3)

Remegade Legace (Book 4)

Renegade Guardian (Book 5)

Starlight

Invaded

Dragon Mount

Paper Wishes

Sorcerer's Reign

Fire in the Woods

Fire in the Woods (Book 1)

Ashes in the Sky (Book 2)

Embers in the Sea (Book 3)